CONTROL
BOOK 1 OF THE LOCKWOOD TRILOGY

CONTROL

BOOK 1 OF THE LOCKWOOD TRILOGY

MELISSA CASSERA

CHAPTER ONE

NATALIE

BREATHE.

Anxiety coils through me. I peer out from backstage at this ridiculous spectacle, knocking my head against a twelve-foot flower tunnel of white roses and wisteria. Petals shower to the ground. My eyes scan the room, praying no one noticed me bump into it, and scoop up the stray petals, shaking a few from my hair in the process. I can't believe they designed this fancy tunnel for the Lockwood student election. It shouldn't surprise me, though.

Lockwood is a bit like posh purgatory—a one-year transitionary school for "offspring of the elite." Not my words—that's actually what it says on the website. Most of us grew up with some type of privilege and a direct path to an Ivy, but turning eighteen and getting to spend your final year of high school at Lockwood is a special privilege only afforded to one hundred and seventy five students each year. Except we don't really learn anything or *do anything* that special. This is more of a well-branded holding cell before we head off to college.

I glance over at my boyfriend, Jack—about to swear in as president of our class. He recites his speech in the corner, murmuring the words even I have memorized after hearing it so many times. And here I am by his side, like some dutiful political wife. Except, I'm not his wife—I'm his girlfriend. And not exactly by choice. We were practically set up by our fathers right out of the womb. Pretty sure they ship our romance more than we do.

Ugh, what am I even doing here?

On the other side of the stage, my fellow students shuffle into their seats. A live orchestra readies in the corner, because of course they didn't want to use a student band. Lockwood spends our $100,000 tuitions to bring in the MET Orchestra from Carnegie Hall. As if there's nothing better to do with our parents' money. Hurricane relief? Foreign aid? Nope. Let's blow all the money on an orchestra for a student election.

I pluck a stray curly hair from my black uniform jacket and flick it onto the near-spotless floor. Rumor is that the previous uniforms were white Ralph Lauren, but so many kids spilled lattes, liquor, or got period blood on them, they decided to switch to Tom Ford black. Crystal-embossed wool peplum jackets for the girls. Itchy as fuck.

I pluck another brown hair from my jacket and start to walk away. Jack clasps my hand, hard. "Where are you going?"

"Nowhere," I mumble. Jack has that intimidating presence that makes you immediately feel like you've done something wrong when he talks to you.

"I'm about to go on," he says, still clinging to my arm like I'm his lifeline. I guess maybe I am. "I need you here."

Words like this should feel romantic, and maybe they would if Jack were that kind of guy. He's not, and instead of sounding sweet, he's bossy. I sigh. I wish I was one of those girls who slaps a guy for bossing me around. I even picture myself doing it sometimes. My hand raising. A hard smack across Jack's perfect cheekbone. Watching the shock and embarrassment on his face. I giggle out loud at the thought.

"What's so funny?"

I shake my head. "Nothing."

Jack shoots me a pissy look, like everything is totally my fault and why can't I just get it together and be there for him. I immediately feel guilty for shitting all over his day, even though I really didn't do anything wrong. I just had some *thoughts*.

I study his face. He's already back to reciting his speech, desperate to perfect every word. I let out a long, deep sigh—sure, he's being annoying, but this is his big day. And I guess he's not that bad of a boyfriend. I should focus on his good qualities, right? Maybe make a list...

Okay, I admit it. He's gorgeous, in that preppy, country club kinda way.

He's got a bright future, no doubt about that.

He's tall and athletic.

He's smart, sometimes—when he doesn't let his ego get in the way of learning.

He's also rude. Cocky. And he couldn't care less about *my* future and what I want. Whoops. I guess those aren't his most endearing qualities.

Oh, and he's obsessed with Josephine.

Yeah, that.

I look out from behind the curtain again. And there she is, right in the front row.

Josephine Stanton. Originally from Marseille. She's everything I'm not. Perfect hair. Perfect body. Crystal blue eyes against my muddy brown ones. My mom had brown eyes until she was nineteen and then they turned this gorgeous shade of green. I secretly wish I'll have the same fate.

I can't help but notice Josephine's cleavage popping out of her uniform blouse that's unbuttoned just low enough. How does she have such insane curves? What the hell is in the water in Marseille?

Jack's voice snaps me from my envy. "Are you going to do something with your hair?"

Offended, I rake my hand over my curls. My hair is half pulled back, smooth and polished on top. "I did already."

"Pull it all back or something. They're going to take our picture when I swear in," he says, frustrated.

Okay, now I might slap him. I suck in a deep breath, forcing myself to stay calm and understanding. Jack's dream was to become class president of Lockwood. Lots of Lockwood grads go on to become politicians, and Jack has bigger dreams to become president of the United States one day. People say that, but I really believe Jack could make it happen.

All he wants is for this day to be perfect. I get it. Or at least, I'm trying to. I know the pressure is on him—on *us*. Is it really that big of a deal to pull my hair into a bun if he'll relax? No. I can at least do that much.

I head off to the bathroom as Jack calls after me, "Hurry up!"

Inside the bathroom, I find Ciel pouting in the mirror, applying shimmery pink gloss. I've known Ciel on and off for years, exchanging pleasantries at high society parties, smiling for the cameras. Now she's basically my closest friend at Lockwood. Which isn't saying much because Lockwood friendships so far are fickle and fleeting. People are always looking over their shoulder for the next best person to befriend who might further their popularity or aspirations.

"You ready for today, Jackie Kennedy?" she says in a sing-song voice.

My pulse skitters. "Please don't call me that. I'm not trying to be the first lady."

"Why? She had amazing style," Ciel says. I study her boho-chic school uniform makeover—a scarf draped in that effortless way, layers of vintage jewelry, and bohemian designer boots. She's wearing the same uniform as mine, yet hers looks like it's styled for the pages of *Vogue* and mine looks straight off a home-shopping network. How I manage to make Tom Ford look frumpy, I'll never know. Ciel also seems to have constructed a flower crown from the rose petals on stage. *Did she just do that right now?* Only Ciel can turn a student election into Coachella.

I glance at myself in the mirror, scowling. I pull out my clip and my hair puffs out in a hopeless cloud of curls. I bet Ciel could pull off this look.

I search the counter for a hair tie. Lockwood bathrooms rival upscale spas—La Mer face cream, eucalyptus steam on a timer, wellness supplements that promise we are one pill away from excellence or a faster metabolism. Guess hair ties are too low-class.

"Did you see the new guy?" Ciel says, while tousling her beachy waves.

"What?" I'm only half-listening. Ciel is always into some guy. Or girl. I can't keep track.

"The new guy. *Scholarship kid.*"

Ciel puts that in air quotes, which means his parents aren't rich enough to send him here, so he got into Lockwood on some other merit. Most people put the scholarship kids into a different social class, dub them losers. I find them a lot smarter, and a lot nicer, than the kids who can afford the tuition.

"He's hot. Probably poor, but hot. And kinda weird." I can see her brain working hard to figure this all out.

"Weird… how?"

Ciel stretches out like a cat. I can tell she's already bored by the conversation she started. "I don't know. He just keeps to himself."

"*That's* your definition of weird?"

She shrugs. "I mean, yeah. He's not outgoing like Jack."

Ugh, here we go. Jack is the standard by which all the girls at this school measure every other guy. If they only knew how imperfect he is. How he keeps you up all night while he paces your room in a rage-sweat about an exam. How he always seems to get "distracted" when you have good news to share. Or when he comes back horny from a party, his breath smelling like sour beer. We'll lie in my bed making out, while he runs his hand up my shirt or teases his fingers over the top of my underwear—which I would probably be into if I didn't feel like dry heaving from his terrible breath.

I finally find a hair tie hidden behind a cluster of cooling gel eye patches and quickly scrape my hair into a bun. At my reflection, disappointment flutters in my heart. Here I go, caving to someone else's wishes again.

Fuck it.

I rip out my bun and leave my hair completely down. Curls tumble all around my face. This small act of defiance makes me grin, and for the first time in as long as I can remember, my reflection doesn't bore me. I even feel a little sexy.

"You want some lip gloss?" Ciel holds out the tube.

"I'm good."

I race out of the bathroom and manage to get backstage just before Jack is announced.

Jack is facing away from me, shuffling his feet and swinging his arms like he's preparing for a boxing match. It would be almost comical if I couldn't see the desperation and fear radiating off him.

Headmaster Rochester announces, "Let's give a Lockwood chant for our class president, Jack Carter!"

Jack looks back at me, but his delighted expression morphs into horror when he sees my hair. There's no time for him to say anything as he's shooed onto stage. I can't help but smile as I follow him out, reveling in my single act of rebellion.

As I step onto the stage, I'm immediately blinded by a camera flash. Deafening roars and cheers ripple through the student body.

Another flash in my face. My voice drops to a harsh whisper. "Stop, I can't see."

The photographer shoots me an annoyed look and backs away.

When I finally regain my vision, I spot Jack at the podium in all his glory. He raises his hand with a powerful wave and the crowd erupts into even louder tremors of excitement and applause.

I take my place behind him, just to the right. I tune out when he launches into his speech—which is fine because I know it word for word. I have to distract myself to stop the urge to mouth the words along with him.

I scope the crowd. A sea of beautiful faces in designer uniforms. I wonder if they are as uncomfortable and itchy as mine. I'll never know anyway—no one tells the truth at Lockwood.

Then, my eyes land on something strange. A line of guards block the back of the concert hall. *That's weird.* They're all dressed in military-type uniforms, not unlike the Queen's Guard, minus the bearskin hats. It looks like they're holding rifles? *Why?*

I squint to try and make out the details. They weren't here before. We don't have guards at Lockwood. Sure, we get the occasional bodyguard— but those guards are in plain clothes and are much less intimidating. They don't barricade an entire student assembly.

Add this to list of strange things about Lockwood. The campus is situated on the private Lockwood Island on the coast of Washington state. You can only reach the school by ferry, and there's nothing else on this island but our campus. The iron gates encircling our school are locked, caging us further from the outside world. Our phones are snatched from us when we enter. Social media? Forbidden. Scheduled weekly phone calls with family and friends on the outside only. Monthly visitations. Like I said, *strange*.

As Jack continues his speech, I can't stop staring at the guards. Six of them. Stone-faced. Blocking the exit. They almost don't look human. I can't be the only one who notices them, but no one else here seems bothered. A needle of fear prickles the back of my neck. My uniform feels even hotter, itchier, than usual.

I tune back in to Jack's speech when I notice his words trail off and a loud gasp erupts from the audience, followed closely by several shrieks. The guards immediately point their rifles at the commotion.

I crane my neck to try and see what's going on. Shoes screech against the hard floor as students scurry from their seats. Jack whips his gaze around the room, annoyed by the interruption.

As the crowd parts, I'm finally able to get a clear view of what's happening.

It's a student I don't recognize, standing and clutching his chest—it looks like he's having trouble breathing. He staggers backward, eyes popped wide, a look of sheer terror on his face. No one is helping him. *Why is no one helping him?*

I rush to the edge of the stage, heart thundering in my chest. I can hear Jack shouting after me. I turn back to him—his glare makes my skin crackle with anxiety, like I've been caught doing something illicit. Normally this look would crush my soul, but something—adrenaline, fear, the desire to make my own fucking decision for once—catapults me off that stage.

My shoes smack to the ground below and I bolt ahead, shoving my way through Lockwood's elite, and get to the student just as he crashes to the floor.

I lean over him and grab onto his arms. His eyes are squeezed shut, like he never wants to open them again.

"Hey," I whisper.

He stirs. His eyes flutter open and clash with mine. They're deep green with flecks of gold. Intense. Like he's staring into my soul.

"Are you okay?" I say.

His breathing accelerates, then his fingers snap around my wrists, his nails digging into my flesh as his gaze darkens. His jaw clenches, nostrils flared—the savage pounding of his pulse strums against my skin.

Every alarm sounds in my body—*get out of here!*—but all reason has just left the building.

I can't move. I can't think. There's something about this stranger that I just have to know.

CHAPTER TWO

HENRY

NATALIE FUCKING COVINGTON.

Of all people to make some grand gesture and "save" me—*she's* the one who leaps off a stage for fuck's sake. Why her?

Her eyes water with concern as she stares me down. And she's speaking in this hushed, breathless tone I can barely understand. "Can you talk? I just want to make sure you're okay."

I begin to tremble with her so close—like I can't control my body's impulses around her. I have this intense need to warn her… save her.

She squeezes her hands into mine. An electric bolt pulses through my body and then I see…

Natalie's face—eyes wide in horror. She seems to be straining, trying to breathe. *There's something tangled in her hair.* Is it leaves? Grass? It looks dirty. No, not dirty, muddy. Like she's lying on the ground. *Something red—bright crimson, even.* Blood? It doesn't look like blood. I search for details. *Her scream cuts through the eerie silence. Piercing.*

I can't handle us touching anymore. I need her to stop. Need *it* to stop. I shove her off me and she crashes back on her ass, limbs flailing.

What the hell? I didn't mean to shove her that hard. I didn't mean to shove her at all. I barely touched her.

As she gathers herself, she looks up at me. Her eyes seem to change color with her mood, shifting from brown to green. It takes all of my willpower not to pull her into my arms and tell her I'm sorry. Tell her that everything's going to be okay. Even though I know it won't be.

I turn my focus away from her and take in my surroundings. Everyone is staring at me—whispering about me. I see her boyfriend on stage, glaring—livid, probably because I just ruined his big moment. Or maybe he doesn't like that I just shoved his girl. Either way, he's pissed.

Something catches the corner of my eye—the gleam of metal. I turn and see a line of guards, all with rifles pointed… at me. A sharp chill leeches through my body. As if on cue, they all point their rifles up, now aimed away.

Were they going to shoot me—a guy who looks like he's having a panic attack? If they only knew what was really going on, my body would be full of bullets. I shudder at the thought. Lockwood is pretentious, but I would have never guessed it would be so dangerous. My foster dad sent me to this school in some stupid attempt to get me to socialize before heading off to college. So much for that.

One of Natalie's friends rushes over to her. I don't know who she is, which isn't that surprising because I've made it a point not to get to know anyone here unless I absolutely have to. The only person that fits that bill so far is Natalie, unfortunately for her.

Her friend shoots me a look of death, and my eyes drift to Natalie, who still hasn't removed her gaze from mine. It's like she wants to say something—maybe call me an asshole, which I deserve—but she doesn't look mad. She looks… intrigued? No, that can't be right.

Natalie looks over at her boyfriend, then back at me. He doesn't seem to like that. He plows ahead, jumping off the stage. I'm one hundred percent sure he wants to punch me. I know I can easily take down this preppy-ass punk, but I definitely don't need to draw any more attention to myself.

I jump to my feet and race to the doors. He's shouting at me, and Natalie's voice rings in my ears—soothing, calm, like she's trying to stop him from freaking out. She's far enough away that I shouldn't be able to hear her, but it's like my senses are dialed up to a million.

I push past the creepy guards to get outside. What the hell are they doing here at a student election anyway? Maybe someone's family hired them. I wouldn't put it past them. I've been at this school for five days, arriving a month after the other students, and I can already tell that Lockwood parents think their kids are the next coming of Christ.

I tug my uniform jacket around me as the cold air stabs my skin. My eyes water in the wind. And then I see…

The back of Natalie's head, her curls whipping in the wind. She must be running. *It's dark. Night.* Late night, maybe. *She's running through a bank of trees, wearing something black. A coat with a fur collar.* What is she running from? Or who? *She whips her gaze around, a look of sheer terror on her face.*

I   slow   my   breathing   and   count   backwards.
10...9...8...7...6...5...

The vision stops.

Counting backwards doesn't always work, but right now, it's all I've got. A Band-Aid, until it gets ripped off and bloodied by a new vision.

As I close in on my dorm, my eyes latch on to a camera tucked onto the top of a building. There are cameras everywhere at Lockwood. Supposedly, they were turned off last year after their little surveillance attempt went to shit. Even a moron could have guessed that would happen. The cameras covering every inch of this campus ended up catching so many students having sex and doing drugs, Lockwood could have produced its own network. Students and—more importantly—their parents complained, and since it's their money paying for this overhyped joint, the cameras are done.

But I don't trust that they're not watching.

When I asked the school administration about the cameras, no one seemed to be able to answer my questions. Not one person had a good excuse as to why they were even filming the students, much less filming their private spaces, like our dorm rooms.

The only place I know for sure there are no cameras are the bathrooms, specifically my bathroom. That's because, I'm one of the lucky few that has a private bathroom, not a communal setup like other students. I ripped the entire camera setup out of the wall, just in case. I haven't been able to budge the camera from my bedroom, so that'll have to stay—for now.

I make my way up the steps to my dorm, taking them two at a time, all the way up to the seventh floor. My suite isn't really a dorm at all. More like a room on the maintenance floor that's sometimes used for staff. I was on a mission, cleaning oceans in

Istanbul, and got to Lockwood after all the other students, so I snagged this spot. A score, if you ask me. Though, I wish I was back in that ocean rather than swimming in a sea of these assholes.

My room is the only dorm room on the floor, and that's why I'm the only student with my own bathroom. The rest of the floor is made up of janitor closets. It's noisy early in the morning when the cleaning crew gets their supplies, but it's a small price to pay for decent privacy.

I shove open the door to my room, toss my keys onto the desk, and flip open my laptop, angling it away from the camera in my room. Just in case.

On-screen is a slice of my research from last night—a photo of Natalie smiling with some other volunteers, celebrating a mission with a humanitarian eye care organization that gives free optometry services to people in Peru. Just great—on top of everything else, she's basically a saint.

I arrived at Lockwood last Monday. It's now Friday. I saw Natalie my first morning. Well, not in real life. I saw her in my mind. Just a flash of her face.

On my way to meet the guidance counselor later that day, I saw her in real life. She was standing in the hallway, talking to a friend. My heart raced and my breath stopped. I've never seen the subject of one of my visions before in real life. She didn't notice me looking at her, which was good—because that's when the second vision happened.

Her face, crushed and sad. Not in a broken-hearted way, more like she was scared or wounded. *A tear leaks down her face.*

That vision was intense, like I could feel her pain. I had this inextricable pull, this rabid need to take her pain away. How ironic that today she tried to do the same for me.

Natalie Covington.

I went on an all-night binge researching anything I could find about her online. There were tons of photos of her with her boyfriend Jack. Candid photos from parties, and charity events, and school functions. And plenty of staged—probably photo-shopped—snaps of them kissing on beaches, and meadows, and other bullshit locations. I felt… jealous. Like, because I had a vision of her, I somehow owned her. Or at least, I owned a fucked up fragment of her future. I know it's wrong to feel like that, but I can't help myself.

My visions are never clear enough for me to piece anything together. Just splices of meaningless life. But my visions of Natalie are different. They're pointed. Still fragmented, but they're all about the same event.

Since arriving at Lockwood five days ago, I've had thirty-seven visions of her, each one revealing a new and more dangerous piece of the puzzle. That's more visions than I've had in the last three years, and those were all completely random about complete strangers. It's fucking terrifying, like a horror movie looping in my head 24/7—one that's actually going to come true.

And I can't tell her.

Not that she'd believe me if I did.

I've got an entire folder of research on my laptop—all of Natalie. I'm smothering my brain with her like some psycho who belongs on a true crime show. I send the folder to trash, hoping this might tear apart all my thoughts and visions of her. But it just triggers another one.

Natalie on the ground, a knife plunged into her chest—scarlet blood encircling her body.

Fuck. She's going to die.

My heart thrums, then speeds. Sweat beads on my forehead and slicks my body. I tear off into the bathroom and clutch the side of the bathroom sink, dying to shatter something—wanting to crack this porcelain in two.

I need to cool down.

I strip off my clothes and turn on the shower full blast. I step into the stream of water and let out a guttural scream. The release helps me feel a bit better. I stand under the water, hoping it will wash away some of my tension.

I have to do something. Have to get away from her.

I have to get the hell out of this school.

CHAPTER THREE

NATALIE

MY PULSE RACES as I spin my underwear-clad body to face the full-length mirror. A purplish bruise covers a nice area of my behind.

I trace my finger along the mark, and my heart thunders the more I fixate on it.

Henry Thorne.

That's his name, and I whisper it out loud as I study my bruise. I try to avoid my urge to know more about him, but my mind keeps whining.

I wonder what happened today, and why he panicked. I wonder why he shoved me. I wonder what it might be like if he spoke to me, or I spoke to him. I wonder what will happen the next time I run into him. I wonder why I care—why it feels like he's clawing through my brain no matter how hard I try and push him out.

I've been back in my room for less than fifteen minutes and I've already learned several things about him. Chalk that up to being raised by a mother who was a journalist.

Henry Thorne.

Eighteen years old. He got to Lockwood a month late after some humanitarian mission overseas. Now he's sorting out his classes. Maybe he'll land in one of mine. *I hope he lands in one of mine.* That'll make it easier to figure him out.

The longer I stare at the colors and edges of my bruise, the more something pulses inside of me. I can't explain it, but it's too hard to ignore. *Henry Thorne.* Those eyes—panic mixed with longing, like he wanted me to help him. I shiver with some kind of viral desire, eating through my brain and body. What the hell is happening?

My dorm room door swings open and Ciel bursts in. Her mouth gapes open when she catches me standing in my underwear, as if she knows what I'm thinking.

"Natty, you have a bruise on your ass!" she shrieks. "You should tell somebody. That's abuse. Scholarship kid abused you."

I breathe a sigh of relief that she can't read my thoughts and roll my eyes. "I'm pretty sure it was an accident. He seemed like he was having a panic attack."

Ciel ignores my sentiment and races to my closet. "So what are you wearing to the inauguration party tonight?" She combs through my closet, picking out a dress. "How about this?"

Lockwood doesn't seem to offer much in the way of academics, but they sure know how to pack a social calendar. There's some kind of dance or ball or uptight brunch happening every week. I take the dress from Ciel and slip it over my head, making sure to catch another illicit glimpse of my bruise.

My mind is already bubbling with what I want to say to Henry tonight as Ciel zips up my dress. I scrutinize my reflection in the mirror. My dress is blush pink, spaghetti straps, flirty, a bit too short for my liking, and so not me.

"I look like a ballerina."

Ciel tucks her fingers under my straps, adjusting to perfection. "Stop it, Natty. You look so hot—totally fuckable."

I audibly groan. "I definitely do not want 'fuckable' as my personal brand."

Ciel ignores me and digs into my makeup drawer. "So Jack's pissed at you, huh?"

She's right. Jack is mad. But I ran off after the spectacle earlier today, not even providing the chance for him to give me shit. I already know what he'll say—that I don't care about his future, that I don't take his dreams seriously, blah, blah, blah.

But he definitely doesn't know that my mind has been consumed by the stranger who ruined his event.

"He'll get over it," I say as Ciel twists up the tubes of various lipsticks to find the perfect shade.

"Adip told me that Jack was embarrassed."

I roll my eyes again. "Why because someone had a panic attack? He needs to get over himself. And what, you and Adip are back on now?"

I've known Adip for years. We went to three years of private school together before transferring to Lockwood and he was widely considered the hottest guy. Seems nothing's changed since we got here.

"No, we're not back on. We dated half a summer and that was years ago." Ciel shakes her head, clearly not wanting to talk about it.

I tug down my dress, my fingers brushing across the bruise. I close my eyes and imagine being touched. Rough hands caressing me—not smooth. Calloused even, like Henry's were when I grabbed them earlier. Maybe he uses them a lot, knows how to use them.

I know I shouldn't obsess like this. I shouldn't bother trying to learn more about him—should give him privacy, leave him alone.

But it can't hurt to look into Henry Thorne... just a little bit more. *Can it?*

CHAPTER FOUR

HENRY

I SIT IN the damp basement of a rickety building, picking at the button on my uniform coat. The air is thick and moldy, but I can still breathe better in this crappy room than at Lockwood.

After the whole mess with Natalie earlier today, I made an emergency call to my dad—well, I made a call to my *foster* dad, Oliver. I have no idea who my real mom and dad are.

I was desperate to get into a chapter meeting—it's like a support group for people with precognitive abilities. Precogs. The closest meeting is in Seattle, which is about two hours from campus, but I don't mind. It means more time I get to spend away from Lockwood. *From Natalie.*

Lockwood doesn't like students fleeing campus on a whim, so Oliver made up some excuse about my needing to see a specialist in the city to refill an important medication, then scheduled a ferry to pick me up. I told him I was thinking of leaving Lockwood, that I thought I'd made a huge mistake, but he encouraged me to stick it out.

I tuned out the rest of our conversation because my visions of Natalie were unrelenting. *Her body lurches ahead, darting between trees.* The place she's running in seems familiar and unfamiliar at the same time. I've already combed the entire campus looking for it and came up short. *She pitches forward onto the cold dirt, spasming with terror. Black spots scatter across my own vision and I taste something metallic and bitter. Blood. Her blood?* I wipe my mouth out of habit, but it's dry. The line between my future visions and current reality have blurred beyond what I can handle.

And that's what brought me here, to this shitty basement far outside of campus.

About a dozen people mill about and file into the room, sitting in a circle of chairs. No one I know. But that doesn't matter—at least they'll understand.

I scan the other precogs, focusing on the guy sitting next to me. He looks spent, compulsively scratching the stubble on his jaw. That's the thing about precogs—we all do something to cope with our visions. With our secrets. Like learning karate because it takes mental stamina and focus. Or smoking weed to relax your mind enough to make the visions tolerable. Or, if you're me, you try everything and still can't figure out how to deal.

A man clears his throat and takes his seat, introduces himself as Leonard. He holds up his hands to get our attention. "Welcome, everyone. Glad you could make it. Please repeat after me. 'Thou shalt not share his visions.'" We all repeat. "'Thou shalt not share his abilities.'" We repeat again. "'Thou shalt not attempt to change a vision.'" We repeat.

I get a sinking feeling in the pit of my stomach. If I'm being honest, I want to break every one of these rules, but that's why I'm here.

"Let's begin. Who would like to share?" Leonard says.

A woman raises her hand, meek and timid. She tells us that her visions have increased lately, she thinks due to stress. Her husband isn't a precog, and because he's not one of us, he can't know about our ability. She's been distracted by her increased visions, and her husband thinks she's having an affair. I feel guilty for tuning out quite a bit of her story. My mind keeps flicking to Natalie. To what's going to happen to her when my vision becomes a bloody reality.

"Son, would you like to share?"

I look up and realize Leonard is addressing me, and I wonder how long I've tuned out. I hesitate, knowing group is supposed to help us feel better, but I still feel uncomfortable sharing these specific visions with total strangers. It's like I want to keep this a secret, keep her a secret, keep her all to myself. Damn, I'm fucked up.

"I'm good, thanks." I fold my arms, a defense mechanism to close off from the world.

Leonard stares at me with empathy. "The more uncomfortable it is to share, the more you need to do it."

I shift in my seat, knowing he's probably right, swallowing my nerves. "I'm Henry. And I've been having a lot of visions since getting to my new school. Visions about one of my classmates."

Several gasps ripple through the room. Leonard motions for everyone to be quiet and leans into me, concerned. "So you know the subject of your vision?"

I nod. "Yeah, I see her around campus."

I notice Leonard's body tense. A vein bulges in his neck, his jaw tics. It's obvious he's bothered by my share. Definitely not how I expected the group leader to react. I immediately go on the defensive. Maybe I can't trust these people after all.

I only came to support group once before, back when I was ten years old and struggling with a vision of a boat capsizing. I had no idea where this boat was, who it belonged to, or any identifying information—unlike my current visions where I know everything about the subject. At the time, I thought this vision of a random boat was the worst thing ever. Now, I'd rather watch thousands of fucking boats sink instead of seeing Natalie get killed.

"What are your visions?" I snap back into focus, and swear Leonard's voice has trailed up into a higher octave. This is definitely making him nervous, and his reaction is making *me* more nervous. Suddenly, I wonder if I should be sharing this at all.

So… I lie.

"I just see her fighting with her boyfriend. Nothing crazy. It's just weird to see the person in real life and know what's going to happen."

Leonard nods. "And do you talk to this girl? I mean, are you close?"

I shake my head. "Nah. I don't even know her except for what I see in my head." I look around at the group, reading the room. Everyone's acting like I'm holding them hostage.

I try a different tactic to diffuse the tension. I lean back in my chair, cocky and confident. "She's not exactly my type, if you know what I mean." I leave that off with a wink. Nervous laughs, tension breaks—except for Leonard, and for me. It's like we're the only two people in the room, locked in a battle of truth and lies.

"So how are you dealing with the visions of this girl?" Leonard says.

I detect a hidden meaning in his words, like he knows—or at least suspects—how I'm dealing with it. Isn't that why I'm here?

"I'm dealing with it fine. Like I said, I'm not into her, so I couldn't care less about her boyfriend drama. Just needed to get it off my mind here."

Leonard's stare indicates he doesn't quite believe me. "That's good." His expression is heavy, disturbed. I wish I could see inside his head, know exactly what he's thinking, but we don't have that kind of power.

He stands and rakes his hand through his hair, pacing a few steps. "Well, this goes without saying, but you are aware that even if you know the person, you can never reveal what you see."

I nod to him like I'm saluting a captain. "Yes, sir. Very aware of our rules."

"And you know that you cannot warn her, or do anything to attempt to change the visions?" I detect a slight threat in his eyes.

"Yeah, I have no interest in doing anything with that girl, much less help her." I chuckle, but Leonard remains stiff. I try to appease him. "Of course, I'm forever bound to our rules, and wouldn't even think of breaking them."

Leonard watches me closely. "Good, that's good. I'm really glad you shared with us today, Henry. I'm going to give you my cell number in case you need anyone to talk to."

Leonard hands me his business card. I take it with a grateful nod, knowing I'll toss it in the trash the minute I leave. Then he whips out his phone. "Why don't you give me your number so I have it?"

My nerves spike. I'm not down with his pushy behavior. "My school doesn't allow cell phones. Something about fostering a better environment for learning. We have phone privileges sometimes, so I'll make sure I call you if I need anything." I tap his business card to reassure him.

He stares at me for a moment too long before moving on to the next person.

∾

I'm completely on edge during the ferry ride back to campus. What the fuck happened back there? That was like some weird interrogation, not a support group. Something's definitely not sitting right with me. Now I feel worse.

Back in my dorm room, I yank off my shirt and pull on a pair of sweatpants. As I change, I realize I'm starving and take out a plastic cup of Kraft macaroni and cheese—my favorite. I fill up the electric kettle and turn it on to boil the water. Maybe this day won't be complete shit after all.

I jump when I hear a knock on the door. No one ever comes to my room. Maybe the cleaning staff just got lost. "Who is it?" I call out.

Another knock. Why aren't they answering? My nerves spike.

I peek through the keyhole. I don't recognize the guy, but he looks my age. What the hell does he want?

"I'm busy," I grunt.

"Hey man, I just wanted to talk for a second."

Jesus, I guess this dude's not going to give up so easy. "Who is it?"

"Name's Wes. Mr. Fiore told me to hit you up for some help with calc."

I don't recognize him and wonder why the hell this teacher would recommend me. Sure, I'm decent at math, but I don't know what would give him the idea that I'd want to tutor other students. "We in class together?"

"No, I'm in pre-calc. That's why he told me to talk to you."

Ugh, fuck. I hope he doesn't have any stupid ideas like wanting to study right now. Or, like checking up on me to see if I'm okay after the scene I made earlier. I open the door, blocking the entry with my hand. I'll make sure he's gone in ten seconds.

"This couldn't have waited until tomorrow?"

Wes laughs. "Damn, warm welcome, buddy." He eyes my sweatpants. "You taking a nap or something?"

"I said I'm busy," I snap, hoping my cold demeanor will scare off this idiot trying to encroach on my privacy.

"Oh, I get it. You gotta girl in here." He cranes his neck over my arm, trying to catch a peek. I don't even give him the satisfaction of an answer, losing patience with this fool. He picks up on my annoyance. "Look, I don't wanna interrupt what you got going. I just need to talk real quick." He looks at me with pleading eyes, like I'm supposed to read his mind or something. Hate to disappoint you man, but that ain't my gift.

"I'm not interested in talking." I try to slam the door shut, but Wes blocks it with his hand. He's stronger than I thought.

"What the fuck?"

He pulls up his sleeve to expose his forearm. A tattoo of the twenty-third letter of the Greek alphabet—the psi symbol. Except it's not just a tattoo, it's a marking. I glance down at my own psi symbol, marked on my forearm. Same size. Same ink. Same exact location.

Holy shit. He's a precog.

CHAPTER FIVE
NATALIE

"NATTY, RELAX," CIEL says as we head to the inauguration party inside the school banquet hall. "You look like dead girl walking."

Ciel assumes I'm twisted up in knots, wondering if Jack is mad at me. That's definitely the last thing on my mind.

"This song is hot," Ciel says. It's the first time I register that rap music is pulsing from inside the building, some Turkish hip-hop song that Adip found, and now everyone at Lockwood is obsessed with it. Ciel chants the wrong words and writhes her body around as we make our way closer to the entrance.

I swing open the door and we're immediately assaulted by the air, thick with sweat and perfume. Cirque du Soleil performers twirl and flip on the stage while trays of champagne float through the room. One thing Lockwood seems unbothered with: underage drinking.

My stomach backflips into my throat as I crane my neck, searching the crowd for Henry. I don't see him anywhere. An instant pang of disappointment stabs at me. My mind clouds with questions. Who is he? Why did he shove me? Was he having a panic attack or something else?

And more importantly, *why do I care so much?*

My thoughts crack when, next to me, Ciel bursts into giggles as Adip picks her up. She wraps her legs around his waist and he plants a deep, passionate kiss on her lips. I watch for a brief second as his hands cup her ass.

Ciel and Adip have a tortured relationship that goes from hot sex to screaming and fighting to hotter sex to breakup, and back around again. I'm kinda envious of it, to be honest. It would be nice to have a little drama in my life. Sure, most people would consider a cheating boyfriend drama, but Jack messing around with Josephine feels kinda cliché. Almost boring.

Adip sets Ciel down and curls his arm around my shoulder. "You took some spill earlier. You good?"

I swallow and nod. "Yeah, I'm okay." Just when my thoughts finally dipped to something else besides Henry…and now we're back.

"If you need me to kick that guy's ass, let me know," Adip says.

I quickly defend Henry. "He didn't do anything." Sometimes I blurt out things before thinking, a side effect of living so much in my head. A coping mechanism, I suppose.

Adip shoots me a look, like a protective big brother, then gives me a quick squeeze on the shoulder before rushing off.

I twist my gaze to Ciel, who is spaced out and swooning. "So you and Adip are back on."

Ciel shakes her head, acting offended. "No, he doesn't do girl-friends. But I can have sex with him without catching feelings. This time, *I'm* using *him*." Ciel nods, clearly victorious about having the upper hand. There's no investigating I need to do here, no clues to suss out—I can already tell this will be a disaster.

I spot Jack across the room talking to a group of guys. He locks eyes with me and motions me over.

As I make my way over to Jack, Henry flashes into my brain. Not just him, but the same memory of him shoving me to the ground. A shudder runs through my body.

"If that asshole who ruined my inauguration shows up tonight…he's gonna pay," Jack says, interrupting my thoughts.

I stifle a laugh. Truth is, Jack's never been in a real fight in his life. Kids that get into Lockwood fight with their words and wallets, not with fists. Even Adip is full of shit. The closest he's ever come to a fight is watching a few guys go at it in his dad's hotel. I don't know Henry, but if physical form is any indication, it looks like he could throw a serious punch. He certainly used a lot of force to push me away. A rush of heat slides over my skin, burning me up so much I need to blow out a breath to calm down.

I don't really have the energy, or focus, to fight with Jack right now. But I'm tired of backing down. "I'm pretty sure that guy was having a panic attack. I'm more worried no one tried to help him but me."

Jack huffs, folding his arms over his chest. "You should have let him sort it out himself. Do you know him or something?"

I shrug, not wanting to give him any indication that I'm thinking about Henry. "No, I don't know him. Ciel says he's a scholarship kid." I feel awful as soon as I say it, but I know Jack will think we're on the same page and stop asking about him. Yeah, I'm being an asshole.

Adip interrupts, clapping Jack's shoulder. He looks back and forth at us, worried. "Trouble in paradise?"

Jack doesn't answer. I shrug again, awkward. Adip rakes his hand through his hair, nervous. Something's off about his mood. He's always so cool and casual, but now he looks completely freaked out.

"Look, there's a… um… surprise performance for you, Jack."

Jack looks over at him, confused.

Before Adip rushes off, he mouths, "Sorry," to me.

What the hell is going on?

Jack looks intrigued as Adip makes an announcement over the mic for everyone to take a seat. Jack and I sit front and center. Our knees knock together and Jack places his hand on my leg. Something about it feels slimy, but I close my eyes and pretend it's Henry. I know that's bad, but it's just fantasy. I'm not even sure I'll get to talk to the guy again, even though I desperately want to.

Ciel shimmies into the chair beside me, breaking my concentration. "What's happening?"

I shrug, mildly annoyed she interrupted my fantasy.

The lights dim and the place goes silent. The music blares and Josephine slinks out from behind the stage, wearing a costume I can only imagine she stole from an old Victoria's Secret fashion show. Skimpy black lace bodysuit, garters and stockings, and sky-high heels. She wears a choker fashioned with Lockwood's emblem.

She begins to dance, sultry and sexy—with actual choreography. She grinds and twirls around the stage, never taking her eyes off Jack. I look over at him, praying he finds this as absurd as I do. But he doesn't. I can tell he likes it, loves it. He crosses his hands over his lap, cracking the tension out of his knuckles. I can see him holding in his breath, then slowly blowing out the pent-up frustration.

Whispers ripple through the crowd and I know everyone is talking about her, about Jack, and about me.

My ears grow hot. I can't believe I'm watching this. And Jack is just sitting there watching her—like I'm not even here.

Unable to take anymore, I push out of my chair so hard it

crashes to the floor, but the sound barely registers above the pulsing music.

I storm out of there, hurrying down the path towards my dorm. I wouldn't even be dating Jack if it wasn't for my father. And I bet he secretly feels the same about me. We're both fulfilling a legacy our parents set out. But the least he could do is not humiliate me in public.

Fast footsteps crunch on the leaves behind me. "Natalie, wait!" It's Jack. I forge ahead, ignoring him. I don't want to talk. Not now.

"Natalie! Can we talk for a minute, please?"

I keep walking, not giving him the satisfaction of looking back. His footsteps pound closer so I speed up. Then I hear the crunch of gravel and a howl of pain.

I whirl around and see Jack sprawled on the ground. His perfect hair is shook loose, a strand dangling awkwardly in front of his face. He looks up at me and bursts out laughing. I can't help but break into laughter right along with him. I don't know what it is—all the tension, anger, hurt—but we both just need to laugh. Besides, he tripped and fell and looks ridiculous.

I walk over and kneel next to him. It finally registers how cold it is outside. The freezing air slices into my body, making me shiver. Jack takes off his suit jacket and wraps it around my shoulders.

"You should really watch where you're going," I tease, pinching his arm.

"Shut up. Don't tell anyone. I'll forever be known as the fallen president."

I laugh again. "I won't."

There was a time when Jack and I were just friends. We met when we were eight years old. Our parents were already plotting our future, but we just wanted to race around the neighborhood and get into trouble. I used to rope him into all my schemes, dragging him along as I hunted for clues about my neighbors, swearing I could uncover all their dark secrets. Most of the time I was successful.

Jack wraps me in his arms, and as we lie back on the ground, a flush of warmth teases my insides. In a strange way—as if something, or someone, has taken over my body—this actually feels good.

Jack traces his fingers along my neck, and I glide my leg up, wrapping it across his lower body. My brain feels foggy with a kaleidoscope of emotions and I can't think anymore. All thoughts drain away until all that's left is desire.

I press myself up and lean down to kiss him. My skin flushes and swells with goosebumps. I'm turned on. Really turned on. Something about the biting air, the dirty ground, and the fact that anyone could walk out of the party and see us feels exciting, dangerous, illicit. I don't know what's come over me.

Jack flips me over and lies on top, trailing kisses down my neck. I close my eyes, taking in every sensation. His hand runs up the side of my hips. I gasp and blink open my eyes and... *Henry is on top of me.*

I jerk my body and shove Jack off, my heart hammering in my chest.

"What's wrong?" His concerned eyes rove over my face.

I peer up at him, panicked and aroused at the same time. It's ice cold outside, but sweat glistens down my spine. The words dry out on my tongue, rendering me speechless, as I struggle to process everything.

A dangerous concoction of feelings swish around my brain that I don't understand. I know I'm physically here with Jack, that's the reality.

But seeing Henry was so damn... real.

CHAPTER SIX

HENRY

WES PUFFS OUT a cloud of smoke, choking on his words. "You want some?"

I shake my head no. "Not a fan of weed." I grab a stray branch off the ground and crack it into pieces. The sky is pitch black, and the small flashlight I managed to find doesn't really light up shit out here. An annoying, faint thump of music plays in the distance. My skull throbs—exploding from all the visions, all the thoughts, all the general mind-fuckery this day has provided.

Wes pops his eyebrows, curious. "Weed helps you focus." He takes another hit. "At least, it helps precogs focus."

"Yeah, I've tried it. Doesn't work for me."

I sink back against a tree and let the air leak out of my lungs. At least I can breathe better out here than in that stuffy ass school. We're hiding in the woods just outside the Lockwood gates. They're always locked—big, ornate, steel contraptions that are impossible to break open without a key. You could climb it, but again, I don't trust those fucking cameras.

Wes has as much interest in being alone as I do, and he found us a place in the far corner of the school property, a small section where you can climb the gate and dart back into the woods, if you know what you're looking for. Now I do. Finally, a place to escape, even if it's a bit tricky to get to. No cameras here.

"You're missing the big party," he says, smirking.

"I'm not much of a party guy. You?"

Wes shrugs. "Sometimes." He motions in the direction of the music. "But that's not the kinda party I'm into. That's just a circle jerk for Lockwood's finest."

A laugh escapes my throat. Jesus, that might be the first time I've laughed since I got to this school. I lodge my thumb between my eyebrows and press hard, trying to erase some of the tension.

"So, you gonna tell me about your vision?" Wes says.

I was waiting for him to ask, but I hesitate to talk about it. After how well it went in group, I'm not sure I want to tell anyone at all about my visions. Like if I say it out loud to him, it makes it true.

The cold wind whips and burns my face, and my eyes start to water. "Nah, I don't really wanna talk about it."

"Must've been a bad one," he says. "What'd you see? Someone get hurt?"

I shake my head no.

"You see someone die?"

His words sting. The throbbing in my head intensifies, a shooting pain stabbing my temple. Maybe it's the migraine, but I have a sudden impulse to blurt out everything.

"Yeah, I saw someone die," I grunt under my breath. The stabbing pain begins to dissolve, like some weird release.

"Someone you know?"

I swallow. Should I tell him? What if he reacts the same way Leonard and the rest of the group did? The dull ache in my head still festers. Maybe spilling everything to this dude will finally give me some damn peace. Even for one night. Shit, at this point, I'd take thirty seconds of peace.

"I saw that girl Natalie Cov—"

"Natalie Covington?" he says, as if he knows her well. I instantly regret telling him and feel a deep pang in my gut. Jealousy climbs through my brain. I don't like that he knows her. *Why don't I like it?* My head is feeling better, but my heart feels like it's prepping for the apocalypse. And then I see…

Natalie's eyes, widening in sheer terror. She must be looking at something. Or someone. *A black coat lies on the ground.* That was the coat she wore when I saw her running in an earlier vision. Why isn't she wearing it? Where is she?

I attempt to shrug off the vision, focusing on finding out what the hell Wes knows.

"You know her?" I ask Wes, bracing myself for his answer.

"Nah, not really. I see her around campus. Her and her boyfriend are the golden couple. Like royalty, or some shit. She's more like his property—required to be on his arm at all times." Wes chuckles. There's another twist in my gut when he talks about them together. He continues to pry. "So, what's gonna happen to the first lady of Lockwood?"

I look over at him, puffing on his joint, so nonchalant. What a dick. Must be nice to feel so relaxed when you're not plagued with visions of a girl being murdered. "All I can piece together is someone chasing her, then attacking her, killing her."

"She's gonna die, huh? Well, now I feel like an ass for talking about her. What are you gonna do?"

"Nothing," I snap, almost offended he would even ask—even *think* I'd do something other than keep it a secret.

"Really?" he says, and makes a face, as if he would do something different. It pisses me off.

"Yeah, really. We can't fucking do anything." Like I should even have to tell him that. My headache's now completely gone, but the stabbing pain has moved into my chest.

Wes stubs out his joint and stands, bouncing on his feet to keep warm. "If you wanna believe that."

Okay, now he's really pissing me off. I have a deep desire to punch him in his smug hipster face. Talking about my vision got rid of my headache. Maybe punching him will get rid of my chest pain, and as a bonus—get rid of this idiot.

"It's not about what I *want* to believe. And you know that," I say.

"Actually, I *don't* know that," Wes says. "I don't buy into all the repressive shit we're fed."

I stare at him, stunned. I've met hundreds of precogs, and never once have any of them questioned the authority. My anger starts to dissolve and I'm sorta intrigued by this guy. At least intrigued enough not to clock him in the jaw. "So what? You're some rogue outlier?"

"You can call me whatever you want, man. Outlier, truther, conspiracy theorist—I don't care about labels. I just know we don't have the whole story," Wes says. "What if there are no consequences to changing a vision?"

I laugh, incredulous. This guy is insane. Great, not only am I stuck at this piece of shit school, I'm now stuck with some conspiracy theory wacko who's about to tell me the earth is flat.

I consider leaving, maybe take a walk in the woods alone to process all this shit, but I decide to stick around and entertain Wes's theories. What else am I going to do to pass the time? At least it's momentarily distracting me from these fucking visions.

"Okay, so what's the whole story?" I say, amused.

Wes looks at me, his expression suddenly serious.

Oh, this is gonna be good.

He crouches down and leans forward, like he's about to tell a campfire ghost story. I suppress the urge to burst out laughing.

"I know someone who changed one of his visions."

My stomach plummets. The only stories I've heard about precogs changing visions are in our precog scripture, and those stories do not go well. Like the time some guy from the eighteenth century—Alcott, I think his name was? He changed a vision and was captured by the townspeople who swore he was into black magic. They stripped him and tied cement blocks to his feet, tossing him in the lake to drown. Another precog from the nineteenth century was caught by a group of scientists who conducted horrific experiments on her until she escaped by committing suicide. These stories rattle on for about 500 chapters, and I read them enough times growing up to scare the shit outta me.

I'm not naive to think that no one has tried, or will try, to change a vision in modern times, but I've never heard a story from someone I know. I'm betting Wes is bullshitting me and doesn't know anyone, either. "Like, some guy you heard a rumor about? Or someone you actually know?"

"My older brother," he says.

Well, shit. My nerves spike. He could be lying. But something tells me there's a kernel of truth to this. "What happened?"

"He had a vision of his girlfriend dying in a car accident. He reacted the same way you did. He couldn't piece together exactly when or how it would happen, but he ended up telling her."

My curiosity spikes. "And then what?"

"She just started avoiding cars. She walked, rode her bike, took the subway. It was easy, they lived in Manhattan."

I process this for a second. "You said 'lived.' Does that mean they no longer live there?"

"I don't know where they live. Once he told her about his vision and she tried to avoid it, weird shit started happening."

"Like what?"

"My brother would say he felt different—like stronger, or clearer, or… I don't even know."

I shake my head and laugh at how insane this sounds. I'm about to just get up and clap him on the back, thanking him for the joke—he made me laugh twice today. Even my chest pain is starting to go away.

"And then, they both disappeared," he says.

Disappeared? I sit with his grim story. Disappeared, how? I roll the tension out of my shoulders, suddenly aware of how stiff I am. On the one hand, this sounds like complete bullshit. On the other, it sounds… possible? "What do you think happened to them?"

Wes shrugs. "Don't know. Maybe they just ran away together. Everything was fine before that, like I said. The only way to find out is to change a vision and see what happens."

I shift my body off the cold ground and stand, shaking the dirt and leaves off my coat and sweatpants. "Then why don't you just do it?"

"Cause I don't have any visions worth changing. Mine are so fragmented, I don't even know what, or who, they're about," he says. "If I had a vision like yours, I wouldn't sit on it."

His words slam into my brain. This is the first time in my life anyone's encouraged me to change a vision. It sounds crazy, but now I can't stop thinking about it—curiosity is murdering my soul.

"Okay, let's say I told Natalie. She'd never believe me," I say. "I don't know her—don't have any relationship with her. Your brother's girlfriend would be inclined to believe him because they were together… but Natalie?" I shake my head at the ridiculous thought. I can just imagine her glaring at me like I'm insane, spreading it all around school—*guess what that freak told me?* Then she'd probably call her rich daddy and tell him, he would call the cops, and who knew what would happen after that? Nope, I'm not even gonna chance it. As much as I want to.

"Maybe you can convince her, give her a reason to believe," Wes says. He looks at me, challenging, daring me, but this isn't a game. At least, not one I think I want to play.

CHAPTER SEVEN

NATALIE

I PROMISED MYSELF I wouldn't do this.

I follow behind Henry at a careful distance to make sure he won't notice me. It helps that most of the students at Lockwood have their head so far up their own ass they have no clue what's going on around them. Maybe he's like that too.

Henry's taking his sweet time making his way down the winding path. I typically clip down it at a crazy speed, mostly hoping to avoid talking to people. It's not that I don't like people, I just don't enjoy small talk, like, "Wow, it's rainy out here!" Yes, genius, it's the Pacific Northwest. We know this.

I exhale into the frosty fall air and yank down my emerald green beanie, tucking it further down over my ears while raking my eyes over the back of Henry, noticing the way the fabric of his coat stretches over his broad and muscular shoulders—far more muscular than the other kids at Lockwood, really. Impressive, actually, to be able to make out someone's physique under a thick, puffy coat—but clearly he's pulling it off.

He's not wearing a hat and his dark, unruly hair gleams in the sun. It's thick and wavy, unfussy—like he just steps out of the shower and lets it dry on its own.

I check my watch—only ten minutes until class. I should be there already, scrambling over my notes for today's exam, but instead, I'm here, following him. I'm not sure what I expect to learn from this little mission. He doesn't speak to anyone, or even look at anyone. His belongings are all zipped up in a backpack slung over his shoulder. He doesn't have a vice like smoking, at least not that he's indulging in now. He just keeps striding ahead at an annoyingly slow pace. Maybe he doesn't want to go wherever he's going?

He's headed to the north side of campus and I need to go south. Dammit. Do I risk being late to class and keep following him? Or just pick up this investigation later?

I can't seem to answer my own question, so my legs make up their mind for me. I forge ahead through the dense trees lining the path, bombarded by the chatter and laughter of Lockwood students. The campus is buzzing today, perfect for when you want to blend into the crowd.

A brisk shot of wind blows through my curls and I tuck my coat tighter around my body, looking down for a second before I smack into someone.

Just as I'm about to apologize and keep up my Henry investigation, I look up and meet Jack's eyes.

"Where are you going? Aren't you gonna be late for class?"

And just like that, I've lost track of my mark. My mind whips together an excuse. "I forgot something in my room."

Jack eyes me, and I can tell he's skeptical, but he rarely questions me. Sometimes I wish he would, because it would mean he cares, but one thing I know about Jack—he's way too self-absorbed for follow-up questions.

⤫

After completely losing track of Henry after Jack's interruption, I race into French class just in time. "Veuillez vous asseoir, s'il vous plaît," Madame Whitney says.

Or Ms. Whitney, as I know her. She doubles as a student advisor and French class teacher, and she's one of the few people I really like here so far. As a teacher, she's formidable—a stickler for the rules. As an advisor, she's nurturing and encouraging.

Students shuffle into their seats. I peel open my textbook and get lost in my notes. I'm decent at most subjects, but foreign language—not so much. French class is my special kind of nightmare.

"Nous accueillons un nouvel élève—we have a new student," Ms. Whitney announces. I barely register what she's saying as I pore over my notes. "Bienvenue, Henry Thorne."

Jolted by the mention of his name, I snap my head up as he saunters in. He catches me looking at him. I immediately put my head back down, my cheeks burning, my breath choppy. He was headed in the opposite direction—why is he here? Why the hell am I so flustered? Did he know I was following him?

Ms. Whitney motions for him to take a seat near the front and I exhale a big breath, happy that he's not sitting near me. I couldn't even try to get clues about him—it would be obvious, sitting so close. He'd probably think I was interested in him, and I can't have him thinking that.

As my head floods with rationalizations, he turns and looks right at me with a mysterious expression that causes goosebumps to ripple across my skin. I break his gaze, pretending to be bored, even annoyed, that he can't stop looking at me. Even though that's total bullshit.

Ciel giggles in the chair next to me. I glance over. "What?" I whisper.

She winks at me and scribbles a note, passes it over. I take it, trying to be discreet. I crinkle it open as Ms. Whitney begins her lecture about today's exam.

Scholarship kid is so into you.

I crumple the note into a ball and shake my head at her, mouthing, "no he's not." Ciel looks at me with disbelief.

"Madamoiselles, is there something you want to share with the class?"

Ciel and I look at Ms. Whitney with innocent wide eyes. Henry's neck is still craned and I'm in full view. I put my hand over the note, scared he might be able to read it from across the room, even though I know that's ridiculous. And, why am I even scared of this guy? *I* was following *him*.

"No passing notes. Next time, I'll send you to the headmaster."

Ciel and I nod in compliance. I tuck the crumpled note under my textbook and yank at one of my curls, a vice to shake out some of my nerves.

"Henry, you have some catching up to do. Perhaps you can study with another student," Ms. Whitney says.

Great, now all I can think about is being chosen as his study buddy. It's the most horrifying and exhilarating proposition I've heard this year. Hell, this lifetime. Imagine what I could learn about him if I could just get into his room.

Henry leans back in his chair, cool and unbothered. "Je parle français couramment," he says.

Ms. Whitney looks at him, confused. I don't know a lot of French, but I know he just claimed to speak it fluently. Laughter rings out through the classroom. I never would have pegged this guy as the class clown type. Huh, Henry Thorne is surprising. I jot that on my mental whiteboard.

"Je ne devrais pas suivre ce cours ridicule mais tous les autres étaient complets," he says.

Everyone looks around in shock—most of us have no idea what he just said, but he sounds pretty damn good at this language.

He stands and faces the class. "I said I shouldn't be in this stupid class, but all the others were full," he translates. His eyes flick to mine before he takes his seat, draping a bored arm over the empty chair next to him.

Ms. Whitney clears her throat, obviously flustered. "Well, Mr. Thorne, perhaps you can shift your attitude about this class and use your flair for the language as a mentor to your fellow students."

Interesting. The humanitarian also speaks fluent French. Also adding that to the very brief list of things I know about him.

Suddenly, brief isn't cutting it.

I need to move this little investigation along.

⮜

The bell rings to signal class dismissal. I keep my eyes on Henry as he collects his unopened textbook and storms out. Then I gather my things in a messy pile and don't even bother putting them in my bag so I can scramble after him.

His long legs quickly eat up the distance as he moves down the hallway. I race after him, bumping into a few other students along the way.

Finally, I catch up. I know he sees me, but he doesn't acknowledge it. He certainly had no problem staring me down in class—why is he acting like I don't exist now?

"Hey, I'm Natalie," I say, trying not to come off like some breathless groupie, but it's hard when I'm speed walking to keep in step with him.

"I know who you are," he says.

He still doesn't look at me or make any attempt at conversation. Heat rises in my body and my blood starts to boil. Maybe Jack was right and I should have just let him have a panic attack and pass out. *Jerk.*

"I just wanted to see if you were okay after what happened the other day, but clearly you're fine."

He doesn't answer, just keeps walking—increasing the pace with his long, muscular legs until he shoves the door open and we're outside. The cold wind rips through to my bones. Why am I still following him? I stop walking, but he advances on… like I don't exist.

I shout after him. "You gave me a bruise, you know!"

He freezes and turns back to me. I wait for an apologetic glance, a surreptitious "I'm sorry." Anything that shows remorse.

None of that happens.

Instead, he storms back to me—coming so close to my face that I can smell his warm, minty breath. Without a word, he yanks the books from my hands.

"Hey!" I shout, trying to wrestle them back. My textbook slams to the ground and I manage to rip back my notebook, leaving him holding Ciel's note.

I swallow, horrified, as he unfolds it and reads the words to himself—*Scholarship kid is so into you.* With anger dancing in his eyes, he crumples the note and throws it at me. The paper bounces off my chest. My mind races with fury, but I'm too shocked to say or do anything.

He leans into me, his lips hovering close to mine. I should

back away, scream at him, smack him, throw the note at him—but I don't. I'm frozen, paralyzed with intensity and electricity, sweltering with emotion. I can't stop staring at his lips—plump, red, moist. A centimeter from touching mine.

"I'm not into you," he says in a throaty, choppy groan.

Then he walks away, and I swallow the retort stuck in my throat. I want to scream after him—tell him I don't give a shit how he feels because I would never be into someone like him.

But I won't. Because that would be weakness. And I'm not fucking weak. I am curious, though.

Who are you, Henry Thorne? And why do you hate me?

You can run away all you want, but I'll find out the truth.

CHAPTER EIGHT

HENRY

I CRINGE AS I walk away from her. Why am I such an asshole?

I couldn't even manage two civil words to her. I could have just lied, told her I was fine, moved on. But who am I kidding? There is no moving on from her or this entire fucked up situation.

I look back to see if she's still standing there. She's not. All that's left is an empty patch of grass, crisp orange leaves circling in the wind before settling where she stood. I clench my fists, equal parts relieved and disappointed. Really, more disappointed. Angry, even. Maybe it's because I'm so used to seeing her in my head, I expect her to be there every time I look.

I turn and race down the winding path to the dining hall, hoping to forget the whole incident. Warmth hits as I shove open the door and take my place in the line for coffee that's about twenty students deep. Coffee is my one and only vice, necessary since I spend so many of my nights wide awake and can barely keep my eyes open during class. I keep my head down, alone with my thoughts.

I bruised her. She couldn't have fallen that hard. Where the hell does she have a bruise? A dull tension stings my head and I pinch the bridge of my nose. Can this line move so I can get some fucking caffeine?

It was an accident. I didn't mean to shove her. I certainly didn't mean to leave a mark. It's dirty and disgusting, what I did. Like an abusive husband who makes excuses after beating on his wife. What kind of darkness is bottled up inside of me?

I only meant to lightly push her away—a touch to indicate that I wanted to get up because I couldn't form words. I didn't even put any muscle into it. How did she have such a violent, visceral reaction to my touch?

I try to shake Natalie from my mind as the line inches forward, but within seconds, I'm fisting my hands again, frustration brewing. Whatever my intention with Natalie, it's no excuse. It was shitty of me to push her, and I need to apologize. But what am I supposed to say? *Oh, I'm sorry, Natalie, but I was having a vision about your murder, so I hope you accept my apology.*

I look up at the line snaked around the dining hall, moving so fucking slow. I just want a black coffee, but everyone's ordering their fancy lattes with twenty different swaps—almond milk foam with just a half pump of sugar-free vanilla-caramel-hazelnut-some-other-shit swirl. By the time they're done, it's not even coffee. Why bother?

The line moves another inch and frustration singes my skin. I close my eyes to exhale some anger and I see…

Night. The ground—broken branches and soggy orange leaves. It looks wet. Maybe it's raining. Screams. Natalie's pleading, muffled. A hand wearing a white glove grips her arm.

I blink open my eyes. The line has moved a bit and there's an empty space in front of me. Bile rises in my throat as I piece together another part of Natalie's horrific attack.

Some idiot behind me starts bitching for me to move up in line. I have to get out of here. I pivot to leave, accidentally bumping into him.

"Yo, watch where you're going, bro."

I grumble an apology, having no desire to argue with this whiny douchebag. I'm desperate for a different sort of release.

❧

I slam my fist again and again into a dusty punching bag. I'd rather my pain be physical than mental. It's easier that way.

The Lockwood gym is filled with saunas, state-of-the-art equipment, and those stupid Pilates machines that look like medieval torture devices. When I asked the fitness director if they had boxing equipment, he led me to a room in the basement filled with stuff that no one uses. Punching bag, gloves and wraps, and a bunch of mismatched free weights. My kinda place.

As I crash my fist into the bag over and over, I remember flashes of my vision.

Natalie running away, gripped with fear.

Punch.

The knife plunged into her chest.

Punch.

Her garbled screams.

I throttle the bag one last time, nearly knocking it off the chain as it swings and creaks.

This is insane. How am I supposed to keep this a secret? How am I supposed to sit in front of her in class, just waiting and watching until she's fucking dead?

The door flings open and the fitness director enters the room. I forget his name—Jim? John? Jeremy. It's Jeremy. "Thorne, your dad's on the phone."

I rip the Velcro and remove the gloves, stretching out my sore hands. "My dad? It's not family phone day, or whatever they call it here."

❧

I'm led by some Lockwood administrator into the room where we're allowed family calls once a week. Or in this case, when your family demands it.

The room is a bizarre setup—like prison meets yoga center. There are twenty phone banks, kind of like cubicles—but instead of two-way glass, you're facing a wall with motivational prints of doves and oceans with empty self-help platitudes like, "Don't follow your dreams, chase them."

Side panels flank each phone bank for privacy, but who are we kidding—everyone can hear your conversation. I'm betting the phones are bugged too.

Each station houses a brightly colored journal and pen, a vase of fresh flowers, a French press of hot coffee, and a bottle of sparkling water. I'd give up all this fancy shit for some privacy. Though, I guess it's cool to have coffee, since I couldn't get some earlier.

The administrator points to phone bank number sixteen. My face still drips with sweat from the gym and I lift my shirt to wipe it off, exposing my stomach. When I re-open my eyes, I catch a girl staring at me. I didn't realize anyone else was in here. She's talking quietly on the phone across the room, eyes glassy with tears. I feel bad she's crying, but I have no energy to worry about anyone else right now. There's only one girl on my mind… and she's about to die.

I slump down in the chair and pick up the phone. "Hey."

"Henry, um—how are things?" I'm struck by how strange he sounds. Oliver is usually collected, the kind of guy who thinks before he says anything. Not necessarily in a calculated way, just intentional.

"Things are things. What's up?"

"I want to make sure you're okay. Especially after hearing what you spoke about with Leonard."

My pulse races. What does he mean what I talked about with Leonard? Group is supposed to be confidential. Did Leonard tell him what I said?

I decide to play dumb. "I don't know what you mean."

There's an ominous silence on the end of the line, a moment that seems to trail on for eternity. "Henry, Leonard told me. I can't stress how serious this situation is."

Annoyed, I rake my hand through my sweaty hair. *Yeah, Oliver, I'm aware this is serious. You have no idea how serious this is.* "Why did Leonard tell you? I told him I was fine. Isn't the point of sharing in group to have confidentiality?"

"I'm sure you can appreciate that something like this needs to be shared with your guardian," he says.

I grit my teeth, anger ricocheting through my veins. I hate when he says he's my guardian. I fucking hate it. It reminds me that I'm a disposable piece of trash. I have no idea who my real mom or dad is. Sure, I feel incredibly lucky that Oliver raised me, but the point is, no one really wanted me. Oliver didn't want me—he didn't choose me. He was saddled with me by the precog authority to make sure I learned all the ways and rules of our kind. Maybe that guy Wes is on to something after all.

"I'm fine. Is this the big emergency you called for?" I can barely conceal my disdain for him and this entire conversation.

"Yes. It *is* an emergency. You need to understand the gravity of this situation. Are you still…?" I know he can't finish the sentence, in case these phones are tapped—but I know what he means. Am I still having these visions?

"No," I lie. I have a fierce need all of a sudden to protect my secret—and most of all, to protect Natalie.

"Perhaps you should finish your senior year elsewhere."

My heart leaps into my throat. I can't leave. Can't leave her. Every inch of my body panics, and the need to save her overwhelms any rational thought. Oliver's reaction and impingement on my privacy tells me he doesn't trust me at all. He has a right to be worried—I don't trust myself. But at this point, I'm not sure I trust him, either.

"I'm staying. What I shared in group isn't happening anymore. Besides, I don't want you to go through the trouble—you're just my guardian." I had to get in that dig.

Oliver huffs in disappointment. "Henry, that's not what I meant."

"It's cool, Oliver. Lockwood is where I belong. Thanks for checking in, though." I hang up before he can say another word.

I sink back in the chair and pour myself a cup of pretentious coffee from this French press, taking a huge gulp. Why was Oliver so freaked out? If Leonard told him what I shared in group, then all he knows is that I saw a random girl have boyfriend trouble. It seems bizarre that he would react like this over a mundane vision.

I chug down more caffeine. Something's not sitting right with me, and I'm suddenly more steeped in loneliness than ever. My foster brothers and sisters are spread out across the world, and I never bonded enough with any of them to confide in them. I guess that's always been one of my biggest issues—I don't bond with anyone. Oliver was the closest I've come to bonding and, well, maybe that was just surface-level shit too.

"Trouble at home?"

I look up, and the girl who was crying on the phone is standing in front of me, dabbing her eye with a tissue. She's short, tiny, almost doll-like. Her blonde hair so light it appears to blend into her porcelain skin. There's a sparkle to her eyes but not because of the color or the tears. She's got a single rhinestone under each lash line—I'm guessing it's some kind of makeup trend.

"Eh, not really. Just a misunderstanding." I hope she gives up with the prying. She seems nice and all, but I'm not in the mood for sharing. And she's clearly going through something I'm not equipped to handle.

"I'm Josephine." She extends her hand to mine.

To be polite, I shake it. "Henry."

She squeezes my hand and bites her lip, and I'm pretty sure she's flirting with me. I don't want to give her the wrong impression or lead her on, so I pull my hand away. Defeat washes over her expression and her pouty red lips curl into a frown. Great—this is the last thing I want to deal with right now.

"Look, I don't mean to be rude. I'm just having a shit day. I really need to head back to my dorm and get a shower." I stand, abrupt, hoping she doesn't take offense.

"It's fine. I can understand you not wanting to talk to me after what happened. No one wants to be anywhere near me."

I stare at her, confused. "Why don't people want to be near you?"

She stares back at me in shock. There's a glimmer of hope and happiness in her eyes, and a ghost of a smile plays on her lips. "You don't know?"

I shake my head, no clue what she's talking about.

"I'm basically the school pariah. I did something that seemed like a good idea at the time, but it didn't go over so well."

She's vague, and I get the vibe she wants me to coax it out of her. I really don't have the patience or interest, even though I feel bad for her. "Well, I'm an eternal pariah. The trick is to not give a shit about anybody. Just worry about you." I gulp down the last sip of coffee and give her a light, friendly squeeze on the shoulder. "I gotta run. Nice to meet you, Josephine."

I race out of there before she can rope me into any more conversation. I speed walk down the campus trail, grateful that it's pretty empty right now so I can be alone with my thoughts.

I laugh at myself and the advice I just gave that girl. What a fucking hypocrite. I'm telling her not to care about anybody when literally every second of my life is spent obsessing and caring about a girl I don't even know.

I'm the pariah. I hurt people, even if I don't intend to. Maybe my mom and dad were right for giving me up. I'm a selfish asshole, and I'm keeping my vision of Natalie a secret because I want to save myself instead of saving her.

She's not a pariah. She's a good person. I have a desk full of proof.

Natalie deserves better. She deserves to live. I just need her to trust me… to believe me when I tell her what's about to happen.

CHAPTER NINE

NATALIE

TALK TO YOURSELF *like you would someone you love.*

That's the sign hanging on Ms. Whitney's office door. I hate these empty platitudes. I talk to myself all the time. And I love myself. I guess. So take that, dumb sign.

I look down and realize I'm picking my cuticles raw—a terrible habit. And now it's multiplied ever since I met Henry. Why does it bug me so much that he said he isn't into me? I hate that I keep replaying his words in my mind, over and over. And I hate even more that I care. I lick a droplet of blood from the corner of one of my fingernails and scrutinize the stubby, chapped mess I've made.

Ms. Whitney's door flings open and Adip saunters out. He spots me and winces like I'm going to hit him. What's his deal?

I start to head inside the office when Adip blocks the way, staring at me with his apologetic, soulful brown eyes that tend to get him anything he wants. "Natty, I seriously had no idea Josephine was going to do that weird dance, I swear. She just told me to announce her 'performance.'" He puts the word "performance" in unfortunate air quotes.

I nearly forgot about Josephine's little dance, and at this point, it's kind of the last thing I care about. "It's cool. You don't have to make such a big deal of it."

"Really? So you're not mad?"

I shake my head no, willing this conversation to be over.

"Good. Cause you're a friend and I care about you. And you give the best advice. So, I found out that Ciel is into someone else."

I cut him off, holding my hand up to his mouth. I should have known that soulful, brown-eyed stare meant he was after something. And that "something" is free therapy from me. Normally I don't mind listening, but my brain is too clogged.

Adip keeps talking, muffled by my hand. "But she said she wanted to give this a real shot."

I remove my hand, so over their drama.

"Did she mention anything to you?" he says.

"I'm not getting in the middle of this. But no, she didn't say anything. Just *talk* to her."

I do know that Ciel has a thing for novelty. It's like the moment the dust settles and things normalize, she'll find someone new to dominate her interest. But it's not my place, nor do I want to get involved.

"I gotta go," I say, pointing to Ms. Whitney's office. Adip gives me a quick hug and lets me off the hook.

I step inside Ms. Whitney's office. It's like a Pinterest board come to life—bright white walls, pops of color, stripes and polka dots. Her decor is a stark contrast to the rest of Lockwood, which looks more like a goth Roman cathedral.

I plop down onto the sunny yellow couch and smile. Ms. Whitney smiles back. "How are you enjoying your first few weeks at Lockwood, Natalie?"

I lie. "I like it."

She believes me. "I thought you'd be interested in this." She hands over a small stack of papers.

It's an application for Unite for Sight, a volunteer organization of community-based assistants for eye doctors—my stomach gets that familiar tight pull of desire. I've always wanted to be an eye doctor. I know that's weirdly specific, but I love eyes. You can see the truth in them, and when you're surrounded by a bunch of rich people who are basically liars for a living, seeing into someone's eyes is important.

When I was little, my mom took me to a small town in Indonesia to help eye doctors give exams to kids without medical care. Several of them had childhood glaucoma and were at serious risk of losing their vision. It really smacked me in the heart, realizing these kids didn't have access to basic medical care and their vision was nearly ruined due to the harsh conditions they lived in. After we left, Mom paid for corrective surgery for all the kids in the village, and those kids still send letters every year thanking her for the gift of sight. I wish she was still alive to read them. She's been gone for one year, nine months, and twelve days. I count every single one.

Mom was like no one I've ever met. Her eyes were magical, and you could see everything she was thinking. They were the most glorious green color, and changed shades depending on her mood—emerald when she was mad, light jade when she was happy.

Her eyes were so similar to Henry's.

"What do you think about the opportunity?" Ms. Whitney snaps me from my thoughts.

I quickly collect myself and look over the forms. "It looks amazing, but I'm here in school on these dates."

Ms. Whitney smiles. "Well, this particular volunteer initiative is in northern France. I've decided to put together a handful of students from our French class, so it will be a school-sanctioned trip. It's only a week long, so I should have no problem getting it approved."

My heart thrums. School sanctioned. French class. Henry. "Um, so it's just students from our class?"

"If we can get enough. We only need four."

My heart is now in my throat, practically choking me. A week in France…with Henry. Surely she'll want to take him. He does volunteer missions, he speaks fluent French. My desire for this opportunity clashes with the idea of being trapped with him and his smug face on a volunteer mission for an entire week. He probably thinks I'm into him too. Just a pathetic girl pining after Mr. Tortured. Fuck off.

"It sounds great, but I should probably just focus on my schoolwork right now. I have so much to study. Maybe they'll do another one over the summer."

Ms. Whitney shoots me a look of deep concern. "Is everything okay, Natalie? You seem a little distracted."

I nod fervently, trying not to give myself away, but making it worse. Guess I'm not as good of a liar as I thought.

"This is a great opportunity for you, and you'll have plenty of time to study on the trip." Ms. Whitney ditches her chair and sits next to me on the couch. "Do you not want to go because of Jack?"

I'm so relieved she didn't say Henry, word vomit takes over. "No, Jack wouldn't care if I went. He's focused on being class president. It's awesome to watch him achieve such a big dream, and of course he's already planning his future speech for when he becomes class president at Harvard. Did I tell you we're planning a visit to Harvard soon to meet the dean? And he's already researching all the organizations he wants us to join."

Ms. Whitney shoots me a stern look. "I thought you wanted to go to Princeton because they have the best optometry program?"

"Oh, I'm still undecided." The truth is, my father has a big problem with Princeton. He's a Harvard man, too, and he's waving my tuition over my head. Unless I can figure out a scholarship situation, it's probably Harvard or bust. I get that this is a total privileged girl problem and everyone should give me a collective eye roll.

"Natalie, if you want to pursue your dream, you can't follow someone else's path. I know Jack is an important part of your life, but couples attend different universities all the time. Let Jack chase his own dreams at Harvard. Don't give up on yours."

I don't want to give her any more ammunition, so I let her think the problem is Jack. But Harvard is a foregone conclusion. I've been wearing Harvard sweatshirts and chanting the fight song since I was five. It is what it is.

⁓

Hours later, I'm stuffed into an all-purpose room on campus while Ciel twirls in front of the mirror in a silky red gown. A bunch of other girls from my class try on dresses around us. It's a madhouse of shiny fabric and beads and sequins, and I want no part of it.

Ciel cranes her neck to peek at her backside. "It doesn't show off my curves like the blue one. Why aren't you trying on any dresses?" Ciel taps her foot at me, annoyed.

I despise all of this pomp and circumstance. The Lockwood Ball is coming up, and since we can't leave school property, designers send in gowns for us. I know that sounds extravagant and dreamy, but it's ridiculous. A bunch of Lockwood girls gathered in an empty classroom, clawing over the best dresses on the racks. It's all-out war.

The dresses are, of course, beautiful, but I'm just not all that into dressing up. I'll wait until everyone fights over the dresses they want, and pluck from the leftovers.

Ciel slips off the red dress and hands it to me. "You try." I make a face, but she shoots me a glare indicating she's not giving up.

I groan as I disrobe and glide on the silky material. Ciel zips it up behind me. It's a little too big, but fits okay. I guess it's not the worst thing I've worn.

"See, it looks amazing on you! Red is so your color." Ciel secretly whips a burner phone out of her purse.

My stomach sinks as I conceal the phone with my hand. Cell phones are forbidden at Lockwood, punishable by expulsion, and if Ciel gets caught, she's fucked.

"Where did you get that?"

"Shhhh." She quiets me and shows me the screen. "Look, someone made a Girls of Lockwood account and it's got almost a million followers. They made me the featured pic."

I grab the phone from her and scroll through the weird account. Photos of Ciel and a bunch of other girls. "This is bizarre."

Ciel rips back the phone. "No it's not. People love looking at what they can't have." Ciel scrolls through the feed, eyes sparkling with delight. "I wonder how they get these photos."

Amateur hour. "I'm sure people here just send them in. It's like when celebrities call the paparazzi on themselves. It's just for attention."

"Well I didn't send anyone anything, so I guess someone is secretly photographing me." Ciel can't wipe the grin off her face.

I know Ciel likes this stuff, but I'm not into yet another revolting version of Hot or Not.

The flash goes off in my face from Ciel's phone. "What are you doing?"

"Taking your picture in this sexy red dress and submitting it to Girls of Lockwood."

I practically tackle her. "No, you're not. I don't want to be on that profile."

"Why? You're totally hot. You're like the angry girl in glasses in every romantic comedy, minus the glasses."

"Stop!" I manage to wrestle the phone from her grip and delete the photo. Ciel huffs, taking back her burner phone.

I slip the red dress onto the hanger and put it back onto the rack.

"Why aren't you taking that?" Ciel asks.

I shrug. "I'll just wait until everyone makes their choice." I slump back into the chair and pick at my fingers again.

Ciel rips the dress off the rack. "Why are you being so weird today? Is it because that stupid scholarship kid said he wasn't into you? Who cares? You don't want him anyway."

Damn, I knew it was a mistake to tell Ciel about that. I was just so irritated—more irritated than I want to admit—and I needed to blurt it out to someone. I should have kept my mouth shut.

I'm not into you.

His words are seared into my brain in that raspy, choppy voice. My body heats in rage.

I climb out of the chair. "I don't care about him. I'm just tired, and we have another stupid French exam tomorrow that I'm totally gonna fail if I don't study."

Before I can escape with my lies, Ciel plops the red dress in my hands. I don't have the energy to fight with her.

I trek back to my room, wrangling the stupid dress in my arms. Ugh, I wish I didn't care about what Henry said. I wish I didn't care about anything except getting good grades so I can get a damn scholarship to the university I want. Maybe that should be my new focus—homework, school, studies, college, optometry. Yes, that's what I should concentrate on. Forget Henry. He's not worth an investigation, or my time. Who needs that asshole?

I'm not into you. I let his words loop around one more time in my mind.

Well guess what, Henry Thorne?

I'm not into you, either.

CHAPTER TEN

HENRY

I TOSS MY French exam onto Ms. Whitney's desk, and it takes all my willpower not to roll my eyes. I could have taken that in my sleep. As I turn back to my desk, I flick my gaze to Natalie, who appears to be sweating this test. She's rubbing the back of her neck with her hand and breathing out in soft, frustrated exhales.

Her eyes catch mine. I quickly look away from her and sit back down in my chair. I've decided to tell her, warn her. Now the trick is to get her to listen to me… to believe me. I'm a complete stranger, and an asshole at that. Likely the last person she wants to talk to, or even see. I cross my arms over my chest, biding time until everyone finishes their quiz.

Another fifteen minutes grazes on before Ms. Whitney makes everyone stop, and she grades the exams on the spot. I ace it, obviously, since I'm fluent in this shit. Ms. Whitney tosses me a look of remorse when she hands me my exam. Guess she feels bad that this class is so boring for me. She's right, but it's also my only shot at getting close to Natalie—so I'll deal with the boredom.

The other students rumble with anything from minor groans to utter defeat as they peek at their scores. I have to admit this class is pretty advanced if you don't speak the language, and I feel a little bad for everyone else.

When class is dismissed, I turn back to Natalie. The other students couldn't escape the classroom fast enough, but there she is—still paralyzed at her desk. My guess is that she's one of the people who failed the exam. Perfect.

I walk over and look down at her. She doesn't look up at me, but I can tell she knows I'm there. She's pissed at me, and I don't blame her. I already lied and told her I wasn't into her in the worst possible way, and now here I am hovering over her. Talk about mixed signals.

I spin a chair around and sit backwards on it, staring right at her. She still doesn't look at me. Okay, she definitely hates me. Gaining her trust might be harder than expected.

I look at her exam—ouch. She failed spectacularly. "Need some help?"

She still won't look at me, and shakes her head no. I move in closer, craning my head under hers to try and make her look at me. It doesn't work. Damn, she's tougher than I thought, but I'm not giving up.

When she can't avoid my gaze any longer, she cranks her head to the side and stares out the window, fixating on I don't know what. A tree? The sunlight catches the sprinkle of freckles across her nose and cheeks. They're only visible when you're really close to her. *Fuck, she's beautiful.*

"You sure you don't need help?" I smirk, trying to make light of the situation. She can't ignore me forever.

"No." She continues to stare out the window in defiance.

I point at her test. "Okay, 'cause this looks like you need help."

She puffs out a frustrated breath. A laugh escapes my throat. She whips her eyes to mine in fury. "I'm glad my failure is so funny to you." Her beautiful brown eyes start to morph into a shade of emerald the madder she gets. I've never seen that happen to someone before.

I hold up my hands in playful surrender. "I'm not making fun of you. I'm just trying to help."

"What, are you going to crumple up my exam and throw that at me too?"

She stands, and I know she's about to storm out on me. Without thinking, I grip her wrists to hold her in place—the gesture sending a bolt of heat through my body, and I'm scared I'm about to have another vision.

I remove my hands and realize she's now frozen in shock. Maybe she had the same reaction, the same heat, from my touch. Or maybe I just completely fucked up and she's about to slap me.

I clear the tension from my throat. "I can tutor you, if you want."

Now she looks even more pissed off. I almost worry that she knows something… about me, my ability, what's going to happen. No, that can't be.

"I don't need a tutor." She pulls herself together and makes a scene of collecting her things. I can't let her leave. The classroom is now empty—even Ms. Whitney is gone.

She slings her backpack over her shoulder and starts to race to the door. I block the doorway with my body in one swift move, extending out my arms. She glares up at me, annoyed. "Move."

I cock my head at her, and it's hard not to stare. I inhale and catch a hint of her scent—she smells amazing. Like cinnamon, sweet and a little spicy. I have an overwhelming urge to bend down and nuzzle into her neck, inhaling more of her, but I know that will just drive her away for good—and drive me even more insane.

"I'm sorry that I shoved you. And threw a note at you. And whatever else I did to piss you off. I was an asshole. I *am* an asshole."

She looks away from me again and folds her arms over her chest. I can't tell if she just despises me, or if there's an ounce of interest buried somewhere deep.

"Let me make it up to you. I'll tutor you, and I promise you'll ace the next exam." I try to catch her gaze, but she still refuses to meet my eyes. I want to clasp her face in my hands and make her look at me, let her eyes tell me everything I need to know. My hand tweaks as I keep restraint, trying to maintain a carefree facade.

"Maybe," she grumbles, her voice defiant. "If you're lucky."

I brighten—I got a "maybe," so there's a chance I cracked her shell after all. "We can start tonight, say eight o'clock? Library?"

There's a gleam in her eye and her mouth twitches. Do I sense a smile? "I don't know if it's a good idea for people to see us together."

I nod, understanding. Her stupid boyfriend won't be happy that we're studying together, that I'm sure of. A tinge of jealousy surges through me, assuming she's making her decision based on what he wants, and not what she wants.

"How about your room?"

Her suggestion stirs something inside of me—excitement, anticipation, I don't know what—but I keep my cool.

"Yeah, we can use my room. I'm in dorm seventeen. Top floor."

"Fine," she says, pursing her lips and, again, not looking directly at me. I can't help but smile that she keeps up her aggravated stance, especially after suggesting we study alone, in *my* room.

She finally looks into my eyes. My breath grows ragged the instant she locks her gaze with mine, and now I'm regretting that I wanted her to look at me so much. Even though I put up a decent front, it's clear I'm not the one in control here—not when she looks at me like…

"Can you get out of my way?"

Oh. My emotions are so intensified around her, I completely forgot I'm blocking the door. I laugh to release some pressure and step aside. She storms by and I watch her go.

Step one. Now I just have to figure out how to get her to trust me before it's too late.

◆

I watch the clock ticking. It's 9:17 p.m. She's one hour and seventeen minutes late, and I'm convinced she's not coming. Fuck.

I give up and figure out what else to do with my night. I could go to the gym, but I already went twice today. Wes wanted to sneak out to that secret spot, but I don't really feel like hanging out with him. Besides, I haven't told him yet that I plan to share my visions with Natalie—and I'm sure he'll annoy me about it the whole time.

I strip off the remains of my school uniform and put on some sweatpants. Might as well get comfortable since she's a no-show. My stomach grumbles and I remember that I haven't eaten all day. I pour some boiling water over dried macaroni and powdered cheese. I flip open my laptop and suddenly my fingers start navigating— searching for Natalie. I blow up a photo of her from some charity event, wearing a white, strapless dress.

It's hard to tear away from her photo until I'm interrupted by a knock on the door. I groan, figuring it's got to be Wes. Since we met, he's been especially persistent about hanging out, all the fucking time. The only reason I entertain him is because he's a precog. I would never hang out with that dude by choice.

I open the door, surprised to find Natalie standing there. She seems surprised to see me too—which is strange because she came to my room. Her eyes rake over my body and then I realize her reaction—I'm wearing thin sweatpants… and nothing else. Luckily, I keep myself in good shape—not because I'm trying to impress anyone, exercise is just a good release. I get a sudden urge to stay half-naked around her the whole night.

"You're late." I smirk, playful. She scrunches her nose and turns to leave. "I'm kidding. Come in." Before she can change her mind, I grab her hand and pull her inside. That same heat ricochets through my body when I touch her, but I try to ignore it and keep a tight grip so she doesn't run. I shut the door behind her.

I grab a T-shirt and slip it on while she peers around my room in curious awe. I'm not sure what she's looking at because it's completely barren in here. Then I realize her photo is still on my laptop screen. Shit. I quickly slam it shut, hoping she didn't see.

"What's that smell?" she says.

"It's mac and cheese—the Kraft kind. Want some?"

She makes a disgusted face and shakes her head no.

"Hey, don't knock my mac and cheese. What—do you only eat it with truffles or something?"

She slants her eyes at me. "It's not exactly hard to make boiled pasta and cheese."

I laugh while I grab the cup and stir around my fake orange cheese pasta while she makes another face. "When you live on a fishing boat in the middle of the ocean for a few months, this is the kind of stuff you have to eat. Regular cheese doesn't keep that long."

I shove a heaping forkful into my mouth. She watches me eat, her eyes wild with curiosity.

"That's right. You were in Turkey on an ocean cleanup mission, right?"

How did she know that? Did she do research on me?

She immediately seems to realize she said too much and quickly covers. "I mean, that's what someone told me anyway."

Sure it is.

I sit on top of my desk and continue eating. "Yeah, the cleanup was hard work, but I wouldn't trade it for anything. We were on the Black Sea, and my favorite part was Giresun. It's the greenest place I've ever been. You see every shade of green on that island, it honestly took my breath away." I take another bite and notice she's watching me closely. Figuring she's hungry, I motion to my bowl. "Sure you don't want some?"

"Nah, I'm good." She tears her gaze away from me, and I wonder why it's so hard for her to look at me now. Maybe I should take my shirt off again. I suppress a laugh at the thought.

"Come on, try it. It'll change your life."

I walk over to her, extending a forkful. Reluctant, she tries taking the fork out of my hand, but I hold it up to her mouth to feed it to her instead. I'm not sure why I do that, it just feels right.

She opens her lips and takes a bite, getting a little cheese sauce on the side of her mouth. I watch her reaction as she eats. I can tell she likes it.

"You're right, it's good," she says with her mouth still full.

"See? Never doubt me." I smile and wipe the stray cheese from her lip with my finger. She covers her mouth with her hand. Maybe revolted by my touch?

She turns away from me and backs up, putting more distance between us. That familiar sense of longing creeps up again—even though she's in the same room with me, I want her closer. It's clear she likes the distance, so I resolve to keep her comfortable. At least, until I can tell her…

"I was late because I didn't know anyone lived up here. I

thought I went to the top floor of the building, but apparently this is the top floor. I didn't know how to get a hold of you, so I left."

I look away to suppress my grin. She wanted to be here after all. "What made you come back?"

"The exam."

Oh right, that. I try to focus and not think this is more than it is.

"Well, welcome to my palace. I'll show you around and then we can study." I motion my hands around my small but clean room. "This is my room."

"I see that." Her lips curl into a smile. I love watching her lips.

I shake off all thoughts of her smile. "Let me show you the best part," I say, motioning for her to follow me. She does, curious. I lead her to my bathroom, the one place with complete privacy. I hold the door for her as she walks inside and looks around in awe. As soon as we're both inside, I get an immediate urge—there are no cameras, no one is watching us. Should I tell her about my visions, right now?

No, she barely knows me—there's no way she'll believe me. She'll just run and tell someone—her boyfriend, her parents, the police. Maybe she'll even think I'm the one who's going to hurt her—or, at least, think I know who is behind it. I'll be locked away in prison or maybe a psych ward and she'll still die, and I won't be here to protect her.

"It must be nice to have your own bathroom," she says. I barely register her words as I play out this entire scenario in my mind. What was I thinking? I'm immediately freaked out at the prospect of telling her at all. My heart skitters and I can feel sweat slicking my back. Then I see...

Darkness. The crunch of leaves. Maybe someone is walking? No, running. *Screaming. Muffled.* It sounds like her, but I can't make out what she's saying. *Something black on the ground. Is it a blanket? A dress? Coat?*

"Henry?"

I blink and I'm staring right into Natalie's eyes, regaining awareness that I'm in this bathroom alone with her. My back is pressed up against the closed door, blocking us in. What the fuck am I doing?

"You okay?" Her eyes search mine, combing over my face. They're specked with gold and green now—not brown or deep emerald like before. This must be the color they turn when she's worried.

I shake my head like everything's chill. "I'm good. I was just— never mind."

She's staring at me, her eyes encouraging me to share more. Not now. Not yet. I need to divert her attention away from me.

"It's cool how your eyes change color with your moods," I blurt out.

Her expression morphs into pain, like what I just said sliced her heart. She must know her eyes do that, so why is she so upset?

"No, they don't," she creaks out the words.

I detect a deep, raw anger in her voice. I'm familiar with that insidious feeling, when there's so much pain you can barely string words together. I wish she would tell me more. Tell me why she doesn't see what I see.

"They do. Look." I point at the mirror and she studies her eyes.

"They just look brown. Same as always." She turns away, like she can't stand to see her own reflection. I wonder why—she's so beautiful. If I were her, I'd stare in the mirror all day.

"Maybe brown is just the color when you feel comfortable." My eyes float to her hands gripping the sink—noticing a new tension that wasn't present before. "Or maybe they turn brown when you're not comfortable?" She doesn't relax, and I wish I could read her mind. Why can't that be my gift?

"Please don't joke about my eyes."

I'm struck by the pleading despair in her voice, and I feel like a monster for hurting her again. I don't know why bringing up her eye color causes her so much pain, but it does. "I wasn't joking. Your eyes were deep green in class today, maybe because you were upset over the exam. And when you're worried, they get these gold flecks."

She looks up at me with tears glistening in her eyes. If she can't handle me talking about her eye color, how the fuck am I supposed to tell her she's going to die?

My entire body tenses. This was a terrible idea. Add this to my bank of terrible ideas since coming to Lockwood. Fuck my life. I crank the door handle and push it open, desperate to get us out of this stifling cage of sadness.

"Never mind. Maybe it was just the light that made your eyes look different. Come on, let's just study."

She takes one last look at herself in the mirror. An indisputable sadness has consumed her entire body. I want to take it away. I want her to be happy, and yet I know that soon, when I tell her about my visions, I'll be the source of all her pain.

But not tonight.

Tonight, we study.

CHAPTER ELEVEN

NATALIE

"TOUT VA BIEN, merci. C'est un plaisir de faire votre connaissance," Henry says.

I honestly have no idea what he's saying, but he looks really good saying it. We've been studying for hours but it feels like minutes. I'm not even sure what time it is.

And I hate that I feel this way. Maybe hate isn't the word. Annoyed? Confused? After that earlier display in his bathroom where he made that weird comment about the color of my eyes, maybe I should just stick with hate.

Anyway, it's scorching in this room—what's the temperature? When I showed up, Henry had his shirt off, so clearly he's not cold. Maybe he should turn the damn heat down and put on a sweater.

His room is small and without much furniture, so he sits at his rickety wood desk while I sit on the bed. I offered the opposite, but he insisted I take the cozier spot. A nice gesture, I guess.

I yank off my sweater so I'm just in a thin, white tank top.

Instantly I feel better, cooler, until I notice his eyes boring into me. There's a tug in my stomach as he sweeps his gaze over my face and down my body.

Is he attracted to me? Is that why he's acting so weird? After his bold claim that he isn't into me, I didn't really consider that maybe he's just super immature and doesn't know how to handle dealing with girls.

This could be fun.

I trace my eyes along his face, noticing the crinkle in his eyes, the hint of a dimple in his cheek, his forearms—muscular, veins bulging, like he's tensing them. Is he trying to hold himself back from climbing onto this bed with me?

"Did I lose you?"

I'm snapped back to reality. Have I misread this whole thing? Maybe he was just waiting for me to repeat the phrase in French back to him. My brain bubbles with frustration. Why is he so hard to figure out?

"Yeah sorry, you lost me." I curl my lips into a one-sided smile, hoping we can lighten this up a bit. But he's clenching his pen so tight I'm waiting for it to crack in half and splatter ink everywhere.

Henry closes his textbook just a touch too hard. I try not to jump as the pages smack together. "Break time."

Perfect. This is a great opportunity for me to figure some things out. He clenches his hands and cracks his knuckles, like he's prepping for the torture of having to socialize with me. I fight the urge to giggle.

"You want something to drink?"

"No, I don't really drink," I say. What I really mean is that I don't drink *often*. I get buzzed quickly, and I need to be on my game here.

He shoots me a strange look and heads to the fridge. "I meant water. You want some water?"

"Oh. Water is good. Thanks."

He grabs two bottles and hands me one. I don't know why it didn't occur to me that he meant water when he asked if I wanted a drink. Maybe because everyone here drinks alcohol, pretty much every night. Glass of whiskey or wine, or both, with homework. That kinda thing.

I sneak a glance in his fridge and notice there's nothing but bottled water. Interesting that he doesn't drink alcohol with homework either.

He sits down on the bed in front of me and goosebumps ripple on my skin. My finger brushes against my textbook as I attempt to curl my fingers around it and pick it back up. Our gazes linger for a second too long, and I almost forget what I'm doing here. Oh right—answers. *Snap out of it, Natalie.*

"So I get that you're not into French. What classes do you like?" he says.

His question surprises me. Maybe because I'm used to being the one asking the questions. "Science—chemistry, biology. I want to be an eye doctor one day."

"Eye doctor?" He seems intrigued. "Why?"

I could launch into a typical long-winded explanation about all the reasons I'm pulled to that career path, but that would eat up too much time. I'm not here to talk about me, I'm here to figure out his deal. "Long story."

He takes a sip of water, and I can't help but notice the moistness left on his lips. God, I really need to focus.

"Okay. Well, when did you first know you wanted to be an eye doctor?"

I'm immediately struck by a memory of my mom and her beautiful smile as she curls one of the children into a hug after their eye surgery.

But then, I'm hit with a different memory—like a flashback in a movie. I'm lying on the blush-colored sofa in my childhood home. My head is in my mom's lap and she's stroking my hair, telling me a story in her soft, sweet, and breathy voice. Thinking of my mom brings back a sort of innocence inside of me, sending me to a time before I developed my signature jaded exterior.

"My mom used to tell me these stories. She loved Greek mythology and my favorite was the story of Argus. He was a giant who was covered head to toe with eyes—some say he had more than a hundred of them. Some of his eyes could sleep while others were awake, so he was an excellent watchman. His job was to guard Io, who was the first priestess of Hera. But Zeus, Hera's husband, fell in love with Io, and he was the one who hired Argus to watch over her and keep her safe."

Henry listens, fixated on me, and I wonder if he's actually hearing anything I'm saying—or if he's just trying to see through my tank top. "Let me guess, Argus fell in love with Io while watching over her?"

Okay, I was wrong. He is listening.

"I don't know if he fell in love with her. Maybe he did. But if that was the case, he didn't tell her before all his eyes were tricked into sleep and he was killed with a stone."

Henry goes completely silent. Something's changed in his expression—like his earlier nerves have frayed into something different. *Darker.* I notice a small movement in his jaw and a flare in his nostril. Is he angry? Suddenly I'm consumed by the need to apologize and diffuse this.

"Sorry, I didn't mean to ramble on with that stupid story."

He stares at me, pained and crumbled—and now I'm getting worried about him. "It's not stupid. It's… beautiful. Sad, but beautiful. He died trying to protect her."

There's a palpable shift in the air, and heaviness blankets the room. Coming here was definitely a mistake. Why do I need to know anything about Henry, anyway? Can't I just mind my own business?

I pretend to care about the time. "Oh my god, it's after two in the morning." I gather my things as quickly as possible. "I should go."

He's still sitting there on the edge of the bed—his mood hasn't improved. "Don't go."

I freeze, and there's a blip in my heartbeat.

"I don't sleep well anyway," he says.

I wonder why that is, but I don't bother to ask. Alarm bells go off inside of me and I just need to get out of here.

"Thanks for helping me study." I'm not quite sure how to say goodbye to him, so I just stand there, awkward. He doesn't make any moves and I extend my hand for a shake. He laughs, breaking the tension, and I force a laugh along with him.

"Truce." I play it off like I'm forgiving him for being a dick before—a gesture of friendship. He stands and shakes my hand. His skin is warm, scalding even. Guess I'm not the only one who was hot. His grip is strong, like he could crush my fingers in a second. I realize I'm just standing there like an idiot, clutching his hand, and I pull mine away. Before I can release, he tenses his grip on my hand—like he doesn't want to let go.

"I'll see you in class." I grab the rest of my things and twist the doorknob, racing out of his room. Before descending the stairs, I can't help but peek over my shoulder. My heart skitters when I notice him leaning in the doorway, watching me leave.

❧

I'm a mess of nerves as I maneuver down the dark campus path. I didn't even bother putting on my sweater, or my coat. The wind is unrelenting tonight—harsh gusts nip at my face, but my entire body feels like it's on fire. Like I'm on a heated high from my time with him. I've never felt like this before, *ever.*

Before I know it, I'm standing at the iron gates of the school property. I must have made a wrong turn. I trace my fingers along the ornate curves of the gate, taking note of the intricate pattern. I've never noticed it before.

The gate slams at the far end, and two guards enter. The sound rattles my core, and I'm struck by the instinct to hide—like I'm doing something wrong. Maybe they'll think I was trying to escape. One guard notices me and we lock eyes, his expression unreadable. After a tense second, he stares ahead and a shiver runs through my body.

I race to my dorm and whip up the stairs to my second-floor room. As I unlock my door, heels clack behind me.

"Natty?"

Shit, it's Ciel. I turn to see her standing behind me.

"Are you just getting home?"

Shit, shit, shit. "Uh, yeah. I was out studying."

Ciel snorts. "Okay, I know what *studying* means."

Refusing to give into her sex-fueled interpretations of normal words, I walk inside my room—but she follows me. She flops onto my bed and twirls her hair. I get a whiff of something and realize she's been drinking. "I know you weren't with Jack because we were hanging in Adip's room. Who were you with?"

I plunk my backpack on the floor and turn on my electric kettle. I'm desperate for my favorite cinnamon tea—the perfect remedy to calm my nerves. "I told you I was studying. I'm basically failing French."

Ciel looks confused, then her eyes snap with recognition. "French, huh? Until two in the morning? Hmmm… well, you weren't at the library because it's closed. Or the dining hall. So if you weren't in your own room, you had to be in someone else's."

Thanks, Ciel. This isn't a true crime podcast. I don't add any fuel to her deductions. "I'm tired. Can you go please?"

She rolls onto her back, getting more comfy. "Everyone in French class is barely passing… except scholarship kid. Oh my god, were you with *him*?"

Shit. "No, Ms. Whitney was helping me."

"Liar. I saw her leave campus around seven."

Good lord, of all the times for Ciel to pay attention. I'm completely out of lies and excuses, but I'm not telling her about Henry. Instead, I take a long sip of tea and feel the heat zigzag through my body.

Ciel jumps off my bed. "Fine, don't tell me. But I'll find out. I'm watching you and what's-his-face." Ciel wags her finger at me.

"He has a name." The impulse to defend Henry knocks me off-balance and I take a shaky sip of my tea, wishing my cup would swallow me. Ugh, I'm so off my game.

"See?! I knew you were with him." Ciel revels in her victory and I kick myself for blurting out such a dumb clue. She giggles in a drunken whisper. "I totally love this match. His weirdness is sexy. And don't worry, I won't tell anybody." She practically skips out of my room and I sink into my bed with a groan.

❧

I'm trembling in moonlit woods—panting from the cold. Henry is in front of me, holding out his hand, but I don't take it—even though I desperately want to. He gives up on waiting, grips my arms and hauls me against a tree—hovering over me. "Let me go," I say, but I don't really mean it. The last thing I want him to do is let me go. He leans closer, ratcheting up my pulse.

I jostle awake at a knock on my door—my dream ricochets through my mind. I'm still warring between dream and reality when someone knocks again—louder and more impatient this time. My entire body sags with exhaustion as I drag myself to the door.

Marta, one of our least-friendly school administrators with eternal resting bitch face, says, "Natalie, your father is here to see you."

I blink. Maybe I'm still dreaming. Why is my father here?

"There's a car outside the gates waiting to take you to the ferry. He's already taken care of permission for you to leave for the morning to have breakfast in the city."

Guess it's not a dream.

I nod and shut the door. My father didn't even bother to call me the last time we were allowed family contact. Now he came all the way here on the ferry from Seattle just to take me back to the city for breakfast? I get a sinking feeling as I yank my hair into a bun, swipe on the bare minimum makeup, and throw on some jeans and a sweater.

By the time I hit the front gates, my body is dancing with nerves. Two guards block the entrance. I'm not sure if they're the same guards as last night—they all kind of look the same. The guards stare ahead, not registering my presence. I peer up at one of them—his expression blank, which somehow makes him seem even more menacing. "Excuse me, my father is—"

Before I can squeak out another word, he unlocks the gate and steps aside. He still doesn't say anything or look at me. I really want to poke him in the chest or step on his foot to get a reaction.

A black limousine idles ahead, waiting to take us to the ferry. I ignore my impulse to get a rise out of this scary guard. As I climb inside the back of the car next to my dad, I'm assaulted with all the familiar smells of my world outside of school. Freshly polished leather seats. Dad's cologne, musky and earthy at the same time.

He's on the phone—he's *always* on the phone—and his tone is dominant and unrelenting. You never question whether he's the one in control. I hate it.

He hangs up without saying goodbye and flicks his glance to me. "Hungry?"

I nod. He doesn't make any moves to hug or kiss me, but that doesn't surprise me. He doesn't show affection in physical ways. Or verbal. Or, at all.

He presses a button and the privacy screen rises between us and the driver. His fingers type fast and furious on his phone while he makes a weak attempt at conversation, like usual. "How's school?"

"It's good." That's always my answer to his questions. *Good.* My father doesn't like extremes—if I tell him something is great, he'll want to know what "great" thing I've accomplished that meets his impossibly high standards. If I tell him something's bad, he'll use all his connections to fix it in the most embarrassing way possible for me. I learned to keep things even with him. Everything is just… good.

"How's Jack?"

"Good." Yep, I'm sticking with what works.

He turns off his phone and sets it down, looking directly at me. My pulse pounds, and I have a feeling he's about to deliver terrible, heart-wrenching news. The last time he put his phone away and looked at me like that, he told me Mom was killed in a car accident.

"Is he happy?"

I'm struck by his strange question. "Jack… happy? Um, I think so. He just got elected student president—"

"I'm aware of Jack's political accomplishments, Natalie. I'm asking if he's happy with you and your relationship."

His words blur together as my body wrenches with irritation. I have no interest in talking romance with my father and answering his intrusive questions. "You should probably take Jack to breakfast instead and ask him."

His expression shifts, and I know that look—it's the look he gets when a deal he's worked on for months doesn't go through. Or when his lawyer alerts him to yet another suit threatening his company. Or when the IRS comes knocking. I'm intimately familiar with that look, and it's never good.

When he's done staring me down with displeasure, he looks ahead. He doesn't look at me again while we drive in silence.

Finally he speaks—his voice is calm, cold, and even. The scariest of his tones. "I have a business issue, and Jack's father is the only person who can help me resolve it. Without his cooperation, things will not go well for us. And we both know how much his son's happiness means to him. I don't need to explain this further, right, Natalie?"

No, he doesn't need to explain. My anger swells—did Jack run to his daddy and whine that I'm not being a good, compliant girlfriend?

I nearly combust with anger as I picture this scenario. I roll down my window—the air in this car is so stifling I want to vomit all over these pristine leather seats.

Tap, tap, tap. He's back on his phone, fingers smashing into the keypad. I clench my fists to keep myself from ripping that stupid phone out of his hands and throwing it out the window.

There's a tiny spot on the leather seat of the limo where the stitching is starting to fray. I pick at it, allowing my frustration to tear a hole in something my father actually does love—material possessions.

I'm not sure how I'm going to make it through an entire morning with him. He'll just speak to me in that condescending way, trying to manipulate me to align him with Jack and his politically powered family.

But he's in for a rude awakening because I'm no compliant princess. Sure, I can smile and nod when I need to, like when my tuition is due, but if he thinks I'm going to carry on this charade forever and marry Jack, he's got another thing coming.

Besides, there are far more interesting people out there to spend time around. People like…

Henry.

CHAPTER TWELVE

HENRY

MY CLASSMATES SWARM with excitement as I make my way down the hall. There's some stupid dance—or ball, or whatever they call it—tonight. It's all anyone seems to care about—an annoying alarm clock of chatter that won't stop ringing.

I walk into French class and slump down in my regular seat. I sneak a peek behind me and notice Natalie hasn't arrived yet. I promised myself not to keep staring at her, but I find myself constantly drawn to doing it, again and again—those stolen glances have become my drug.

My urge to see her has only gotten worse since having her in my room to "study." What a terrible idea. She couldn't get out of there fast enough, and the most we bonded was when I handed her a lukewarm bottle of water. I'm not even sure she'll look at me again, much less believe me when I tell her about my visions.

Visions. My fucking visions of *her*. I barely got a second of sleep last night because, after she left my room, it was like my mind was set loose. Visions of her splattered my brain in rapid succession for hours and hours and haven't stopped until now.

Without Natalie in-person to look at, I turn my focus out the window. The sky is gray, nearly the color of charcoal, casting an ominous shadow over campus. A stark contrast to the excitable mood that seems to permeate the halls.

The bell rings and Ms. Whitney delivers an announcement—half the class is a no-show, primping for the ball. Guess that means Natalie's not coming. A shot of disappointment crowds my brain, but I file it away.

The class drones on, and I tune out Ms. Whitney and sink into my thoughts. There's a certain sense of peace without my visions, but that peace also terrifies me—because I've momentarily lost the compulsion to tell Natalie. I can even fool myself into thinking maybe the visions were a mistake. Maybe they won't come true. Maybe I can just ignore all of this and it will go away.

Bullshit.

When class ends, I race outside—in a hurry to go nowhere. I have a lot of time on my hands at Lockwood. Besides homework and the gym, there's not much else to do. There are a few student-run clubs, but they're nothing more than extracurricular popularity contests. It's astounding how this school has such a coveted reputation. My theory is that it's just some elaborate scheme of privilege.

A familiar voice shouts out behind me—Wes. Before I can duck off somewhere, he falls into step. "Hey man, you wanna hang later?"

Fuck, this dude really doesn't take a hint. You'd think after telling him I don't wanna hang no less than fifteen times this week, he'd give up. I almost admire his persistence.

"Can't, I'm busy. Sorry."

"Don't tell me you're going to that dance." He cracks up laughing. "They've got a roomful of tuxedos in that building, some red-carpet Hollywood shit."

"Hell no." Dances are definitely not my thing. Nor are any other social gatherings where you have to dress up like some fucking fairytale prince. No thanks.

"Wait with me while I have a smoke and we can get something to eat—I'm starving."

I'm not interested, but what else do I have to do? He is a precog, after all, and I feel an innate duty to at least put up with him.

I lean against the exposed brick wall while he lights up, and that's when I notice Natalie—standing with a few other girls. Her friends buzz with that same excited energy that doused the hallway, but Natalie seems uninterested. She's not wearing her school uniform, which is strange.

Jack approaches their group and leans into her. He runs his hands over her hair and seems to say something that disappoints her because her face curls into a frown. Something stirs inside of me—it's subtle, but possessive. And just like that, my visions are back.

Natalie whips past trees at a dizzying speed. I've seen this before. *She's in full view now, not just her face. She's wearing a black coat, red fabric visible under the bottom of the coat—probably a dress. A white-gloved hand grabs a fistful of her coat. She's pulled backward but manages to wrestle free of the coat.* Who is that behind her? *She forges ahead, now only wearing the red dress—moving faster and faster, screaming. The same hand grips her arm and yanks her back. She falls to her knees. An arm grabs at her. A man's arm, wearing some kind of suit jacket, or a uniform. It's black. No, blue. Navy.* It's hard to see the color with shadows drenching everything.

"Bro, you good?" Wes's voice rings in the distance, but my

vision won't let up. Panic presses on my body and mere breathing feels like punishment.

Natalie is dragged backward. She's jamming her heels into the ground, but her attacker must be too strong. Why can't she kick him, fight harder? *She's pressed against the gate. The click of a lock. She's pulled through. He's carrying her off school property.* Where is he taking her? *The gate slams behind her, her expression that of someone who has lost all hope.*

"Dude, let's go," Wes says.

❧

When Wes and I reach our secret spot off campus, I'm vaguely aware that he dragged me all the way out here. I don't even remember climbing the fence or being careful to avoid the cameras. It's like I completely blacked out.

The visions finally stop, and my head is splitting—like the worst kind of hangover. I sink down onto the cold ground, pinching my nose to alleviate some of the pain and nausea.

"What did you see?" Wes asks.

I can't even form words to answer him. I don't want to talk about this at all. I just want the pain to go away and to figure out what I saw. "Nothing."

"Bullshit, it's not nothing. You freaked out back there. Was it about her?"

I nod, my eyes still squeezed shut, losing the will to lie.

"What are you going to do about it?"

Before I can answer, another vision slams into my brain.

Natalie walks out of a building wearing that same black coat. She's clearly distressed, but still put-together. This must be before the attack. Where is she? It's definitely on campus, the architecture undeniable—but I don't recognize the building. *She bundles her coat around her tightly and wipes a stray tear.* She's upset, why? What happened to her? *Music thumps in the background and she stares back at the closed doors for a moment, a sense of longing.* Does she want to go back inside? Why is she even out there alone?

As I piece together the scene, realization hits. "Do you know which building they're having the dance in tonight?"

"Uh, I think it's in the Snyder Building. Why?"

Panicked, I sprint back to campus—Wes shouting after me.

⁊

The Snyder Building sits at the far end of the campus and looks like a gothic cathedral—dark and menacing. The windows are colored with crimson glass that only amplifies the tortured architecture. Not exactly the place I'd expect some fancy ball to happen, but what do I know?

Workers shuffle things in and out the massive double doors—the same doors from my vision. The same doors that Natalie was standing in front of—contemplating something. *She's going to leave this place alone and get attacked.* My stomach churns and sinks. One of the workers bangs into me with a steel catering tray and apologizes. I barely register his presence, my mind completely fucked with the grim realization—Natalie is going to die, *tonight.*

Unless I do something about it.

I pace, furious. What's the plan here? Should I track her down right now, beg her to go somewhere private with me, and then tell her? What do I even say? *Think. Think.*

A gust of chilled wind whips against my face, blurring my vision. I rub away the moisture from my eyes and crouch down—maybe I can focus better if I tune out my surroundings.

"You okay?" The worker who banged into me now looms over my body, concerned.

No, dude, I'm not okay. I am most definitely the opposite of okay.

"Yeah, all good."

He shrugs and continues on with his work.

Maybe I should just go to her room, see if she's there. I can figure out what to say when I get there. One step at a time.

No, that won't work. It will freak her out that I even know which room is hers.

Okay, so checking on her hasn't been limited just to French class. I may have followed her back to her room, once. She seemed troubled that day, something was off, and protection kicked in against my better judgment. I kept my distance, but I still followed her—like a total creep.

Maybe I can lie? I'll say someone told me where her room was. No, that won't work either. This is so damn complicated. *Fuck, fuck, fuck.*

I fist my hand around a patch of grass and yank it from the ground. Why did I let this slide? Why didn't I tell her last night? Now she's going to pay the price because I didn't get my shit together.

"Do you want me to call someone for you?" The same worker is back—the crease in his forehead deeper and he's clutching a cell phone, fingers hovering over the keys. He's probably watching me cowering over here on the ground like I'm having a mental breakdown, and is considering having me committed. Can't blame him.

I pull myself together, tossing off a "no worries" glance before continuing down the path to my room—feet smashing into the gravel. My mind rattles through a million scenarios of how tonight will play out—all of them end with me either in prison, dead, or worse.

I go even faster as the trail slopes uphill, and before I know it, I'm out of breath. This distance is usually easy for me to tackle, but it suddenly feels excruciating. I take a moment to catch my breath, leaning against a small, rickety wooden bridge. I don't even know why this bridge is here—there's nothing under it but shrubbery, like a rotting skeleton.

The sky darkens as more clouds float into place and I can taste rain in the air. The moisture triggers another vision…

Natalie's heels dig into the ground, but her attacker is still dragging her away. I saw this already. *Her heel gets jammed and her foot shakes loose—the ground wet and muddy. She can't catch her footing, or fight back, because she's sliding.*

A drop of rain splashes onto my cheek. Then another. Dark clouds loom and the sky opens with big fat raindrops that soak the ground in an instant. I tug my coat over my head to block the onslaught as I race to my room.

⌘

I strip off my soaking wet clothes—shivering to the bone. I take a long, hot shower while looping in my mind about how the hell I'm going to pull this off tonight. By the time I step out of the shower, I've rolled through every emotion, and now I'm just left with outrage. It takes every ounce of strength not to punch the mirror. Maybe the pain of the broken glass will feel better than the misery I'm experiencing inside.

I clutch the counter as an alternative, bracing and grounding myself. The best option I have is to find Natalie at the dance and tell her there—hide in plain sight. It's a masquerade ball—at least my face will be partially concealed and I can tuck her away for a quick conversation without raising too much attention.

My mind races back to a conversation with Wes—his brother warned his girlfriend, right? Yeah, and they disappeared. My chest tightens.

The more thought I put into this, the more defeated I become. Natalie will have a million questions—questions I can't answer without telling her about my ability. And there's no way she'll believe me if I tell her that.

Back in my room, my energy is completely sapped. I flop back on my bed and peer around—everything an affirmation of my new reality. In a few hours, things will be different, and it might not even be safe to return to this room.

My shoulders tighten and I push myself off the bed, yanking a suitcase from the closet. I don't have a lot of things to pack. My uniform can stay here… guess I won't be needing it anymore.

Run away. It's the only viable solution. Tell Natalie, and leave. She can't ask questions. She'll survive. I'll move on… or face the consequences. *Consequences.* A sharp ache stabs through my gut.

I ditch the suitcase and decide just to pack my important belongings in my backpack. What do you need when you're so uncertain about tomorrow—tonight, even? I decide to pack like it's my own personal apocalypse.

My muscles clench in angst and I suck in a deep breath. I have a plan—a shitty plan, but a plan, nonetheless.

I'll tell Natalie tonight… then leave this place for good.

CHAPTER THIRTEEN

NATALIE

IT FEELS SO right to hide.

As I slip the diamond-encrusted Venetian mask over my eyes, I kinda wish it was mandatory to wear them all the time—a way to stay shrouded in secrecy. I never understood why people want to live their lives so publicly, posting every second on social media and then filtering the hell out of it so it's not even real.

I shove open the heavy door, entering the Lockwood Ball. Candelabras vomit light all over the room. The Saint Petersburg Philharmonic Orchestra has been flown in for the occasion—the oldest Russian orchestra, the conductor a good friend of our school's headmaster. And then there are those weird guards, lining the room. Six of them. They don't fit in here at all—honestly, they're killing the vibe. Which I kind of love because everyone here is so obsessed with elegance.

I nearly bang into a tower of violet-dipped roses and realize they're everywhere. Overkill, if you ask me.

All I care about is if *he's* here.

I spot Ciel and Adip huddled in the corner, her legs wrapped around his waist. I guess it's a good thing she picked the dress with a high slit. He's whispering something to her—and it must be good because her fists clench his tuxedo jacket.

A tower of champagne glasses covers a table to my left, and in a mindless move, I swipe a glass from the top—sucking down the tart, bubbly liquid. I'm not sure why I do it—I rarely drink—but it just feels right to do it here, now. My insides sizzle at the liquid, making me crave more. I take another sip, just a small one this time—and that's when I notice him.

At least, I think it's him. Tousled dark hair peeks out from a gold and black Venetian mask. His broad shoulders and muscular arms fill out that tux so damn… *yep, definitely him.* Suddenly, my glass of champagne is empty.

I trade my empty glass for a full one and chug down way more than a sip. It occurs to me that hanging over here alone, wearing a mask, downing champagne, and watching Henry is the most satisfied I've been in a long time. Is that fucked up? That's fucked up.

We haven't spoken since our tutoring date last night… okay, it wasn't a date. Session is more accurate. I missed French class and considered "accidentally" bumping into him somewhere on campus today, but I stopped myself.

Somehow, I have a third glass of champagne, and it's already almost empty. Damn, when did I take this? When did I drink this?

I down the rest and set the glass on a nearby tray. That's it, I'm cutting myself off. I wobble slightly—this champagne must be strong. Or I'm not meant to suck down three glasses in less than ten minutes.

A giggle escapes my lips as I teeter on my heels. Gripping the side of the table, I blink and focus my gaze—locking eyes with

Henry across the room. A tremor races through my body. He walks forward with purpose. Shit, he's coming over here.

Panic and desire swirl through my body, mixing with my champagne haze. He's getting closer, maneuvering through the crowd, and I'm rendered paralytic.

Someone bangs into me—jolting me out of the moment.

"There you are." Jack's voice slithers through my foggy brain.

He curls me into his arms and plants a kiss on my lips. I don't kiss him back, my body still frozen from my almost-encounter with Henry. Jack pulls back and studies me, amused. "Have you been drinking?"

I slur out a few words. "How can you tell?" Damn, this champagne is really messing with my head.

Pulling myself together, I pretend to fix my mask so I can sneak a look at Henry, but he's gone. There's a dark, needy hole left in his absence.

"Come on, let's dance." Jack holds out his hand. I take it, hesitant. I hate dancing, but he twirls me into his arms. Well, less of a twirl and more of a stumble on my part.

He studies my dress. "This is a new look for you."

Annoyance bubbles in my brain—I don't know if it's the champagne, or his tone, or because he interrupted my run-in with Henry.

There's no time to think anymore when the band strikes up a Volta and everyone rushes into formation. La Volta is a Renaissance dance—an annoying staple for us prep school kids. We learn it when we're young and perform it over and over at every function like a prissy version of a wedding line dance. Jack bows to me and I curtsy back with a grimace.

At the beginning of the dance, you face your partner and perform a series of moves, then you press together and your partner lifts you by the waist and spins you. When Jack attempts to execute the perfect lift and spin, I fumble. He frowns at me in frustration, but I really don't care about my dance skills right now, or ever.

I'm off to my next partner, Adip. I can tell he's already pretty wasted, so our moves are choppy and grow messier with every step. We both burst into laughter.

"Are you drunk?" he says.

I nod and Adip slaps me a high five. A few classmates snap their heads to us in horror. Come on people, who cares? It's a stupid Volta. Get the stick out of your ass.

When it's time to switch partners for the last time, Adip flings me into the next guy. I'm dizzy from our ridiculous dance moves, and the champagne swirls faster in my brain. I don't even register who my new partner is, until he grips my arm and yanks me close.

Wait, I recognize this body, this heat, this…

Through his mask, Henry pierces me with his stare—his green eyes intense, serious. His breaths are sharp, quick, panicked. My breath hitches, getting swept away in his emotions.

He hauls me off into a dark corner in the hallway, away from the crowd. My back presses against the cold stone wall, but the temperature almost feels like relief. He places his palms on either side of me, caging me in. He rips off his mask and hovers over me.

Goosebumps prickle my skin as I fixate on his lips making tiny motions, as if he's trying to say something, but the words won't come out. He's silent, watching me for what seems like hours—until finally he speaks in a raspy whisper.

"You're in danger."

The song hits its crescendo the same moment he speaks, and I'm pretty sure I didn't hear him correctly. "What?" Did he just say I was in danger?

"I saw…" Panic illuminates his eyes and he backs away.

I'm struck by the sudden absence of his heat. "You saw what?"

He pinches the bridge of his nose—is he in pain? What did he see?

The song ends—claps and cheers erupt. The band is no longer playing and the noise from the ball becomes soft background chatter to our conversation.

Henry stares at me with desperation. "Please don't leave here alone tonight."

"Why? What are you talking about?" I fold my arms over my body, getting frustrated.

He turns to leave, but pivots back to me, abrupt—maybe even angry. He grips my arms, his body taut with anguish. My head spins and my body rushes with fire at his touch. What the hell is going on?

"If you see a man wearing white gloves, I need you to run."

What? Before I can even respond to his insane request, he races off without another word.

⁓

I shuffle through the crowd in a daze—the air is thick, the music screaming. Overwhelmed, I down another glass of champagne and head back into the hallway. The scene of the crime. Okay, not a crime… I don't even know what the hell that was.

I brace against the wall, trying to piece together what's real and what's fantasy. Everything blurs—what was Henry trying to tell me? Was it some kind of elaborate prank? Or was my mind fucking with me?

A giggle erupts from a nearby room followed by a familiar guy's voice. Jack.

Curious, I curl around the corner—the door is slightly ajar and I peek through the slat. Josephine is perched on a desk, dress riding up. Jack slips between her legs and she's pulling at his shirt. He seems to be telling her to stop, but his actions don't match his words.

This is it, what I've always wanted—to march in and catch them, make a spectacle out of what was going on behind my back all this time. But now that I'm faced with that fantasy, I'm shocked that I feel… nothing. Blank. Empty.

At least, that's how I feel about *them*. They can have each other.

My mind whirls in a hazy mess of confusion as I stumble off. I grab my coat from some elegant armoire the school rented and burst outside. The cold air should be bitter and painful, but it feels refreshing after all the shit that just happened in the last five minutes. I wrap my coat tight and stare back at the double doors.

Maybe I should march back in there and tell Jack that it's over, that I don't care if he wants Josephine because I don't want him anyway. That'll really piss my father off.

But I'm too drunk, and if I'm going to make a scene, I want to be sober enough to crush it. I laugh at the idea, and my stomach churns. I try to recall the last time I ate something today. After losing my appetite with my father earlier, I don't think I've consumed anything but tea. But I'm not even hungry, my skin is just throbbing and pulsating with too much energy. A bead of sweat trickles down my spine. Must be the alcohol.

I scan the empty school grounds and realize how peaceful it is when there's no one out here. Everyone's cooped up at the ball, even the guards, making this the perfect time for a walk back to my dorm, alone.

As I wander through the desolate campus, feet crunching in the crispy fall leaves, my thrumming heart returns to a steady beat, and my nerves lower—cool and temperate. I suck in a long, deep breath of cold air and it feels like the best breath I've taken in my life. Maybe it's escaping the ball, or escaping Jack, but things in this moment just feel right.

The ground crunches behind me, and I'm suddenly aware that I'm not as alone as I thought. Probably a drunk classmate stumbling back to their dorm.

I check behind me, but nothing's there. Maybe it was a squirrel. Are squirrels out at night? Maybe I'm just hearing things.

I advance a few more steps and the ground crunches behind me again, almost mimicking my steps. My chest pounds. Am I being followed?

I take a few more steps… and the sound continues. Either I'm drunker than I thought, or someone is definitely following me. Panic claws at my mind.

Don't leave here alone.

Henry's sobering words flutter into my brain. *You're in danger.* Wait, he warned me not to leave the ball alone. Why?

I saw…

What did he see? He never answered my question.

Nerves get the best of me and I decide to turn around and head back to the ball. The other footsteps seem to stop—maybe I was just imagining things? Just to be safe, I forge ahead.

I only make it a few paces when the crunching footsteps grow louder, closer. I speed up, but my heel latches into a crack in the ground and I slip and fall, skinning my knee. My body throbs with alarm.

"Let me help you, miss."

My gaze locks with one of the weird guards, and I let out a relieved breath. It throws me to hear him speak—the stone-faced man. There's no emotion in his eyes, or his words. Guess he's just carrying out his duty. Well, I can take all the help I can get right now.

He extends his hand out and I clasp his white-gloved hand… *white glove.* Henry warned me about a white glove.

Terror rips through my body. I yank my hand away and scramble to my feet, racing back to the ball.

The guard grabs the back of my coat and I'm yanked backward. I somehow manage not to fall, and wriggle out of my coat. *I'm free.* A crash of adrenaline catapults me ahead.

"Help! Help me!"

I'm gaining ground and am close enough to the ball that someone might be able to hear me. The music blares from inside.

"Help! Please!"

The guard grabs me around the waist and drags me from my destination across the path. I dig my heels into the dirt, hoping to get some traction, but the ground parts and I'm gliding. One of my shoes gets jammed and pops off, rendering me unable to walk with just one high heel.

I scream and kick and try my best to fight, but he's too strong—and before I know it, I'm being dragged to the front gates. My voice grows hoarse from effort. Where is he taking me? He pins me against the cold steel while he unlocks the gate. He's distracted for a split second while he fumbles with his keys.

Petrified, I shove his arm—his keys tumble to the ground. I race ahead, but he grabs me, slamming me against the steel gate once again. My brain rattles on the impact. He manages to open the gate and pull me outside. I beat against him and scream with every inch of willpower I have. Someone has to hear me before my voice gives out.

Then… there's a knife at my throat. I clam up—the sharp blade pressing so hard against my neck I'm afraid to even turn my head a fraction.

I need to leave a trail. Someone will find me. I refuse to give up hope, and shake off my other shoe. He doesn't seem to notice the shoe is gone as he marches me into the woods. Lost slippers work in fairy tales—I don't believe in them, but if there's ever a time for one to come true, please let it be now.

I just have to stay alive long enough for someone to find me.

We descend into the woods—naked branches sway in the wind, a few leaves clinging on for dear life.

I wince as my bare feet drag over sharp and jagged rocks and stones. Maybe I can use one of them as a weapon. If I can somehow manage to distract him, just long enough to grab something and smash it into his skull, I could buy more time. Get away.

My mind spins in circles, trying to figure out a plan. Any plan. Blood surges through my veins in a frenzy.

The farther we go into the woods, the more hope slips away and reality sinks in. My legs and arms begin to turn to jelly. The muddy ground slick from a short bout of rain is like thick, unrelenting sand. But I don't want to stop walking—when this walk is finished, I'm terrified of what will happen.

And just like that, we stop.

There's nothing but darkness. I can't even hear him breathing. My heart nearly bursts from my chest, and it's possible I might have a heart attack before he can do anything.

The atmosphere shifts in an instant—and he shoves me against the ground. My wounded knee slams into something sharp and a searing pain ricochets through my body.

Ignore the pain—just get away.

CHAPTER FOURTEEN

HENRY

I COULDN'T LEAVE Lockwood.

I tried. I really tried. But it wasn't long before second thoughts clawed through my mind. The visions of Natalie are gone, replaced by real horrific flashes of what might happen if she doesn't listen.

I have to make sure she's safe.

What an epic shit show. I couldn't even string two words together—did she even understand anything I said? I swear she had a tinge of realization before I fled, though I wonder if I mistook her emotion for something else. Like confusion over why I manhandled her into the hallway to basically say a whole lot of nothing.

I wind back down the path, closing in on the ball. I've already ditched the tuxedo and changed into jeans, a sweatshirt, and my coat. My backpack is slung over my shoulder. I just need to check up on her... one last time.

Then I'll leave.

Back at the dance, the entire place has morphed from prim

bullshit to a complete rager. Students falling down drunk. Teachers falling down drunk. Even the orchestra looks drunk.

I circle the room at least three times before reality sinks in.

She's not here.

I abandon the ball, pausing outside the entrance. She left. That means she was standing on these steps, staring at these doors. My heart rate accelerates as I piece together my visions.

The school entrance. The man in my vision, pulling her out of the gates.

I race to the school's entrance, challenging myself to quicken the pace—pushing to my absolute max. There's no time to waste. I may already be too late.

I arrive at the gate in full force, nearly slamming into it on impact. It's locked—it's always locked. I hoist my leg up onto the cold steel and begin to climb, noticing a glimmer of gold on the ground in front of me.

Natalie's shoe.

No, no, no.

I power through the rest of the climb and smack down on the other side, desperate to find her footsteps. The path into the woods glistens, making it easy to spot the prints leading into the woods. A shred of hope.

My senses sharpen with every step—the whistle of crickets, the rustle of leaves, the whipping wind. It's dark, but it's like my eyes are a flashlight illuminating everything in my path. Moving faster, farther—fear etches into my brain when I hear her screaming.

As I round the corner—my vision splays into alarming reality. Natalie is pinned on the ground, trying desperately to fight off the guard.

I grab the first thing I can find—a jagged rock—and throw it against his head as hard as I can. A sharp pop rings out and blood spurts on the ground. His body slumps over Natalie, and her eyes widen with fright.

I shove his body off of her and kneel down next to them. Natalie crawls a few inches back.

Holy shit, he's dead.

I did that.

Natalie studies me as I loom over her attacker's body. I have no idea what to do to make this better for her, so I pull her into a hug. She squeezes me so tight, it nearly stops my breath. We stay there for what feels like an eternity until her ragged breathing slows and her heart stops drumming.

I pull away from her just a bit and she clenches my arms. I look her over for injuries, tracing my hands over her hair, caked with mud and debris. "I'll go get help."

She shakes her head in a violent no.

"We can't stay here. You need—"

"No." Her voice cracks, but her tone is firm and unrelenting. How can I argue with her right now? She's probably in shock. She's shivering—quaking, really. I remove my coat and wrap it around her, then start removing my sweatshirt.

"No, you'll freeze," she says, her voice hoarse and strained.

Temperature is nothing compared to what she just went through. I remove my sweatshirt and lay it over her legs like a blanket, spotting a bloody patch on her thigh before I notice that her knee is starting to swell. I know a bit about wilderness survival from one of my missions, and that wound looks like it needs some attention. "Wait here."

She clasps my hand. "No."

"I'll just be over there." I point to small patch of bushes directly in her eyeline. She nods and lets go of her grip on my hand.

I shoot her a reassuring glance as I collect some yarrow—a

wildflower found in most abandoned fields here. It blooms in summer, but extends through the fall. I get to work, rolling the damp yarrow between my fingers to make a paste.

"I'm going to put this on your knee to help with the swelling." She nods. I dab some on her knee—she sucks a painful breath through her teeth. "You okay?" She nods again and I continue applying.

"What is that?"

"It's called yarrow. It's pretty legendary for treating wounds. They used to call it soldier's woundwort." Why am I rattling through the medicinal history of this plant when she just went through a serious trauma?

Silence strums between us as I finish tending to her knee. She's watching me, careful. I'm dying to know what she's thinking.

"How did you know I was in danger?"

Fuck…

Something passes in her expression, the fear gone, leaving nothing but determination. I've played this moment over in my head a thousand times, and there's just no good way to answer her question.

"I can't tell you that."

"Really." It's not a question now—she just doesn't accept my answer. I need to diffuse this, fast. I could run—I know all the twists and turns of these woods. It would take minutes for me to reach the front of the property and hail down a hitch to the ferry.

But I can't leave her here. I won't.

"If I tell you the truth, it will put you in even more danger."

She studies me, testing me with her gaze. She doesn't believe me. "More danger than I was just in? How did you know that man was going to attack me? You said you *saw*. What does that mean?"

I wince at the onslaught of her interrogation. Maybe I was

clearer with her than I thought. But if she understood me, why did she leave the party alone?

It doesn't matter. This isn't a fucking "told you so" moment. She almost died.

We're suspended in time—the atmosphere punctured with accusation and anger. She's pissed at me. Mad that I won't tell her how I knew.

Imagine how she'd feel if I told her the truth.

I'm upright in an instant—what's my plan here? My body aches from the cold, unable to warm my frozen arms. My brain circles in unforgotten cycles of angst.

She's still waiting for my answer, growing more angry with every second I don't respond. The sky grows heavier, blanketing our duel with more darkness.

Here's what I know: I just defied my entire existence and told her about my vision. I just killed someone to save her. Now she's terrified of me. It's the worst trifecta of dread I could have imagined.

But she was the one who was attacked. This isn't about me. She did nothing to deserve this.

I join her on the cold ground and her body shifts away from mine—it's slight, but noticeable. Not wanting to make her anymore uncomfortable, I look away and crumble the yarrow in my fingers.

"What are you thinking about?" I look back at her and she's staring at me, her brow furrowed. Anger replaced with… concern? No, it's probably my imagination. "We need to get you some help. Can you walk?"

"I'm not going anywhere until you tell me how you knew." There it is—her bargaining chip. She's on to me. She knows I won't leave her here.

But I can't bargain. She's already wounded—physically, emotionally. Do I really want to pour salt onto everything she just experienced by revealing that people in this world have powers and visions? That there's an entire secret society of precogs lurking around corners? No, not gonna happen.

"We need to go. Come on, I'll carry you." I climb to my feet and extend my hand. She glares at it, like if she touches me, she'll turn to stone.

Something rustles and cracks in the distance. We both snap our heads in the direction of the sound.

"Natalie! Natalie!"

A search team. I'm certain Jack's is among the echo of shrill voices screaming. What the hell do I do? Hold up my hands in surrender? Try to explain? Lie? Say nothing?

Who cares what I do? This isn't about me. It's about her.

"Run," she says.

The word sends shockwaves through my bones. She's holding out my coat and sweatshirt, extending a lifeline. Why is she doing this?

"I need you to run."

My words to her, thrown right back at me. Every inch of my body screams to stay, but I listen… and I run.

CHAPTER FIFTEEN

NATALIE

SO MANY QUESTIONS.

They pummeled me for hours. Cops. Then detectives. Headmaster Rochester. Jack. Ms. Whitney. Ciel. Adip. My father, by phone. He seemed angrier that the school didn't have proper security than he did about the fact that I'd almost died. I guess I should be pissed, completely crushed about that. But I just felt numb. His reaction felt… expected.

Now, finally enjoying a few moments alone, exhaustion seeps in. I sink back into a hunter green leather chair in Headmaster Rochester's stuffy office and close my eyes. What I'm really thinking about—what my mind oscillates between—is the notion that I almost died… and the fact that I lied about how it happened.

Breath tangles in my throat as I curl a charcoal-colored woolen throw around my body. It's itchy, but warm. Good enough, I guess.

My knee pulses with pain, but the swelling has gone down. I trace my finger over the wound, and a memory of Henry's hands bobs to the surface. Touching me, tending to me. A surge of heat firecrackers through my body, but my thoughts thrust back to reality.

He knew I was going to be attacked.

I'm dying to plumb what that means, my mind going haywire with possibilities—but I won't. Not yet. Not until I get my answers from him. He owes me a serious fucking explanation, and something deep and dark inside of me hopes it's a good one… because I want to know I did the right thing. That I didn't tell anyone about him being there because he truly had nothing to do with my attack.

I distract my jangled brain by fixating on the decor in this room. Rich, mahogany wood. Awards hovering in every corner and crevice. It's dark, with one tacky antique jeweled lamp illuminating the space. This is the place they thought I'd be most comfortable, most safe, for an interrogation. It looks like something out of a serial killer documentary.

Ms. Whitney told me in our first meeting that when I feel uncomfortable in public spaces, I should try to ground the room. Close your eyes and picture the four corners of the space. Then imagine yourself, encircled in a protective fence of your favorite flower. I generally side-eye this sort of meditation, but this one usually works.

I squeeze my eyes shut and try… and try… and try… to ground this room, but every attempt fails. Lie after lie, the room feels as if it might swallow me whole.

After hours of their questions, and hours of my ~~lies~~ answers, I'd begged for a few moments alone. Everyone's just outside the door now—hovering… waiting. My gaze latches onto the window. Maybe I can just climb out, run away from this entire mess.

Everyone thinks I fended off that guard alone. I noticed their skirted glances, wondering how, physically, that was possible. I sold them on adrenaline and tears. And they all bought it.

The police already investigated the guard's apartment on campus. Warren Wright. That was his name. Apparently, Warren took a great interest in me—his place was smothered with articles, photos, my student ID. A fucking dossier of my life tacked to his wall. My chest constricts and I suck in as much air as I can manage. I breathe in life… life that I almost lost a few hours ago.

How did Henry know?

A shiver runs through me at the sound of faint rapping followed by the door creaking open. Ms. Whitney peeks inside, still wearing her dress from the ball—her mask pushed up in her hairline. "Natalie, can we come back in?" she asks, cautious. Her brow furrows with concern.

I nod, wishing I could say no—but I have to get this over with. Ms. Whitney indicates to the group that it's safe to enter. Jack rushes in first, followed by Headmaster Rochester, and one of the detectives (I can't keep their names straight). Ciel and Adip are last.

Jack plants himself in the middle of the room, holding court like he's some kind of savior. "Are we done here? I'd like to take her back to her room to get some rest."

He puts his hand on my shoulder and I shove it off. His touch feels grimy and wrong. I'm almost thankful he's messing with Josephine so I never have to feel his touch again.

He places his limp, cold hand on my shoulder again, and I knock it off… again. His cheeks redden and I can tell he's mortified. He sneaks a look around the room, always so fucking worried about what everyone else thinks.

"Natalie's just having a rough time right now. She really needs this to be over," he says.

Anger leeches through my body. How fucking dare he speak for me? I stand and shove off that itchy wool blanket. My body is so hot with rage I don't need it.

"I'm going back to my room, but I'm not going with you. I'm not going anywhere with you," I say. I make sure to deliver that message right into Jack's smug little face so he won't pretend this has nothing to do with him.

I shove past him, making my way to the door. A searing pain slices through my knee when I put weight on it. I wince, careful not to show anyone I'm hurt so they don't slow me down.

"Natalie, what are you talking about?" Jack says.

I spin back to him, my eyes must be wild with fury. "Don't."

Whatever it is, my words or my tone, gets him to back off. Within seconds, I'm outside—the cold wind dances around my body, but I don't mind. It reminds me that I'm still alive.

Ciel and Adip's footsteps trudge behind me. Adip catches up, curling his arm around me. "You should stay off your knee. Let me carry you," he says.

"I'm fine to walk."

His voice catches and I can tell he wants to argue, but he doesn't. That's the thing when you get attacked—people treat you like glass. They're so afraid you'll shatter into pieces. But most of them don't realize, when my mom died, I was already broken.

⸙

Ten minutes later, I'm back in my room. Warmth floods my cheeks and I feel a sense of gratitude that I'm even back in my dorm again. Adip and Ciel follow me inside.

"You want some tea?" Ciel asks.

"I'm okay. I just want to be alone." I flop into my cozy, blush-colored round chair that I hate. The minute I sink down, I notice the blood stains on my dress, the brownish-red hue of it splattered on the cherry red fabric—like a macabre painting.

Adip and Ciel watch me and exchange concerned glances. "I don't think you should be alone tonight. We can stay with you," Ciel says.

"I'm good. You can go."

"Natty…" Adip attempts to intervene.

"Thank you, guys, for everything, but I just want to be alone please." I'm praying they get the message or I'm going to start throwing things at them.

"Okay, we'll be in my room. Knock if you need anything," Ciel says. They leave… slowly, but they leave.

Finally some damn peace. I push myself to stand and begin to slip off my mud- and blood-caked dress. I wince, suddenly realizing how sore I am. Looking in the mirror is like a horror show. Twigs and leaves etched into my hair. My face streaked with mascara and tears. My eyes bloodshot and puffy.

I desperately need a shower, but something stops me from washing the night away. There's a rustling over my skin as my nerves awaken. I attempt to chase off the sensation, but truly, I don't want to. I've never felt this… on edge before.

He knew.

Hot, fierce confusion burns through me. How could Henry possibly have known unless he was involved somehow?

And as horrifying as that thought is, it doesn't scare me. Why? Why didn't I tell anyone? Why did I save him? All rationale vanished and I had some unexplained desire to save him. Why?

Even if he *was* involved, he still killed that guard to save me.

My body is somehow panicked and aroused at the same time, a dangerous concoction of feelings I no longer want to deal with right now.

I finally peel off my dress and make my way into the girls' bathroom. The hot water scalds my body as I wash away all the horrific remnants of the night.

The cold air stings as I step out of the shower and dry off. I slip on a robe, the fabric grazing over my knee. My body heats at the memory—the trauma and sadness and grief drains from my body and something else fills the empty space. Something… *arousing.*

I can feel Henry all over me. Pressing against my knee. Wrapping me into his arms.

My heart pounds as I pad back into my room in my slippers, hoping Ciel doesn't whip open her door and start another poorly cloaked interrogation. I boil some cinnamon tea and sink into my bed, taking a soothing sip. The spicy heat coats my insides, bringing my pounding heart down to a flutter.

As I lie down, it strikes me how my bed has never felt so comfortable. Soft, billowy blanket, clean and smooth sheets, my pillow arching and molding around my aching neck. The comfort is settling, allowing my mind to relax for a luxurious moment. Until something Henry said slips into my brain.

I saw.

He saw… what? My attacker? It's such an odd choice of words that it clings, refusing to leave my mind. The words play in a constant loop as I toss and turn and watch the clock slowly tick.

2:15 a.m. 2:16. 2:17.

There's no way I'm going to sleep tonight.

I should be scared, terrified of what just happened. And I am. But something else keeps winning my mental war—a desperate need to see him.

My legs move at their own volition, out of bed. Getting dressed. Slipping on sneakers. Internal alarm bells blare for me to stop, but something inside of me whines that I need to go to him. A dangerous seesaw between the desire to see him and the fear of what I might discover.

Desire wins.

CHAPTER SIXTEEN

HENRY

MY EYES RIP open. Sweat slicks my body.

I jolt up in bed to the familiar sights and sounds of my dorm room, but everything is amplified. The numbers on the alarm clock are blinding. The hum of the heater that I barely noticed before now seems to whir and whine. A faint drip sounds from the bathroom. How can I possibly hear water from the bathroom down the hall?

And when the hell did I fall asleep?

It's 2:17 a.m. I must have dozed off for about ten minutes. But in those ten minutes, I saw her. This time, not in a vision, but a dream. *Precogs don't have dreams.* At least, I've certainly never had a dream before.

I clutch my head—it feels fuzzy, different somehow, my dream still vivid, assaulting me with images. Maybe it's not a dream after all.

I wander through pitch-black woods, brushing against the scratchy bark of a tree. I don't recognize this place. *The trees are lush, in full bloom—branches and leaves dipping over the path.* What time of year is this? It can't be winter. Maybe spring? *I wear a T-shirt and jeans, sweat beading on my forehead.* It's too hot to be spring, must be summer. *I pull off my T-shirt and wipe the sweat from my face. I continue searching, growing more frantic.* What am I searching for?

I see her—Natalie, braced against a tree. I must have been looking for her. *She wears nothing but a flowing white dress. Her feet are bare, hair cupping her face with wild curls.* What is she doing out here? What are we doing out here?

She spots me approaching, her expression a mix of danger and delight. Her lips curl into a smirk, her eyes begging me to come closer. Were we meeting here—in this secret place?

I walk ahead, but before I can reach her, she spins away from me and breaks into a run. I pick up my pace, running after her. Why is she running away from me?

We weave in and out of the trees. Does she want me to chase her? She's not laughing, and this doesn't seem like a game. Or is it?

Finally, I reach her—my fingers clamp around her wrist and twist her body to mine. I press into her, pinning her against a tree. Her expression is full of pain and desire. Why? Did I do something to hurt her? Am I hurting her now?

"Why are you running away from me?" I say.

She doesn't answer as she studies my face. Why doesn't she answer? Does she want me?

Because there's nothing more I want in this moment than her.

She slips under my arm and escapes my grasp—running faster, farther. Guess I have my answer. *She is running away from me.* Maybe this vision means that when I tell her the truth about everything, she'll flee… scared of me. Scared of my ability.

No, there was something in her eyes. Something that tells me she's not scared. *I struggle to keep up with her, until she freezes and turns to me. I stop, too, leaving inches between us. She wants to tell me something—I know it. Her chest rises, lips purse.*

"*You can't save me, Henry,*" she says. Save her? I already saved her. What does that mean?

She tips backward and I lunge to catch her. Wait… we're on the edge of something. *I reach over to try and grab her hand, but it's too late. She plummets over the cliff and disappears into the rocky, watery abyss below.*

Dream… or vision?

Whatever it was, it feels as if it's holding the functions of my body hostage. I'm crouched on the edge of my bed, muscles aching. An eternity must have passed while I sat here, replaying this scenario.

2:20 a.m.

Three minutes? Three fucking minutes is all the time that's passed. I let out a guttural groan.

Since leaving Natalie, I feel like I can conquer the world and simultaneously destroy it. Apparently, a side effect of telling someone about your vision and then changing that vision, is that you go completely fucking insane.

The smart thing to do would have been to leave, just like I planned. But I chickened out. Or rather, desire and curiosity won out. Because I couldn't leave here… couldn't leave her. Not yet. Something inside me knows our story isn't finished. And my dream, or vision, or whatever the fuck that was, just solidified it.

A knock on my door startles me. My stomach plummets as I realize—this is it. *Someone knows.* The police. The precogs. It doesn't matter who.

I peer through the keyhole, shocked to see Natalie standing there. *Shit.* I'm on borrowed time, and I know she's here for an explanation. An explanation I can't give her.

Her knock grows impatient, and as if my hand is separated from my body, I find myself opening the door and meeting her gaze.

The first thing I notice is her scent. A waft of spicy, sweet cinnamon. I've smelled this on her before, but tonight, it's stronger. More enticing. She's surprisingly put-together after what just happened a few hours ago. Her face is scrubbed clean. Her hair slicked back into a bun. She's wearing sweats and a coat. She's breathing hard, her chest puffing up and down.

Then, I realize I'm not wearing a shirt… again. Just like the last time she visited my room. She doesn't seem affected by it this time. Her stance is purposeful—confident. She's here for answers.

How long have we been standing here, regarding one another? I pierce the bubble of our silence. "Are you okay?"

She shoves by me without a word, stopping just inches away from me. This is not good.

She folds her arms over her chest, penetrating me with a searing look. "I need you to tell me how you knew."

I close the door. How am I going to play this? I can't conjure any lie or an excuse that makes sense.

"I can't tell you that. I'm sorry," I say, pleading.

Her nostrils flare and her eyes pop open with wicked fury. I'm convinced she's going to punch me, and that's cool. I probably deserve it.

Finally she speaks, her voice brooding with anger. "Do you know how long I sat there lying to everyone about what happened? You owe me an explanation."

Maybe I can just grab my things and go. Run the hell away from this interrogation, from her. But what about my dream? What if it was an actual vision? What if I couldn't alter things—and she's still in danger? Maybe my purpose here is to protect her, no matter what. That thought glues me to this incredibly uncomfortable place we're in.

"Please trust me. It's better that you don't know," I say.

She bites down on her lip, not in a sexy way. In a way that she's trying to suppress her rage for me. She looks away and huffs out a frustrated breath. I wonder how long this stand-off is going to continue.

"Then at least answer this," she says. "How is it possible that you *saw* what would happen to me?"

Anxiety burns in my chest. I'm so damn stupid. Why did I say that to her?

"I don't think you heard me correctly. Or maybe I was nervous and didn't say the right thing. But I didn't mean that I *saw*. I just knew, but I can't tell you how."

She pierces me—with her stare, her wrath, her doubt.

"Fuck you then," she says, and storms out.

CHAPTER SEVENTEEN

NATALIE

I'M A MESS.

Light glitters through the sheer pale pink curtains on my dorm room window. I've never hated the sun so much in my life. Or those ugly ballerina curtains.

I yank the covers over my head, desperate not to face the world today. Or maybe ever. Sleep is a distant wish, and I've been trapped in this state of restless exhaustion all night. My limbs twinge and ache—I don't know what to do with my legs, my arms, how to make myself comfortable. Will I ever be comfortable again?

Flashes of last night's attack play out in my mind like a silent movie. My neck still pulses where the knife was pressed, and I swear I can still feel it there. My stomach swirls and churns at the cold metal that still seems so present.

My knee tingles, right at the spot Henry touched when he tended to my wound. Goosebumps prickle my skin as I recall his warmth. The way he held me. The way he looked at me.

All night, I've roiled between disgust and lust—an agonizing combination.

He knew… and he refuses to tell me how.

Every time I remind myself, whenever the cold truth that Henry knew about the attack sinks in, my chest constricts, squeezing all the oxygen from my lungs.

A faint knock on the door jostles me from my thoughts. My teeth grit at the interference. *I don't want to see anyone. Go away.*

There's another knock and the doorknob turns. Damn, I should have remembered to lock it when I got home last night. I was so twisted up from Henry's refusal to tell me something—anything—that I just collapsed.

The door creaks open and the person I least want to see peeks around the corner—Jack. My gaze lands on the half-empty teacup on my nightstand and I consider throwing it in his stupid face, but I really don't have the energy. All that I have left for him is a dull layer of disgust.

He's careful, hesitant, as he pads across the room and gently sits on the edge of the bed. My body stiffens when the mattress dips with this weight. He snakes out a hand and circles his fingers along my back, the same way you'd soothe a crying child. It should be a comforting gesture, but it just feels cold and distant and wrong. As if he's a complete stranger.

Mustering any strength I have left, I shift away from him and sit up, pressing my back against the headboard so he can't touch me there any longer. He leans in to trace his finger over my cheek, but I chop his hand away. He retreats, wounded.

"Leave," I say. There's no wavering or invitation to argue in my tone.

"You've been through a lot. I know you don't mean to hurt me," he says.

Hurt… him? Jesus, could he be more self-absorbed? His girl-friend, the person he's supposed to "love," was just attacked and he's worried about his own emotional state?

I glare at him, pointed and blunt. "I don't care if you're hurt."

"Natalie, don't say that."

My teeth clench down so hard they might crack—it takes everything in my power not to strangle him. "I don't need you to police me. I'll say whatever I want. And what does it matter what I say? You're with Josephine, right?"

And there it is. Guilt creeps onto his stupid, reddened face. "Josephine? What are you talking—?"

I cut him off, sarcasm dripping. "I saw you together last night, so I don't need your excuses. I'm all good on those." I swing my legs off the bed and press myself to stand. I need to get away from him, put some distance between us, before I explode. I've never been physically violent towards anyone, but my palm is twitching, adrenaline surging, and I don't even recognize myself right now.

"Nothing happened," he says. It's the most meek and mild response I've ever heard from him. I wonder what everyone would think of their perfect class president now—a lying, weak-willed snake.

"Bullshit," I say, pacing the room. My pulse races and my energy ratchets with every step. The strangest part is I don't even care that much anymore about him, or what he did. But there's this throbbing inside of my head—no, my stomach? Heart? I don't know, but I'm about to explode.

Jack stands and tries to block my movement. "You should rest."

"Leave," I say. With every retort, there's a deeper churning inside of me. My veins seem to pulse with fire, like some external force is feeding me power and life.

Jack sinks back onto the bed, hanging his head. He can't even look at me. "Can I at least explain?" he says, his voice reduced to a quiet whisper.

I ignore him and put on my tea kettle. There's no explanation Jack can give that would make an ounce of sense, and I'm in no mood for whatever bullshit he wants to dish out. Mentally, I feel like I could run a marathon or go fourteen rounds with a heavyweight fighter, but I know I just need to chill… calm my nerves. So tea it is.

"I swear nothing happened," he says.

Is he serious? I'm about to crack this tea kettle over his head, but I don't want to ruin the kettle.

"Do you think I'm an idiot? I saw you in that room with her."

His eyes widen, knowing he's screwed. I'm not sure if he's more freaked out that I caught him, or by my behavior.

"Listen, she cornered me—"

Oh, he is *not* going there. I'm not *letting* him go there. "So you're just going to blame everything on her? *You* cheated. *She* didn't cheat on me. Take some responsibility for once."

Jack stares at me in disbelief. "I didn't cheat on you. She told me she had feelings for me, but I told her I was in love with you."

His proclamation of love makes my gut churn. "You have an interesting way of showing love."

He looks away and I'm just so done with this conversation and this entire façade of a relationship.

"I felt bad. She was really upset, and I didn't want to hurt her," he says.

I snap. "So you decided to hurt me." It's not a question. He made that choice, but he never thought I'd find out because underneath all that confidence and bravado, he's really just a coward. I wish the security cameras still worked in our dorm rooms so I could release this pathetic conversation to the whole Lockwood student body.

Jack's mute, he can't even muster a response. For a future presidential candidate, he sure needs to work on his debate skills.

"I can't do this anymore. I know you've been seeing her behind my back for a while. We're over. We've *been* over," I say. And it feels really good to finally say it. I should have said it a long time ago.

Jack rushes over to me and clasps my hands in a panic. I yank them away and wipe them against my body, grossed out by his touch.

"No, you can't break up with me," he says, pleading.

"I can do whatever I want."

My kettle whistles and pops, and I busy myself preparing my tea. Jack watches my every movement as if it's the last time he'll see me.

"Natalie, please. I promise I didn't do anything wrong. I love you. We can't break up." His whining grates on my ears, making me wince. "I think you're just freaking out because you were attacked, and that's understandable."

This pisses me off more than anything. How would he presume to know anything about my attack, about how I feel?

"Get out," I say. Rage laces my words. It must be enough to convince him because he obeys, hanging his head as he slowly walks out the door.

There's no emptiness at his absence. No sadness. After all this time together, I'm left feeling nothing for him.

❧

I make it through the rest of my post-attack, post-breakup weekend better than expected. Ciel and Adip dote on me constantly—make me tea, make me laugh, bring food from the dining hall so I don't have to leave my room. I've always had a cautious friendship with both of them, never entirely clear of their motives. But this past weekend has proven that maybe they really do give a shit about me. Maybe I've been too guarded all this time.

When Monday rolls around, I manage to get myself to French class. We have a test, but after what happened, I most certainly would have been excused. My real motivation for going to class is just to see Henry again. Even the anticipation of seeing him gives me a sick sort of illicit thrill.

All weekend, I wanted to rush back his room, chase him down, demand an explanation. But I figured giving him a few days of space might help him come around, even though staying away from him felt like dying a slow and torturous death.

At some point, he's got to talk to me, he's got to tell me the truth. And I'm determined to do whatever it takes to make that happen.

Ciel and I walk together to French class and take our normal seats. Whispers snake through the classroom, and I know they're about me. Gossip ranks at the top of Lockwood's favorite activities, and my attack—and subsequent breakup—is headline news.

When the bell rings, Henry still hasn't arrived. My heart plummets—where is he? I can't get the thought out of my head that maybe he left school. Escaped out of my life forever.

The idea that he might be gone leaves me pained, shivering, numb. I have a strange sense of abandonment, which I recognize is ridiculous, but clearly all rationale has left the building at this point.

I don't even realize class is over until the other students begin shoving their chairs and collecting books— murmuring, gossiping, clicking, zipping.

As if in slow motion, I slip my book into my backpack, my mind clouded only with thoughts of Henry.

"Natalie, can you hang back a moment, please?" Ms. Whitney asks, shooting me a comforting smile. I trudge over to her desk, suddenly feeling weighted and exhausted.

She looks me over. "How are you?" she asks, but clearly already knows the answer.

I shrug. "Not great."

"Why don't you take a few days off? We could call your father."

I shake my head no. That's the last thing I want. There's no way anyone's prying me off this campus until I get my answers from Henry. Until I see him again. *Until I can touch him again.* My heartbeat speeds up. This constant state of panic and arousal is giving me whiplash.

"I feel better coming to class. Otherwise, I'll just focus on the fact that everything fell apart—like my relationship." There. I'll just get Ms. Whitney off my back by distracting her with my meaningless breakup.

"What do you mean by relationship?" she says. Guess the rumor mill hasn't spread as wide as I thought.

"Jack and I broke up," I say, attempting to muster some emotion.

Ms. Whitney's eyes pop open in shock, but she quickly pulls herself together. Ugh, even she's swept up in the gossip.

I excuse myself and trudge down the crowded hallway, ignoring the stabbing gazes of my classmates. Is everyone so bored that they have nothing else to fixate on but my breakup?

Meanwhile, Jack—*us*—is the furthest thing from my mind.

I exhale a pent-up breath.

Where is he? Where is the person who saved my life? The person who is clearly lying to me.

A frustrated quickening rises in my stomach. There's a wrongness to it, a restless tremble that rises and falls in my body.

I have to find Henry.

Please let him still be here.

CHAPTER EIGHTEEN

HENRY

I WONDER HOW long I can survive in my room without coming out.

My bottled water and mac and cheese rations are dangerously low, and I have no coffee. Not that I'm eating and drinking all that much. Or sleeping. I'm constantly haunted by her, dreaming of her, thinking of her.

She's always occupied my thoughts—owned my whole fucking life since I got to this school.

I check the clock, realizing I just missed French class, and a familiar pang of longing creeps in. I missed an opportunity to see her, but seeing her is the worst thing I can do right now. She'll just keep demanding answers I can't give.

I lie in my bed, unspooling a thread from my blanket. It started as a way to shake out my nerves and now this blanket is shredded into oblivion. Feels good to destroy something when the walls are closing in, when my body is aching and restless.

I need to get the hell out of this room.

My weekend consisted of hiding from Natalie, doing whatever exercise I could manage in this small space with no equipment, and dreaming about Natalie. I'm going fucking insane.

Wes stopped by a few times, yelling through the door, but I never answered. He's gotta know by this point that I changed my vision—I'm sure the news about Natalie's attack is all over the school. Wes is probably salivating over what I did, dying to know what happened, what I felt, and what's changed.

I don't want to tell him a damn thing. It somehow cheapens everything—feels wrong to talk about Natalie's attack with anyone because it's her experience. I don't need to co-opt it with my own feelings and fears.

Even hiding in this room, I'm making it all about me. Ensuring my safety, if only for a brief time. God, I'm a coward.

Sure, I can't tell her how I knew. But I can least come out from hiding. Can face her, at least—even though I'm dreading our next conversation. Dreading that all she wants from me is information, an explanation. Understandable, sure, but it's so divergent from what I wish she wanted.

Me.

I know that can never happen.

An hour later, I'm soaked with sweat and feeling maybe five percent better. Instead of being a coward, I went to the gym and pounded out my frustration on every piece of equipment I could find.

I yank my sweatshirt over my head and step outside. It's cold as fuck today, and the wind bites even harsher against my sweat. My plan was to grab some coffee and food from the dining hall and head back to my room, but the faint sound of a girl's voice shouting my name stops me in my tracks.

It's the blonde I met the day I spoke to Oliver. Josephine, I think her name is? She's already heading towards me, her ponytail bouncing as she walks. I manage a smile, not wanting to be rude.

"Hey, Henry. I haven't seen you around lately," she says. Her blue eyes glisten in the sun and she's got those rhinestone things under her eyes again. I detect some eagerness, maybe even desperation in her voice. I'm not sure what that's about.

"Yeah, I haven't been feeling well," I say, shifting on my feet.

"I'm sorry to hear that." She pouts and squeezes my arm. "Is there anything I can do for you?"

She rakes her eyes up and down my body, and there's a hint of suggestion in her voice. Okay, more than a hint—practically a megaphone of desire. I don't sense her attraction is directed specifically at me, though. More like she's a girl who likes to flirt, and thinks she has to act this way to get guys to pay attention. That might be true for some guys, but not for me.

"I don't need anything, but thanks for asking. Nice running into you." I paste on a smile, not wanting her to feel completely rejected. The last time I saw her, she was in tears and I'm not looking to send anyone away crying. I've caused enough pain.

I try to skirt past her, but she clasps onto my arm—almost desperate. It's a strange feeling, comparing her touch to Natalie's. Josephine's grip just feels normal. Skin on skin—no heat, no tingle, no fire. It's almost comforting, because any time I touch Natalie, I can barely exist without losing my mind.

"I was going to get some coffee. Do you want to join me? My treat. You look like you might need it," she says.

Shit, I was already headed there anyway. How bad would it look if I told her no, and still went to the dining hall? Pretty bad.

Maybe it would be good for me to hang out and have a normal conversation with someone. She seems nice enough, and as long as I'm clear that there's nothing more than friendship between us, there's no harm in a cup of coffee.

⌇

The dining hall buzzes with activity, and fortunately no one seems to notice my existence, or previous absence. I get lost in the sea of students, which is a good thing.

I take a long sip of my black coffee and the caffeine feels so fucking good. Josephine sits across from me, drinking some lavender triple foam I don't even know what. I teased her about her order and she instantly took offense.

"What do you think of Lockwood so far?" she says, sucking some foam off her finger. Jesus, I'm really going to have to be blunt with her.

"I don't think much of it," I say.

She giggles at my response. "I looked for you at the ball," she says.

My body pulses with anxiety. *The ball.* Did she see me with Natalie? Maybe that's why she wanted to have coffee—because she has questions.

"I was hoping I could get a dance," she says.

I exhale the breath I was holding. So she didn't see us, thank god.

"You would have been disappointed. I don't really dance," I say, hoping to squash any kind of romantic notions she's angling for.

"I bet I could convince you," she says seductively. I'm about to shut her down when, like magic—or more like a nightmare—Natalie appears.

She's alone, but appears to be searching for someone. Probably her asshole boyfriend. Her uniform is slightly disheveled, her hair messy—which I love. She seems exhausted, lost... distant. Something inside of me is dying to run over to her, wrap her in my arms, comfort her. But I know that's the last thing she wants. She only wants one thing from me, and it's definitely not holding her in my arms.

Her eyes lock with mine and her expression morphs from exhaustion to anger. Extreme anger. Repulsive anger. Like she wants to tear my head off.

"Do you know Natalie?" Josephine asks. I'm not even sure how long I've been staring at her, but it must have been long enough for Josephine to notice.

"Not really, I just have a class with her."

Josephine studies me, jealousy pouring off her. I'm careful to minimize my emotions while still keeping an eye on Natalie. She's frozen in place, glaring at me—not even hiding it.

"She's a little rough, don't you think?" Josephine says.

"Rough? No, I don't think so." I immediately regret blurting that out. It's none of Josephine's business how I feel about Natalie. But damn, I just have a constant need to protect her from everything, including someone else's opinion.

Josephine suppresses a huff and I know she wants to argue, but she doesn't. Her hand grazes across the table and touches mine. Natalie seems to grow even more disgusted by Josephine's gesture. Wait—is she pissed at me? Or pissed that I'm with Josephine?

Whatever the reason, I pull my hand away and lean back in my chair—safe from any more of Josephine's advances. Her disappointment is palpable.

"Maybe we can hang out tonight," she says, her voice laced with promise. It barely registers in my charged stare-off with Natalie.

Then with one final glare, Natalie storms out of the dining hall.

My entire body lurches forward, dying to run after her. I collect my coffee cup and dump it in a nearby trash bin.

"Where are you going?" Josephine says, irritated.

"I have to go, sorry. Thanks for the coffee."

My legs move in panicked bursts. I don't even give a fuck in this moment if Josephine knows I'm chasing after Natalie.

Once I shove the doors open and smack my feet onto the concrete outside, Natalie's gone. Reality hits, paralyzing my entire body.

She saw me—and ran way. Not just ran away, but glared at me—revolted and disgusted—and *then* ran away.

She doesn't want to see me. I'm chasing after her, and she doesn't want that. She didn't ask for that.

And as much as I know I can't tell her the truth, that I can't answer her questions—it's painful, fucking crushing, to know that she can't even stand to be around me.

CHAPTER NINETEEN

NATALIE

I'M TRAPPED IN a bubble of frantic rage. Jealousy is devouring me whole. I hate that I'm jealous.

Seeing him with Josephine… it's like an attack. Worse than my *actual* attack. How messed up is that?

I race away from them, through campus on trembling legs, shifting and changing directions—unable to concentrate on anything but the image of Henry and Josephine together. I'm locked in this spiral of anger and horror and there's nowhere to escape.

When did they even meet? Did she ask him out, or did he ask her? I thought she was obsessed with Jack. Is this a sick joke? My stomach convulses so hard I'm afraid the toast I had for breakfast will spill out. I'm never eating toast again. I've lost my appetite forever until the end of time.

They were just sitting there, so cavalier. So cozy. Just two people enjoying their coffee, getting to know each other. It makes me want to vomit. *They* make me want to vomit.

I duck behind a bank of trees, pacing, not knowing what the hell to do with myself. The sun has almost set and the slickness of fallen rain coats the ground like gunmetal.

And then, just about the worst thing that could happen... happens.

It's Henry, walking ahead with Josephine calling after him. He pauses, then spins back to her, as she closes the distance between them. It all plays out like a slow-motion montage in a horror movie, and I'm numb. Frozen. I slide behind a tree out of view—wanting to die every second I watch this, but I can't look away.

What are they talking about? She seems to be asking for something, maybe begging. My rage boils and I'm completely consumed. I want to fucking scream out loud. To thrash and race over and shake him to his senses.

But why? He's nothing to me, and I'm nothing to him. Whatever fleeting connection we had wasn't about romance. Right? And he owes me an explanation, whether he's messing with Josephine or not.

He walks away and she watches him go. My hands ache, and I realize I've been clenching the straps of my backpack so hard all the blood has drained out while I lurk here, watching them.

Before rationale kicks in, I'm moving in Henry's direction—following him.

What the hell am I doing?

I don't know what I'm doing. I just know I'm burning... for answers. For closure. For beginnings. For him to say Josephine means nothing to him and that I'm the only person he thinks about.

Damn, why am I feeling this way?

I know I should stop. Nothing good can come from following him, from confronting him now.

But I keep going, up the winding path. He doesn't notice

me following behind. Maybe he's too distracted with thoughts of Josephine. That familiar jolt of jealousy takes over and presses me forward.

He's gaining ground, far enough ahead of me that he flings open the door to the hall where his room is housed. The door slams shut behind him. I have a moment—staring at that closed door. If I go in there, nothing will be the same.

I don't care.

I suck in a deep breath and forge ahead, climbing the stairs two at a time.

As my feet smack onto the top floor—there he is. About to twist his key in the lock, pausing when he sees me. My chest is heaving, and I'm out of breath. I want to rush up to him, grab him, hit him. I'm so out of sorts that I can't comprehend my own feelings.

It's dark in the hallway. Empty. Dead quiet. I bet he can hear my breathing.

"What are you doing here?" he says, his voice a low grumble. His chest rises and falls quicker—his breath speeds in my presence.

Say something.

I take a step toward him, my shoe creaking on the old floor. Then another. My footsteps echo in the empty space. He flinches the closer I get.

He studies me, eyes blazing. Drawing me to him. All my anger starts to trickle away in that stare.

"Why won't you tell me how you knew about the attack?"

He flicks his eyes around, nervous. His jaw clenches and he's almost panting. "Because I can't."

That refusal again. It triggers something deep and dark inside of me, acting like a truth serum.

"Why were you with her?" The words tumble out before I can think twice. I instantly regret it.

"Who? Josephine?" His voice dips at her name, husky and sexy. My jealousy invades every inch of the hallway.

"Yes."

He looks away from me, blowing out a frustrated breath. "Why do you care?"

The truth balloons in my chest, lodging in my throat before I blurt it out.

Because I want you. Because you're mine.

I stay silent.

He snaps his wild green eyes back to mine, his body tightens. He's getting angry, I can see it. Feel it. But what does he have to be mad about? He's the one hiding, keeping secrets.

He throws his backpack to the ground and it smacks on the floor. Before I know what's happening, his fingers clamp against my wrist and tug me flush to his body. His fingers dig into my flesh. My veins are on fire as he thunders over me. His nostrils flare, his mouth opens then closes—like he's struggling to say something.

"What do you want from me, Natalie?" he asks in a gruff whisper.

I want answers. To everything. But the words again choke in my throat.

He shakes his head—Annoyed? Angry? Something else?—and lets me go. I'm struck by the coldness of his absence. He picks up his backpack and heads to his door.

Something rumbles deep inside of me, a ticking bomb about to explode. I throw my backpack on the floor and advance on him. I'm shaken, furious.

"I want you to stop playing games and tell me how you knew about my attack," I say, not messing around.

He turns to me with a different kind of intensity—colder, darker. It scares me, but not enough to back down.

"Stop it," he says, his voice harsh and strained.

"No. I'm not going to stop until you answer me." My heart pops out of my chest.

He bends toward me. "Not here."

"So what… I have to wait until you find a convenient place for you to tell me the fucking truth?"

He grabs me again, this time by the shoulders. I reach my hands up and clamp his wrists tight, which seems to make both of us more rabid. We're locked in this physical war of emotions—I've never felt so out of control. So alive. So terrified. We're both burning, about to singe into something dangerous.

"You should be thanking me for not telling anyone," I say. My words are laced with hate and lust and every mercurial emotion possible.

He knocks my hands away and presses his hand against my mouth. Asserting control over me, pressing his forehead against mine.

"Be quiet," he says, growling.

Fury ripples through me and I pry his hand off my mouth. He can't shut me up. Who the fuck does he think he is?

He stumbles back a few steps, his expression filled with disbelief. Like he's not sure what came over him. It throws me for a second—maybe there's an explanation for him behaving so reckless and rude?

Then I notice his fists balling at his sides. No, he doesn't get to be angry. Every ounce of frustration bubbles to the surface and all that's left is a scream.

"I lied to everyone for you. The least you can do is tell me the truth!"

This flares his anger to a breaking point. He lunges at me, and my breath escapes as he yanks me into his arms and hauls me toward the bathroom.

Terror cracks through me, sobering my senses. Is he going to hurt me? Did he know about the attack because he's behind it all? Is Henry Thorne going to kill me?

CHAPTER TWENTY

HENRY

SOMETHING ABOUT NATALIE, about this whole situation, makes me wild—pushes my edges, cracks them, breaks them. It's like I'm hovering above our bodies, watching this all play out—wondering why I've become this. Is it because I changed a vision? Maybe precogs don't need to worry about outside forces. Maybe when we defy our existence and rules, we only ruin ourselves.

Natalie pummels her fists against my arms, fighting me off. I can't let her go. My grip tightens as she shivers and squirms, her breath puffing out in short gasps.

She wouldn't stop talking, questioning me. Does she really believe this school isn't watching us? She's smart—she wouldn't just take them at their word that they shut off the cameras, would she?

I kick open the bathroom door with my foot and haul her inside.

"Let me go!" She's shouting now, and I know I can't force her. What I'm doing… it's horrible. Unfathomable.

This back and forth, push and pull between us has to end—it's driving me crazy.

I lock the bathroom door while clutching her thrashing body against it. At the very least, we have privacy in here.

She pushes against me with her body, her hip bone digging into my pelvis—but I don't pull away. I lean into it. The more she pushes against me, the more I push into her—unable to let her go.

"What the hell are you doing?" Her volume increases, her voice loud enough that it ricochets off the thin bathroom walls. My stomach boils. What if one of the cleaning crew walks by? They'll think she's being attacked, that I'm trying to hurt her when I just want to tell her the truth.

She manages to claw out of my grasp, and the color of her eyes shifts from brown to bright green. I'm lost in her heated gaze for a split second as I finally let her go.

She spins around in a flash, unlatching the door. I knock her hand away before she can succeed and wrap my arm around her waist, dragging her away from the door into the only corner of this bathroom she can't escape—the shower.

She wrestles against me as every ounce of my willpower dissolves for good.

"Let me go," she says, her voice strained.

I grip onto her forearms and pin them above her head against the cold tile. She whines as her body hits the wall, which only amplifies our fire. Her gaze trails to my lips, and for a second, I think she wants me to kiss her, but I banish the thought. *She's scared of me.* She should be—I don't even know who I am right now.

My curiosity around her desire is abolished when she lets out another scream. Panic climbs up my spine. I need some way to drown out her voice before someone hears.

My eyes land on the faucet, and I crank the handle. Cold water pummels down on our clothed bodies, dislodging the heat between us. We both freeze in the shock of it all— then the water warms, encircling us in steam.

She gapes at me as the water cascades down. Her hair is dripping—a few curls clinging to her long neck. Her white blouse is soaked through under her uniform jacket, her pale pink skin visible through the wet fabric. I'm frayed, coming apart, as I take her in—drenched in this lockdown of agony and lust.

Just the sight of her now, our gasping breath heavy, intertwined, is so fucking distracting. My grip softens, just for a second—but long enough for her to yank her arm away and slap me across the face.

My wet cheek stings from the force. She's strong, stronger than I expected. Her slap stirs something deep inside of me, in those dark recesses that you hope never see the light of day.

She tries to shove past me, but I twist her body, shoving her back against the wall. She emits something—a moan, a cry. I'm not sure. Whatever it is, it's intoxicating. I'm drowning here, with the heaviness of the water, the intensity of being so close to her. I wrap my hands around the back of her neck and fist her hair, pressing my body against hers. I know it's wrong. So damn wrong.

"I hate you," she says. Her hands climb to my chest and I'm waiting for her to push me away, but she clenches my shirt. Pulling me closer. *Fuck.*

"You don't hate me. I can feel that you don't hate me," I say.

Her breath catches in her throat and then she cranks her head to the side, refusing to look at me. "I hate you," she repeats. Her voice is laced with disgust. She still won't meet my gaze, which makes my blood boil.

"I don't believe you," I say, that sinister emotion bubbling inside.

"I was attacked *because* of you. You knew." There's so much vitriol in her words. Her refusal to even look me in the fucking eye. The notion that she could think I was the reason she got attacked.

And then, I snap.

I grab her by the face and force her to look at me. If I'm going to tell her the truth, she's going to look me in the eye while I do it.

"I can see things," I say through clenched teeth. "I saw what was going to happen to you."

"That's not possible. You're lying." she says, furious.

I match her tone. "I can see the future."

Her eyes widen in horror and disbelief as that sinks in. I press on, refusing to give her any time to process.

"No one can fucking know about this, and I'm putting both of us at risk by telling you, but you just wouldn't give up, would you?" I'm screaming now, nearly spitting out the words—all restraint vanished.

She's trembling, almost convulsing. But I can't stop. "I risked everything to save you. And now that you know the truth, do you regret saving *me*? Huh, Natalie? Do you regret that you saved a freak… lied to everybody, for me?"

She's speechless. We're frozen, the water bleeding down over us, my hand squeezing her face. I stare her down, trying to process what the fuck just happened. Shame envelopes my body—what am I doing? Why am I treating her like this? Why did I tell her that way, or at all?

I shove away from the wall—away from her.

"Fuck!" My guttural reaction causes her to flinch. I smack my hand against the shower, the glass rattling on impact.

I step out of the shower, heavy with pain, rage, and regret. Water pours off my clothed body, soaking the floor.

Natalie still hasn't moved an inch, panting under the steady stream of water. Guilt rakes through me—I need to apologize, beg for her forgiveness, for treating her like that. For scaring her. I curl my fingers through my hair and start to pace. My feet slosh in the water on the floor as I try, and fail, to calm down.

As I squeeze my eyes shut, fast footsteps race over the soaked floor.

She's leaving.

Every one of muscles vibrates, dying to hold onto her.

But I have to let her go.

CHAPTER TWENTY-ONE

NATALIE

THE DOOR OF Henry's building slams shut behind me. Something about the squeaking metal, the friction, creates a cold crack in my otherwise numb veneer. My brain's completely frozen, unable to process what he just told me without overloading.

He can see the future.

His words ring like a gunshot and a chill rips through my body. No way. He's got to be lying—lying to cover up some darker truth. But what the hell is the truth? Fear smacks into my brain.

No. I have to stay focused and figure this out.

Henry is eighteen years old. He doesn't even know me. My attack was random—at least that's the conclusion the police came to. I suppose they could have made a mistake, that there's some bigger conspiracy at play and Henry is somehow involved with that creepy guard.

Why would anyone conspire to kill me though? Unless I wasn't the target. Maybe they were trying to hurt me to get back at someone else.

My eyes water, blurring the path ahead. Cold water from the shower drips down my legs, my shoes slipping and sloshing on the muddy ground. I just need to get back to my dorm. Focus… and make it to my room.

What if Henry is telling the truth? What if he does have these mystical powers that he buried as a secret and risked everything to warn me… to save me? No, that's impossible. That shit only happens in fairy tales, and I'm the farthest thing from a princess. I don't need—or want—to be saved.

"Natalie?"

Jack seemingly appears out of nowhere, advancing on me. Maybe he was hiding in the bushes like a creep. At this point, anything's possible.

I fixate ahead, quickening my pace. I don't have to talk to him. We're broken up, I owe him nothing, and he's the last person I want to see right now.

"Natalie!"

He's not giving up, his footsteps pounding the path, closing in. His fingers curl around my arm and he yanks me to face him. I recoil, ripping my arm from his grasp.

"Why are you all wet? Are you hurt?" I know he's concerned— who wouldn't be? I'm running through campus in the freezing cold, soaking wet. I must look like a true crime reenactment.

"I'm fine," I say in a mumble. "I have to go."

As I escape the confrontation, I'm surprised, and relieved, that he doesn't follow.

❧

The minute I duck into my dorm room, I brace against the wall, catching my breath. My clothes and hair are plastered against my body. I'm angry—boiling angry—and yet… intoxicated? I don't trust Henry…or do I? No, I hate him. But I can't deny that every time I'm near him, it's like firecrackers burst all over my skin.

At some point in my hazy fog of fucked up emotions, I manage to take a hot shower, change into sweats, and make tea—but forget to drink it. I stare into the mug of cold water where a saggy cinnamon tea bag floats somewhere near the bottom. This is a metaphor for my life. I set down the cup and slip under my covers, shutting out the world.

He can see the future.

And, just like that, I'm full-on obsessing. I bolt upright, almost frantic, and whip open my laptop.

Psychic. Consciousness. Premonition.

Hundreds and thousands of results. Everything from strip-mall fortune tellers to life coaches gifted with "magical psychic abilities" to unlock your abundance (whatever that means) to creepy, monster-like fables. None of these are right. None of these are Henry.

Then I stumble upon something called precognition. It's a Latin derivative about seeing events in the future. *Interesting.* I fall down the hole of stories—one about a woman named Helen Potter who claims her visions have helped law enforcement to pin murder suspects. Her website is all turquoise and soothing and features mantras about taking your soul on a journey and tapping into your inner psychic wisdom. I click around and notice the site hasn't been updated since 2013. A quick Google search of her name reveals the truth—Helen Potter is a sham. Since being exposed, she's denounced her previous mystic lifestyle to join some cult who believes tarot cards are constructed by the devil. Yikes.

I hunt a bit more, landing on a different woman who claims to have precognitive powers. She calls herself a precognitive empath and has premonitions about the future either while awake or in a dream. Her biggest gift is knowing when people are ill, and she's saved numerous people from getting a troubling cancer diagnosis before it was too late. She was on *Oprah*… that's got to mean she's legit, right? It's *Oprah*.

Oh wait… wasn't Oprah conned by that author who fabricated his addiction? So even Oprah gets it wrong sometimes.

Ugh. We're all fucked.

I slam my laptop shut and sink back under the covers.

Why are you lying to me, Henry Thorne?

§

The next day, I make my way to French class, numb. I doubt I'll see Henry. He's probably long gone by now after last night's mess. My eyes are puffy and bleary from no sleep. I've yanked my matted hair into a bun and my uniform is wrinkled beyond belief. I know my classmates are watching me, judging me, but I don't give a shit.

As I get closer to the classroom, the air thickens—almost like it's burning. It's both a familiar and foreign feeling. My entire body tingles with heat, and that's when I see Henry, standing a few paces away. His green eyes are dull and exhausted, his face is pale, and his hair is unruly and messier than usual. He clearly hasn't slept either.

Good.

The tension is excruciating. Whenever we're this close, he's usually staring at me. But not this time. Today he's doing everything to avoid eye contact with me. I wonder if he feels the air, the heat, between us.

My brain sizzles and pops with a million questions. Maybe with a good interrogation, I can get him to admit he's lying, admit *why* he's lying. I'll even promise not to say a word to anyone. We can both finally move on from this toxic bullshit.

I take a step toward him. His chest heaves and falls and he rubs the back of his neck. I'm affecting him.

Another step. Then another.

He still won't look at me, even when I'm inches away. It's as if we're the only two people standing in this hallway.

"Why won't you look at me?" That wasn't what I planned to say, but if I've learned anything from being around Henry it's that nothing pans out as I expect.

He meets my gaze—there's something pleading and pained in his expression, and I almost regret wanting him to look at me. I study his eyes. Maybe I can plumb an answer from those deep, soulful windows. His lips spasm in a hopeless attempt to speak when…

Jack steps in between us, shooting me a glare that vibrates with fury. I've never seen him so angry.

He turns his back to me and confronts Henry, leaning directly into his face. "What did you do to her?" Jack says, practically spitting his words—pointing back at me as he accuses Henry.

Henry flicks his gaze to me and tingles ricochet through my body. God, why does he affect me so much?

"I don't know what you're talking about," Henry says, unflinching.

"Bullshit. I saw her leaving your room upset. I'll give you one more chance to tell me what the hell you did to her."

My heart leaps into my throat. How did he know I was leaving Henry's room? There's no way…

Henry looks over at me again. Jack follows his gaze and his suspicion goes wild, as does his anger.

"What were you doing with him?" he says, his attention now fully directed at me.

"It's none of your business," I say. And it's not. We're no longer together, and no matter what went down with Henry, it has nothing to do with him.

Jack laughs, incredulous. His face is tomato-red and I'm waiting for him to throw himself to the floor into a full-scale temper tantrum. Instead, he hovers over me, crowding my space, attempting to intimidate me. He grips me by the shoulders and starts shaking me.

"None of my business, huh? Well I guess I know exactly what you were doing with him. Never figured you for a slut."

Before I can even react, Henry grabs him by the shirt and shoves him off me. I expect Jack to stumble back, maybe even crash to the ground—I've stared at Henry's biceps enough to know how strong he is.

But in some superhuman surge of strength, Henry sends Jack flying clear across the hallway. His body smashes into the lockers so hard one of them springs open from its lock.

Shock jolts every person in the hallway. Henry restrains himself from doing any more damage, while Jack lets out a painful wail. A few of our classmates crouch down to help him. Everyone oscillates between doting on Jack and glaring at Henry like he's a monster.

I'm unable to tear my eyes away from Henry. He stares back at me, like he's trying to read my mind.

How did he just do that? How could he be that strong to throw Jack across the hallway? Jack's not a small guy, athletic enough from playing polo.

Is it possible that Henry has some kind of power? And if it is possible, maybe he's not lying after all. Maybe he has more than one power. *What is he?*

I stand frozen, unsure what to do—until Henry makes the decision for me.

He clasps my hand and pulls me from the hallway. The other students crane their necks and whisper as we exit, but I don't care. I know this is the moment I'll finally learn the truth.

CHAPTER TWENTY-TWO

HENRY

FURY EXPLODES IN my gut as I drag Natalie by the hand down the long path where we can escape. She must be freaked out, questioning herself—probably seconds from running away. But she doesn't.

She hasn't spoken a word. I'm guessing she's in shock, or maybe she fucking hates me after everything that went down already. After everything I did and said, I wouldn't blame her. But she's still holding my hand. There's hope.

I tighten my grip and race ahead, faster, ducking both of us under the last security camera as we close in on the gate ahead. My mind spins with what happened back at the lockers—what I did to Jack. How did I manage to throw him across the hall when I barely touched him? I mean, I was so angry that he would talk to her like that and put his hands on her. An absurd amount of jealousy flashes through me just thinking about him touching her.

I grind to a halt in front of the iron gate. Natalie slams to a stop behind me, nearly crashing into my back. As if coming to her senses, she yanks out of my grip. "What the hell are you doing?"

I don't know what I'm doing.

"Do you trust me?" I say.

Her eyes widen with shock, blazing fierce and green and breathtaking. She's incredibly ambivalent about me, I get it. But she doesn't say no… she doesn't say anything.

I hop up onto the gate, hooking my foot into the steel slat, and look back at her, holding out my hand. She watches me, confused and curious. Ignoring my extended hand, she grips the steel gate next to me and climbs, quick and agile, and lands perfectly on her feet on the other side. *Impressive.*

As if reading my mind, she smirks at me through the gate. "I used to sneak out of my house all the time. You coming? Or you need a hand?"

I chuckle and climb after her, much less graceful. She stifles a laugh as I stumble a bit getting down. It cracks our tension, and for a brief moment, I think we might be okay.

I clasp her hand again and she doesn't fight as I lead her away from campus. As we move farther into the woods, her grip tenses and her expression hollows. In all the rush to get her alone, I didn't even consider that this is where she was attacked. This place is flush with horrific memories for her. I'm such an asshole.

"I'm sorry, we can find another spot," I say.

She straightens her spine and shakes her head, pulling some stray curls back into the messy knot piled on her head. "No, it's fine."

The atmosphere shifts between us—she stares at me, serious, sizing me up.

"What was that back there?" she says.

I shrug and lower my gaze. She wants answers I can't even give.

"I don't know," I say. Her lips curl into an oval as she puffs out a frustrated breath. I can't stop staring at her lips, wondering how soft they might be. Wondering how she might taste—probably like cinnamon.

"You must know," she says. Her voice is clipped, annoyed. It snaps me from my fantasy, breaking my thoughts and desire for her. That's probably for the best.

"I honestly *don't* know what happened back there. What I *do* know is what I told you already. That I can see the future. That I'm a precog—short for precognitive. That's what we're called."

She crosses her arms, closing off her body, and inches away, distancing herself from me. Understandable, even though it stings. Even though I'm dying to close that distance between us and tell her everything she wants to know while tracing those lips with mine, ripping her hair down and curling my hands into it…

"So there are more of you?"

Again, she breaks my thoughts. Right… *focus*. Answer her questions, she deserves to know.

"Yes, there are more of us. Not many, but we're out there," I say.

"Are you human?"

Her question surprises me, and I don't know why. Of course she'd wonder if I'm human—I have this power and she just saw me fling her ex across a hallway like he was a used Kleenex.

"Yes, I'm human. I just have an ability."

"You can see the future and have some weird superhero kind of strength. I think you have more than an ability," she says. And damn… she's right. I take a couple of deep breaths as realization sinks in—is there something more to my ability?

"It must be nice to be a hero. Going around and saving people you have visions about."

"You're the only person I've ever saved. The only person I've ever told. The only person I've ever changed a vision for."

She's dumbstruck by my response. I wonder if my admission was too much, too intense for her—but then I realize that the weather is a cruel bitch today and she must be freezing out here wearing just her uniform.

I peel off my uniform jacket and wrap it around her shoulders. She doesn't budge as I wind my arms around her, my hands grazing her shoulder blades. As I tighten my jacket around her to create some heat, my hands connect with her arms and the ground begins to stir. The leaves float up a few inches, swirling in a bizarre fall-colored mosaic. No gust of wind, though. Strange. Natalie seems to have noticed it too.

Startled, I stop touching her and the ground settles. All I can hear is the sound of our breaths as they escalate, wondering what the hell just happened. Was it an earthquake?

"What was that?" She reaches out and clenches onto my arm. The moment her hand touches my skin, the ground shifts and rumbles again, the leaves lifting, swirling, and stirring. She quickly releases her hand, and it stops.

What the hell is going on? I peer around—we're still alone and everything is silent again. But something is happening out here, ignited by our touch, and I have to know what it is.

"Can I try something?" I say.

She nods. I circle behind her and slide my hands onto her shoulders. Again, the ground stirs—the tremor doesn't affect our balance, but we feel it. The leaves begin to rise and swirl like a cyclone.

"Henry." I know she's freaked out by the tone of her voice.

"Close your eyes," I say. I don't want her to be scared, but I have to know what's going on. Is this happening because of us, because of our connection? I'm confused… intrigued… terrified.

I'm not sure if she closes her eyes or not, but her neck and shoulders relax a bit. I press my thumb into the nape of her neck and massage as the leaves continue to whip around, cocooning us into a spectacular mass of red and gold and orange. I soften the tension in my hands and the cyclone stops—the leaves flutter, delicate, in the air.

"Open your eyes," I say. She gasps and spins around, staring at this insane atmospheric shift in complete awe.

She faces me, studies me. Her eyes seem clouded with something… fear? Desire? Both? My heart thuds as we lock into this moment, the leaves dwindling to the ground and the atmosphere settling, but everything between us ratcheting up.

Heat washes through me and I'm completely consumed. I fixate on her hair. I long for those unruly curls to be freed, wild. Before I realize it, words tumble out of my mouth.

"Take down your hair." I don't ask, I command.

She eyes me for what feels like forever, then follows my order. She yanks out the hair tie and shakes out those beautiful, chestnut-colored curls.

I slam my body into hers and fist the back of her head, craning her neck so she's looking right up at me. A soft moan escapes her lips. She snakes her hands around my back, and her nails sink into my shirt, raking down my back. I hold back a groan as I cover her mouth with mine. She tastes amazing—sweet and spicy. I've pecked a few girls before, but nothing compares to this… to her. I feel this kiss in every part of my body.

For a moment, her lips are hesitant—inviting, but holding back. Then she seems to explode—perhaps with desire or pent-up emotions or… I don't know what. I don't really care. I only care that she's mine. Right now, she's mine.

We break apart for air, both of us panting. I trace my eyes over her face, unable to read her expression. "Are you okay?"

She pins me with her eyes again, then slams her mouth back into mine—moaning… like she's dying. I can feel how much she wants me and it drives me absolutely insane. I haul her legs around my waist and cradle us down to the ground until she's lying flat on her back and I can settle between her thighs. Our lips never break apart—writhing, shivering, clawing at each other.

And then suddenly…

She begins to go limp. Her lips relax, her head dips back. I catch the back of her hair and cradle her neck so it doesn't smack the ground. Dread races through my mind. Is she okay? What the hell is happening?

"Dizzy," she says through skittered breath.

"Okay, it's okay," I say. But I'm not sure if it is. I climb off her and stroke her hair while she holds onto my hand. What did I just do? Did I hurt her? Did I push this too far, too fast? Dammit, what is wrong with me?

Her eyes start to flutter and roll back.

"Natalie," I say, panicked. "Stay with me."

Her grip flattens and her eyes flutter again. She's quickly losing consciousness.

"Natalie!" I shake her gently, then harder—but it doesn't help.

Her breathing stills… and her eyes fall shut.

CHAPTER TWENTY-THREE

NATALIE

WHERE THE HELL am I?

I stir awake, not quite able to peel open my eyes. Chilled air nips at my skin, and my body trembles with an onslaught of wind. A tightness pulls in my chest, as if my lungs are starved for air.

Am I floating? I'm certainly not walking—my legs are jelly.

Am I dead? Is this what happens when you die?

I blink hard to clear the cobwebs from my sight. There's a familiarity in this space. The trees above—old and twisted and blanketed in colorful leaves with dead edges, the first glimpse of winter just around the corner. A rich mahogany flag flutters in the chilly breeze, our school's emblem dotting both sides with bright yellow.

School.

My memory floods in.

I recall Henry's lips pressed against mine, causing a stir of heat. We'd crashed to the ground, and I felt him everywhere. I lick my lips, noticing my mouth still tastes of him. He devoured me, slow and passionate—nothing has ever felt as good as that kiss. *Nothing.*

Then… what the hell happened?

My senses crawl back into my brain as I look up at Henry, realizing he's carrying me. He doesn't seem to notice that I'm awake. I savor the brief moment to study every angle of his face—the sharp peaks, his delicious jaw, his lips. *Those lips.*

Our gazes clash and concern washes over his gorgeous face. He lies me down onto the ground, as gentle as glass. I normally hate being treated so delicately, but somehow, when he does it, it's a whole other story.

"You're okay." Not a question—he seems relieved.

I nod and attempt to speak, but nothing comes out. My throat is dry and cracked, as if hundreds of tiny knives are stabbing at it.

I study Henry's face, and my body aches with an overwhelming urge to kiss him again—to pull him down on top of me. I try to ignore my desperation for him. I'm not a desperate girl. I bite down on my lip, a feeble attempt to crowd out my hunger for him.

"Can you walk?" he asks. Clearly, he's not picking up on my desperation. Good.

I nod and press up to stand, but my legs are far too weak and give out. In a split second, Henry's there, steadying me.

I manage to croak out a few words. "I don't know what happened."

"Did you eat this morning?"

I shrug, honestly not remembering. I can't seem to concentrate on anything right now—least of all what I ate, or didn't eat, earlier.

⁓

He carries me to the gate, and in some Herculean effort, manages to lift me over and help me land safely on the other side. We try not to make a scene as he helps me across campus, back to my dorm, his arm tucked around my waist—enveloping me. His warmth is so comforting. So… damn… hot.

Once tucked safely inside my room, Henry helps me into bed. He even pulls the covers around me—the sweetest of gestures that only makes me want him more.

He opens the small fridge in my room and studies its contents. A half-eaten yogurt. An avocado. Salad dressing. I can't see his face, but somehow, I know he's disappointed by the lack of food.

"Remind me to bring you some macaroni and cheese next time," he says.

Next time.

That means he wants to come back. My head swirls with all the things we might do in this room, next time. None of them involve macaroni and cheese.

He sifts through my cabinet before settling on some crackers and one of those pretentious jars of nut butter with twenty-seven ingredients.

"Here, this should help settle your stomach." He holds the cracker to my mouth and I can't help but smile that he's feeding it to me. I take a small bite, trying not to get crumbs everywhere.

As soon as I swallow, my stomach churns. Thank God for the trash can next to my bed because within seconds, I vomit. I wipe my mouth, hating that he's seeing me like this. My future fantasies of us dissipate in my pool of puke.

Henry watches with concern. "I should take you to the nurse."

"No," I say. "All they're going to do is give me a shot of some bullshit medicine that I don't need. Plus, they'll have to call my father—and the less he knows, the better."

Henry looks surprised by my choice, but doesn't argue. I get cozy under the covers while he perches on the side of my bed.

"I think this is my fault," he says, his demeanor grim.

"Why do you say that?"

"I don't know. I think something happened—when I kissed you. I may have hurt you…"

I don't catch the rest of what he says because I'm fading again. It's the weirdest feeling, losing consciousness—yet being so aware of what's happening and having such a strong urge to tell him how much I want him…

❧

I snap awake, rocketing forward. It takes me a moment to realize where I am and what just happened.

I'm alone. My body is slick with sweat, but I'm freezing. I realize my window is cracked open, and I climb out of bed, mustering strength to glide it shut.

I peel off my sweat-soaked clothes, feeling gross, and yank on my robe. I desperately need a shower, but I'm too exhausted to walk the few steps it takes to get there. Besides, I might run into Ciel or any of the other girls in the dorm and I'm definitely not up for a chat.

My eye catches something on my nightstand—a bottle of aspirin and what looks like a note. I carefully unfold the letter:

Natalie, I hope you feel better when you wake up, but take these if you don't. - Henry. p.s. Scholarship kid is definitely into you

Nothing can wipe this permanent grin from my face. I reread the note again. And again. I flop into bed and read it once more before clutching it to my chest. My life has somehow become a fucked up rom-com, and I love every second of it.

I take the aspirin and nurse some cinnamon tea, feeling a million times better a few hours later. But I can't shake what Henry said to me—about him being responsible for what happened earlier. Goosebumps awaken on my skin and an uneasy feeling creeps through me. Why would he think that? And why the hell did I pass out while we were kissing?

I finally shower, letting the hot water roll down my body longer than usual. I manage to avoid any run-ins with other students as I duck back in my dorm room and spend a little extra time getting ready. I tousle my curls and swipe on some pink gloss and rub some of my favorite perfume on my wrists and behind my ears, barely containing my excitement. I'm ready to confess… and tell Henry exactly how I feel about him.

⤬

Clutching his note in my hand, I practically skip down the path as I make my way to Henry's dorm. I went from passed out and vomiting just a few hours ago to feeling better than I have in years. Maybe better than I've ever felt.

Rounding the corner, I spot Henry in the distance. He sits on a bench, head hanging, staring at the ground. I wonder what's on his mind. Is he thinking about me? Just the thought of that tingles my heart.

He spots me in the distance and a surge of happiness spikes inside of me. I give him a small wave, but his mood darkens at my gesture. *Strange.* My own cheery demeanor plummets into disappointment.

Within seconds, he's unglued from the bench and standing in front of me—no, looming over me.

"What do you want?" he says—or, more like growls, his voice laced with poison… poison aimed at me.

I stammer in complete confusion, "I was just…"

"Go. Get out of here," he says, his tone cold and distant. He pivots away from me and I'm completely gutted. What in the actual fuck?

I hold up the note he left for me. "Why did you write this?"

In an instant, he's in my face. His breath fogs the air, his chest puffing up and down. "Go, Natalie. Now."

"No! You can't just treat me like this. Back and forth. Hot and cold. I'm not your toy."

He rips the note out of my hand and tears it into tiny pieces, letting them scatter to the ground. Somehow, it's like my heart was just shredded and scattered right along with it.

"There. The note meant nothing. I don't want to see you again."

And with that, he's gone, racing off and disappearing into a sea of students pouring out of class.

I can't move—I'm frozen in time… in space. Trying to process what the hell just happened. How everything could have just gone so wrong in mere hours. None of this makes sense. None of it.

Hot tears spring to my eyes and the last thing I want is to cry, especially in public. Everyone is already so far into my business, and I'm sick and tired of being fodder for constant whispers and gossip.

I wipe the wetness from my eyes and suck in a deep breath as I turn back to my dorm and run smack right into another student.

"Sorry," I mumble, craning my neck up to the tall guy who for sure knows I've been crying.

He stares down at me, curious. His stance, his gaze, is pointed. Unrelenting. I can't help but meet his eyes for a second as he towers over me. His eyelids narrow, almost highlighting the most vibrant green eyes I've ever seen in my life. He's got to be well over six feet, like a basketball player moonlighting as a runway model.

Heat pricks at my spine, that feeling you get when you feel like you're being watched. Maybe because he refuses to look away from me, which is intimidating and oddly compelling. I don't remember seeing him around school before, and he is definitely someone you'd remember.

"Sorry about that," he says. "I'm Wes."

CHAPTER TWENTY-FOUR

HENRY

THIS IS MY punishment.

I knew it was coming. Knew *they* were coming.

There's a reason precogs are taught not to change visions, why we spend years coming to terms with hiding our dark secrets from the world. Because when we defy the authority—they fucking know.

And now they're here… here for me.

I noticed the first one the moment I left Natalie's dorm room earlier. He didn't stick out in a crowd. With his sharp navy-colored blazer, pressed khakis, and horn-rimmed glasses, he could have passed for a visiting teacher, or even an overzealous parent begging to get their kid accepted to Lockwood next year. But it was clear to me that this guy didn't belong on campus. A palpable energy ricocheted around him, unexplainable but undeniable.

I needed to know my instincts were right, so I weaved through campus—making my way up the long stretches past every building. Sure enough, everywhere I went—this guy wasn't far behind. He kept his distance, but he was always watching. Maybe waiting for the moment I'd finally be alone. Well, fuck him. I can play this game. And even if he gets me alone, I could easily take him.

And then, I noticed a woman. How long was she following me—maybe the whole time? Stealthier, smarter than him. I didn't even notice her until I sank onto a bench, taking a moment to process what the hell was happening. She sat across from me, nose in some Tolstoy, tucking her shiny hair behind her ear. But I caught the flick of her eyes, trained on me. I could have mistaken it for attraction, but it wasn't. There was something else in her expression.

And just as I noticed the woman, Natalie appeared. Every one of my nerves spiked in that moment. What would they do if they realized it was her life I'd saved? I couldn't take that chance. Couldn't—wouldn't—lead them right to her.

So I pushed her away, in the most brutal way I knew possible. And I know she hates me now…she'll probably hate me forever.

But I guess that's my punishment for saving her.

If I had the choice, I'd do it all over again.

My feet crunch into the leaves as I make my way down the path to the far end of campus. I don't really have a plan at this point other than to hop the gate and run. It's a terrible fucking plan, but it's all I've got right now. Get off campus, get them away from Natalie. I don't even want to think what's going to happen after that.

The monstrous iron gate isn't far away now. I quicken my pace and take a moment to peek around—I'm no longer being followed, at least as far as I can see.

This thought snags into my brain—if they're not following me, does that mean they're searching for Natalie? I freeze right as I arrive at the gate. *Fuck.* What if it wasn't me they were after? What if…?

Before I can have another thought, everything goes black.

A searing pain rattles through my head. I blink, trying to adjust to my surroundings. I notice two things right away—it's pitch black, and I'm moving.

My body jerks with unnatural movement, pain edging every inch of me. Where the fuck am I? My head throbs, and my neck is so stiff I can barely crane to see anything.

Summoning every ounce of energy I have, I press my arms into the cold steel floor. I still have strength in my hands—that's good. Whatever injuries I may have sustained, at least my hands are still mobile.

I attempt to steady my hazy senses. I'm in the back of a van—a van that's moving, probably across gravel, as chunks of debris seem to be pinging off the metal exterior. I ground my hands onto the floor, attempting to gain some semblance of balance. Clearly, I was tossed back here, haphazardly, after being rendered unconscious. Did they drug me? Knock me out some other way?

A shooting pain slices through my head again, and as I lift my hand to check for a wound—something clinks. I realize I'm chained to the floor. They chained me to the fucking floor—steel shackles around my wrists attach to a long, thick chain.

My heart pounds and complete panic sets in. My instinct is to yell out for help—but I immediately squash the urge and clench my jaw to stay quiet. There's no one to help me now. I'm here, chained up, all alone. I've seen enough of the world to know that when you're in danger, you don't want to draw attention to yourself. Be sensible, don't cause a scene. Follow their orders and clock every fucking escape route possible while pretending to be docile and obedient.

This is my punishment. My consequence, for saving her.

Natalie whips into my mind for a brief second, bringing the only relief I've had since I've regained consciousness. At least they didn't take her, at least she's safe back at Lockwood. I *hope* she's safe back at Lockwood. The thought of her in danger causes bile to rise in my throat.

I attempt again to focus my vision in the dark as the van clatters and clangs along a bumpy road. Did we take a ferry off Lockwood Island? How long have I been unconscious? We can't be on a highway, or any smoothly paved road. Where the hell are they taking me?

Suddenly, a muffled voice sounds in the distance, followed by another voice. There's something blocking my vision of the front seats—drywall maybe? Whatever it is, I'm unable to see who's there.

I can't make out what they're saying either, but those are distinct male and female voices talking… no, arguing. I assume they're the man and woman who were following me, but who knows? Maybe there were a fleet of people after me, just waiting to take me down.

Well, I'm not going down easy.

I begin to note any escape routes. There's no handle on the back doors, so I assume you can only access it from the outside. There is a small, heavily tinted window on the left wall of the van. If I could somehow get out of these chains, I could smash it and leap out. The fall would hurt, but we don't seem to be moving too fast given that we're on an unpaved road.

I pull at the shackles around my wrists, careful not to make too much noise. They're locked, and of course I don't have a key. The chain attached is too thick to break. Maybe there's something I can find to pick the lock. I trace my fingers along the ground, feeling around for a stray piece of metal…anything that might help.

The man and woman in the front seat are still speaking in a torrent of clipped tones, their voices growing louder. I pause my search for a moment, suck in a deep breath, and tune into my senses—attempting to make out what they're saying.

"Demain," the man says.

French. They're speaking French. A brief moment of comfort sinks in—at least I can understand the language and glean some small bit of information.

"Demain ils l'exécuteront," he says.

Tomorrow, they will execute him.

Any comfort I might have felt is now completely fucking gone.

Tomorrow, they will execute him.

It's me they're talking about, I realize.

Tomorrow, they will execute… me.

CHAPTER TWENTY-FIVE
NATALIE

"ARE YOU OKAY?" Wes asks.

I shake myself back to my senses. How long was I just staring into this stranger's eyes? It suddenly hits me how mentally, physically, and emotionally battered I am. How much everything just completely sucks right now.

"Uh, yeah, I'm okay," I say. "Excuse me."

I attempt to shove past him—get out of this stupid frosty air and back to the safety of my dorm room where I can drink tea and forget about Henry fucking Thorne.

"Natalie, right?"

Ugh. Guess this conversation is going to happen. I suppress the urge to heave a sigh, and turn back to him, pasting on a weak smile. "Yeah. And you said your name is Wes?"

He extends his hand. I accept the gesture—he claps my hand with a firm grip and I swear he gives me an extra squeeze, tracing his finger gently along my wrist, which feels intimate… personal.

Maybe I'm just imaging things. Wouldn't be the first time, considering I never seem to know what the fuck is going on anymore.

"I don't think I've seen you around here before."

He seems surprised by my admission. What is that about?

"My bleeding heart. Natalie Covington doesn't even know of my existence."

Is he trying to flirt with me? I suppress the urge to roll my eyes. Sure, he's hot. But the last thing I need right now is to get mixed up with some new guy.

"Sorry," he says. And now I'm surprised.

"For what?"

"I don't know. I'm Canadian, we apologize for everything."

A gust of wind blows as the clouds cover the sky. Rain begins to trickle down. "Well, I gotta go, I have somewhere I have to be," I say, making a quick excuse.

I attempt to slide past him again, but his words lock me back in. "I'll walk you," he says.

I don't have the energy to stop him, so as I pick up my pace, he falls into step. I'm a shitty companion, but I really don't care. Hell, he's the one who wanted to walk with me so… his problem.

"You look like you could use some of this," he says, plucking a joint from his pocket and extending it to me. I shake my head.

"I'm good, thanks."

"You don't smoke?" There's no judgment in his voice like most of the students here, just genuine curiosity.

"I've tried it a few times but it doesn't really do anything for me," I say. "Besides, I don't like feeling out of control."

He chuckles. "Respect." He puts the joint away. "Crazy that fight that went down between Jack and Henry this morning, eh?"

Great. So Wes is Lockwood's version of *Gossip Girl*.

"I'm gonna walk by myself. Good talking to you."

But he doesn't let me get away. "Sorry, I didn't mean to bring up a sore subject. Sorry," he says, looking genuinely remorseful. And all the apologizing is annoyingly endearing. "Why don't you let me buy you a cup of tea?"

I'm immediately struck by his question. "How do you know I drink tea?"

He smirks. "Wild guess."

❧

I sink the tea bag into boiling water and peer around the empty classroom. After buying us both tea, Wes snuck me into this abandoned room in the back of one of the oldest buildings on campus. After today, after Henry, getting to know Wes a bit is turning out to be a decent distraction.

Apparently, the school had plans to renovate this room for some time, but just never got around to it. It used to be an old sewing room—tarnished machines, broken threads, and shreds of fabric litter the space. It's like the rotting skeleton of a time when home economics was the hottest thing. Faint chalk signatures are still etched on the blackboard, as if the ghosts of teachers still meet here. I trace my finger along the writing.

"Pretty beautiful. Bit eerie too," Wes says as the wind whistles through a crack in one of the windows.

"How did you find this place?"

"Natural curiosity, I suppose. Curiosity will be the death of me one day," he says as he leans against the old wooden teacher's desk. "I have a bit of a gift for finding all the secret spots on campus. Maybe I just prefer being alone way too much."

I nod, understanding exactly what he means.

"Like the part of the woods that Henry took you to? I showed him that place," he says.

Shocked, I turn from the blackboard and whip my gaze to his. "You're friends with Henry?"

I had no idea Henry had any friends, or that anyone knew Henry and I had a… whatever we had.

Wes raises one eyebrow. "He obviously didn't tell you about me."

I shake my head no. He yanks up the sleeve of his uniform shirt to reveal a tattoo on his forearm. Recognition flashes in my brain—Henry has that same tattoo, in that same spot. Confusion bubbles in my brain.

"Guess he didn't tell you about this either," he says.

"No, he… didn't tell me much of anything, now that I think about it," I say. "Why do you have the same tattoo?"

"It's not a tattoo," he says. "It's a branding. All precogs are branded."

I swallow, stepping backwards and awkwardly bumping into the chalkboard, knocking an eraser to the floor. There's more than one precog at Lockwood? Does Wes know Henry had a vision about me—that he saved me? That he killed someone for me? And what does being branded mean? I have a million questions and can't manage to squeak out even one.

Get it together.

"What did Henry tell you?" he says. "About us… precogs."

My nerves are on high alert—maybe this is some set up. I promised Henry I wouldn't tell anyone about him and his ability, and I keep my word. Even if he lied to me about his feelings and totally screwed me over.

Wes discerns my silence. "Well, I'm an open book, so ask away." He swaps his tea for a small bottle of whiskey from his jacket pocket and downs a long swig. "Cheers."

He takes a seat and leans back in the chair, strapping in for my interrogation. I'm speechless—trying to get information out of Henry was like pulling teeth. Why is Wes so forthcoming?

"Okay, if you don't have any questions, I'll start. This branding on my arm, got it when I was thirteen. We all get it. Hurts like hell, but it's a rite of passage—means that we're allowed to enter normal society."

"What does that mean—enter normal society?"

"Means we can make our own decisions, go to fine schools like this one. There are rules in place to keep us subservient. We follow the rules, have it ingrained in us until we're good little teenagers, and can go into the world as rule-abiding precogs."

"Are you a rule-abiding precog?"

Wes snorts. "I'm sharing all of our deep dark secrets with a normal. Definitely not rule-abiding."

"A… normal? What is that?" I ask, a bit offended. Is that the precog way of calling me a basic bitch?

"That's… you. Normal just means you don't have our abilities."

I snicker at the thought. Normal. I don't feel very normal.

"Does the word normal offend you?" he says. "Because I don't think the label quite fits you. You're anything but normal, Natalie Covington."

I'm surprised by his words. I'm guessing he's just being nice, but is full of shit. If they really are friends, he probably knows that Henry just tried to humiliate me.

"You don't even know me," I say.

"You're right, I don't. I really only know what Henry told me about you."

I can't stifle my laugh. What he "told" him about me. I can only imagine. Given the way Henry just treated me, I'm already about to punch the wall thinking about what he might have said.

"That's why I convinced Henry to save your life," Wes says.

At those words, everything in my world grinds to a horrifying halt. My mind coils over the possibility that Henry never wanted to save my life after all.

Wes did.

CHAPTER TWENTY-SIX

HENRY

WE JOLT TO a stop, the van lunging forward and then back, nearly knocking my body into the wall. More hushed whispers come from the front seat—but their voices are too muffled and I can't make out any of the words.

They're going to kill me. That much I know.

The loud sound of metal creaks from the front of the van, and I know my captors are exiting the vehicle. Footsteps crunch on the gravel outside, each step sending a slice of terror through me.

The back door of the van flings open and I'm on alert. Surprisingly, it's not the man and woman I noticed on campus. These are different people, both dressed in black coveralls with buzzed heads. There's something eerie about their expressions—something that rings with more horror than the fact that they've kidnapped me.

Were they on campus following me too? How did I not notice them? They don't say a word, and I know I should keep my mouth shut but I can't help myself. "Who the hell are you?"

No reply. Not even a register that I asked them a fucking question—it's like they don't even recognize I'm here. They stand, side by side, expressionless. They're staring *at* me, yet they don't seem to *see me*. Anger stirs inside of me, causing my rationale to fly out the window. I clench my fists, ready to pummel the information out of them. I don't care if I'm chained up, I'll find a way. I need to know who these people are and what the hell they plan to do with me.

"Did you hear me? I'm talking to you!"

Still nothing.

We're locked in a holding pattern of torturous silence. Well fuck this. I'm done sitting here waiting around for these morons to decide my fate. I know I can't physically go anywhere, considering I'm chained to the damn ground, but I stand anyway—the van ceiling barely clearing my height. As soon as I'm fully standing, the woman takes one step forward. Her expression never changes, she doesn't make a sound, but that small movement forward means something. It's supposed to intimidate me… it *does* intimidate me. But I'm not backing down. No way.

I take a few steps forward to the back of the van and my chain locks in place—I'm unable to go any farther. Neither of them makes a move to stop me, which somehow pisses me off more. "Come on, just take me. Kill me. Whatever you want to do. But at least give me the decency and do something besides stand there."

Their silence speaks volumes. I survey the van for anything I might be able to use as a weapon and clock a metal bar within my reach, something that might be used to pry a window or maybe a door that's been wedged shut. Before I can reach for it, I notice a flick in the woman's gaze. It's the slightest movement—but it sticks out because she hasn't even blinked since we've been here. I wonder if she's noticed the metal bar, too…if she senses my intentions.

I've got nothing to lose, so I reach for the bar and in an instant,

I'm rocketed backwards, slamming down onto the hard metal floor—rattling my bones. It takes me a second to realize what's happened—I was flung back by the chain that no one was holding. How did that happen?

My vision blurs and fireworks explode behind my eyes as consciousness slips away and everything turns black.

❧

My sense of smell returns first. I know because the scent of blood fills my nostrils.

Where am I bleeding from?

I press together my chapped lips and flatten my tongue against the roof of my mouth, swiping it across my lips. I don't taste blood.

I fist my hand, open and closed. Okay good, I can at least move.

My head pounds in deafening clunks that make me feel nauseous. Bile crawls up my throat, but I suppress the urge to vomit.

I blink, trying to adjust my vision, but nothing comes into view. It's not even blurry—just completely pitch black. Am I blind?

I immediately panic and jolt upright. The ground is cold, hard, and unrelenting, and my body aches to the point of agony. But I can't focus on my pain right now—I need to figure out where the hell I am. Why the hell I can't see.

Something feels foreign on my face, scratching against my skin. It takes me a moment to realize that my face is covered.

I lift my arms to remove whatever is covering my face, but my arms are locked in place. I yank them a few times before realizing I must be chained against the wall or the floor, my limbs rendered useless. I try to move my legs and realize they're shackled together too. I'm flooded with rage and panic and can't think of anything to do except scream for my life, but I know that won't save me. I just need to keep my shit together, one step at a time.

Then, I swear I hear something—a muffled noise somewhere in the distance. Whatever the hell is covering my face is obscuring everything, hushing my surroundings. My heart is beating so fast, so hard, I wonder if that's the sound I'm hearing.

But there it is again. It's not my heartbeat, it's a voice. I just can't hear anything with this fucking thing covering my head.

"Is someone there?" My voice croaks, and I wonder if they can even hear me.

"Bend your head down as far as you can," a man's voice says. I realize I'm not alone in here now, but who the hell is talking—and why do they want me to bend my head?

"I'm not doing anything," I say, standing my ground. I may be going down, but I'm not going down easy.

"I'm trying to help you, man. Bend your head forward and reach up your arms—I'll tell you when you can grab the hood," he says.

I pause, reluctant to listen to or trust this stranger, but I could use all the help I can get. I do as he says, my fingers finally grazing the rough fabric of what I now know is a hood.

"Okay, now pull the hood down and then to the side, they're a little tricky to get off," he says.

I follow his orders and after a few moments of struggle, manage to get the hood off. Light floods my eyes, like someone just flashed a camera in my face. Blurry circles cloud my vision until it finally clears to reveal my situation.

I'm in a room—not quite a dark basement like those featured in horror movies, but it's not all that far off either. A sudden chill rips through my bones as I realize how cold it is in here.

Across from me sits another guy, the guy who helped me get

this fucking hood off my face. I don't know him, but there's a familiarity in his expression. He's chained to the wall in the same position as me, except he's far more worn and dirty—tragedy soaked on his face and body. I wonder how long he's been here.

"Thanks," I manage. My eyes case the room, noticing that there are no windows and just a single heavy steel door that appears to have about a thousand bolts on it. *Fucking great.*

"They got ya good," the guy says.

"What do you mean?"

"Your head. I didn't think they were supposed to hurt us in transit, but you're bleeding. Guess they broke the rules for you."

Memories splinter my brain and I begin to remember how this all happened. The strange man and woman, staring at me. How I tried to be defiant, planned to do anything to escape that van and somehow was flung backwards and knocked unconscious. But no one was there to do it.

"Do you know why we're in here?" I say.

The guy chuckles—his laugh sounds strangely familiar and tension ripples through me. I have this weird feeling that I know him somehow.

"We're in here because we're the bad guys. We changed a vision. Fucking repressive bullshit," he says, his voice dripping with sarcasm and disdain.

Now it's my turn to chuckle. At least I know who he reminds me of now. "You sound like someone I know."

"Yeah, who?"

"A guy I go to school with. Wes."

His expression darkens and fear sprints through me. Shit. Did I say something wrong?

"Wes Thompson?" he says, his voice barely a choked whisper.

"Uh, I actually don't know his last name, now that I think about it. Tall guy, dark spiky hair, glasses, kinda hipster…"

He looks off and a small sob escapes him, puncturing the silence in the room. What is going on?

"You know him or something?"

He quickly sniffs and steels himself, probably doesn't want me to see him cry. Not that I'd care or judge. "He's my brother."

My stomach sinks and I remember—Wes mentioned his brother, told me he disappeared. And now here I am with him. Damn, how long has he been in here?

"Wes told me about you. He was actually the one who encouraged me to change my vision. Said he didn't buy into the precog authority bullshit," I say.

"Yeah, that definitely sounds like Wes. My fault, really. I'm the one that started it all. Our family was… is… never mind."

I don't press him, maybe another time I will. Right now I can tell he's too broken to talk about his family and whatever happened. And it seems like we're going to have a long time in this place to share our confessions.

"I'm Henry, by the way," I say.

"Timothy," he says. "So what's your story, Henry? What vision did you change?"

I shiver as rage consumes me and my mind is plagued with Natalie. Saving her. Her saving me. Of what could have been between us.

"A girl I go to school with. I had a vision of her dying… well, being murdered." An avalanche of grief hits me, remembering what nearly happened to her, but I swallow it back.

"I can relate to saving someone you love," Timothy says.

Love. When I saved Natalie, I didn't love her. Or did I? Do I love her now? I'm not even sure I know what love is. But whatever I feel for Natalie, I know I've never felt it before.

"I didn't even know her," I say, surprised at my admission. I guess I've got nothing to lose. Might as well treat this guy like my therapist and let all this shit spill out.

He looks at me, shocked. "Wow, man. I can't imagine risking everything for someone you don't even know."

It makes sense, what he's saying. Why *did* I risk it all? I don't regret a second of what I did, or regret saving her. But he's right. Most normal people wouldn't endanger their entire life for a complete stranger. I roll through my mind, trying to find one clear reason—an explanation of what led me here.

"I guess I felt she deserved to live more than I did," I say. The words pour out and actually shock me. But that's really what I believe. She *does* deserve to live and *does* deserve all the happiness in the world. Happiness that I'll never be able to give to her.

"Where is she now?" he says.

"Still back at school." I grimace at the thought.

"At least you know where she is, that she's safe," he says. "I don't know what happened to my fiancée. I've been here for ninety-three days."

Sadness seeps into my brain—I feel for this guy. And I also accept that this... this room, this existence, is going to be my grim fate too. At least until they kill me. Or did they mean they were going to execute someone else, and I'm left here to rot until they're done with me?

"What was her name?" he says. "My fiancée's name is Willow. Willow Spence. She hates her name. Thinks it's the worst combination of hippie and upscale douche."

I laugh, then wince at how much it hurts just to do that simple act. My ribs throb, and I wonder how many injuries I've sustained.

"Her name is Natalie, Natalie Covington," I say.

His expression darkens again and, even though I've only known this guy for about five minutes, I know that look.

"Covington?"

I nod. "Yeah, why?"

"Is her mom Madeline Covington?"

I vaguely remember reading an article about Natalie during my time of incessantly stalking every piece of information about her I could find. In the article, she talks about her mom being a huge influence on her life, but she died in a car accident almost two years ago.

"I'm pretty sure her name was Madeline, yeah. Why? Do you know her mom?"

Timothy's eyes flick around, as if he's trying to process something—piece something together.

"Madeline Covington was a journalist. A big deal. She was secretly planning to do an exposé on precogs. But then she was killed in that accident," he says.

I freeze, piecing together my own conclusions. Was Natalie's attack somehow connected to her mom? Did Natalie know about precogs all along? Was *she* planning to expose us?

No, that can't be. She would have told someone about me, turned me in. She kept my secret, and protected me. But why? Was she planning to extract information from me? Continue her mother's research?

A horrible sinking feeling washes over me. Who is Natalie Covington... and did I ever really know her at all?

CHAPTER TWENTY-SEVEN
NATALIE

"WHAT'S WRONG?" WES asks.

What's wrong? A million things, but I'm not about to share any of them with this guy. With trembling hands, I brace myself against the old chalkboard, dust filming on my sweaty palms. It was never Henry's idea to save me. It was this random dude's idea.

I wonder how their conversation went. Was Henry like: *oh, our classmate's going to die LOL* and then Wes said: *dude, you should do something about this?* Is this how they talked about my impending death? How they decided my fate?

"You good?" Wes asks. He rises from his seat and my body tenses with indignation. I can't manage to take a breath, much less answer him. I'm afraid if I let out even one word, I'll just scream until he thinks I'm a complete mess.

I back away from the chalkboard and rush to the door. I know I'm under scrutiny here, and I hate that. I hate eyes on me—the attention. What would I say to him anyway? Thanks for saving my life, but I need you to just leave me alone.

"Wait, where are you going?" he says, but by the time his words register, I'm already out the door, tearing down the empty hallway like one of those pathetic girls in a horror movie running from a monster. I smash my hands into the metal door and shove it open, finally sucking in a relieved breath and gathering my scattered thoughts.

Wes saved me.

Maybe I should feel grateful or indebted to this stranger. But I'm not grateful. I hate that it was him that saved me, and not Henry. I hate that everything I thought I knew is wrong, ruined. And I hate even more that I feel this way. Anger bubbles inside of me as I storm through the campus grounds littered with students who stare and whisper as I pass.

The path to my dorm winds to the left and rain nips at my face. It's beautiful this time of year on campus, when the leaves fall and fragment with gray skies, but it doesn't feel beautiful right now. All I see are leaves crumbling to the ground, cragged branches winding like claws. Everything just feels like death—including me.

The rest of my walk whizzes by in a blur and, before long, I'm back in my dorm. I slam the door shut and a picture unhinges from the wall, crashing to the ground. I gently pick it up, tracing my finger along a photo of my mom. God, I miss her. My heart squeezes as I study the shot by some famous photographer. As an award-winning journalist, she got to travel with amazing people. It didn't hurt that she was beautiful, and I'm sure everyone wanted to snap photos of her. She looked like one of those classic movie starlets.

The door to my room flings open and Ciel skips inside uninvited, flopping herself onto my bed. I really need to remember to lock my door.

"Thanks for knocking," I say.

Ciel rolls her eyes. "Someone's in a mood. Adip and I are done."

Shocking. "What happened this time?"

"Ridge Jenkins happened," she says.

I suppress the urge to burst out laughing and place my mom's photo back on the wall. "Ridge Jenkins? That sounds like one of those guys in a romance novel."

Ciel shrugs. "I don't care about his name, if you know what I'm saying."

I do know what she's saying, but I don't care to indulge it right now. Though a good gossip session with Ciel is probably what I need, I'm just too exhausted from the nightmare of today.

"You owe me an explanation, by the way," Ciel says, shooting me a glare.

My stomach tightens. "Explanation for what?"

Ciel hops off my bed and grabs some nail polish from my vanity. Ciel's short attention span definitely carries over from romantic entanglements to nail colors. "Well, let's see," she says. "First, your new boyfriend punched your ex-boyfriend like some avenging superhero. I mean, Henry has a good body, but damn, I didn't think he was capable of that."

My heart clenches and I don't want to talk about Henry, or even hear about him. I squeeze my eyes shut, willing Ciel to just shut up.

It doesn't work.

"Talk about romance novel. The way he yanked you out of the hallway, I thought he was going to sweep you into his arms and declare his undying love while confessing that he's ready to give you his seed." Ciel swipes a fresh coat of ballerina pink polish on her thumb.

"His… seed?" I hold back my urge to gag. "No one talks like that."

"Yeah, they do. In all those books, they say that. That's a big turn-on for guys, you know, to like—"

"Please stop." I hold up my hand before she goes any further. "I don't want to hear about seeds, or whatever. Between that gross term and Ridge, you clearly need to stop reading romance novels."

"Don't change the subject. You disappeared for like twenty-four hours. Please tell me you snuck off and had hot sex with Henry."

"Ciel!" I shout, louder than intended. My voice rattles off the walls and Ciel appears genuinely terrified at my overreaction. While I appreciate the fragile bond of our friendship, I just need her to shut up before I lose my mind.

"You made me mess up my nail," she says, pouting while swiping the ruined polish from her finger.

As if I've lost control of my body, I storm over to her and shove the bottle of polish in her face. "Just take it to your room and do your nails there. I need to be alone right now."

I guess my expression, my voice, my stance, hold enough weight that Ciel knows I'm not messing around. She rises, her eyes widened like she's scared… of me.

"Damn, Natty. Fierce." She looks me over before following my wishes and leaving. I even caught an air of respect floating off her.

Fierce is fucking right. I just survived a hit on my life and covered up Henry's lie. I learned there's a whole section of people with supernatural abilities and didn't completely lose my shit. I began to fall for someone… and found out he doesn't really care if I die. I'm alive because of some random guy who also has these weird psychic powers.

⸄

Several hours pass. I crank music in my headphones while I tear through my closet, yanking clothes onto my bed and floor. My hair is wild and unruly and I even swiped on more makeup than usual. Well, let's face it, I really don't wear makeup that often—but for some reason, it felt right to paint my lips with the deepest, glossiest red I could find.

I don't have class today, but I do need to see Ms. Whitney for a student check-in. Luckily, there's no dress code for guidance counselor appointments, so I don't have to wear that itchy, oppressive uniform. As I claw through my clothes, I toss aside items from my pathetic wardrobe on the floor—pink top, another pink top, pink cardigan. I'm like a walking caricature of a chaste high school princess. Just give me some pearls to clutch and I'm all set.

I finally find a pair of ripped jeans. I throw them on with a white T-shirt that I knot in the front, exposing just a tiny part of my stomach. I slip on my mom's leather jacket—vintage from some Italian designer that made it special for her after she wrote an exposé on the garment industry.

I study my reflection in the mirror.

And then… I notice it.

Something about my face, my eyes, just looks strange. I crane my neck forward to get a better look in the mirror. The muddy brown color of my eyes has morphed into this light, glittery shade of golden-green. There's a clench in my chest, as if my heart is shrinking as I remember Henry telling me that my eyes shifted color that day we were in his dorm bathroom. I didn't believe him then. Maybe he was telling the truth after all.

Ridiculous.

Henry… the guy who lied to me about everything. Wes's revelation—that it was his idea to save me—sticks in my brain and heart. Suddenly, my eye color darkens into a shade of emerald—the color of my mom's eyes. A hot prickle shoots down my neck and spine, and my stomach knots as I back away from the mirror.

What's happening to me?

I can't get out of my dorm room and away from that mirror fast enough. I make my way to Ms. Whitney's office in record time and plop down in the small waiting area.

Out of compulsion, I dig some sunglasses out of my purse and slide them on just as Jack steps out of Ms. Whitney's office. His arm is in a sling, and as much of a jerk as he was to me, I feel sorry for him, for what happened.

He shoots me a strange look. "Hey. Something wrong with your eyes?"

My nerves spike. *Does he know?* "Why would something be wrong with my eyes?"

"Umm, because you're wearing sunglasses inside and it's not sunny in here—or out there," he says, motioning to the window.

I exhale in relief, totally forgetting about the glasses I just put on my face. "Oh, right. Um, I just have a migraine and the light bothers me," I say, hoping he buys my lie. Jack would definitely notice the change in my eye color. Or maybe he wouldn't, since he doesn't seem to notice anything that doesn't have to do with him.

"Hey, I'm sorry for what I said to you," he says. "I was a dick."

Wow. Okay, wasn't expecting an apology. "It's okay. Sorry about your arm," I say, sheepish.

"Yeah, well, you didn't do it. Where is your new boyfriend by the way?" he says, and I detect a deep revulsion in his voice mixed with fear.

"He's not my boyfriend, and I have no idea where he is."

Sadness lingers between us, and I strangely feel bad about everything. I mean, sure, he's an ass, but did he really deserve to get caught up in all this mess?

As I waffle over my feelings, a shriek sounds in the distance and within seconds, Josephine is wrapped around Jack, trailing kisses down his neck. Well that didn't take long.

Jack appears uncomfortable and shifts out of her embrace. Josephine notices me and smiles, coy. "Natalie, sorry, I didn't know you were here," she says.

She absolutely knew I was here.

"It's all good. No worries," I say, pasting on a smile.

"I just didn't want there to be any hard feelings," she says.

"None at all. I think you two are perfect for each other," I say before marching into Ms. Whitney's office.

⤚

My appointment with Ms. Whitney is easy and drama free—just what I needed. I sense that she wants to pry about my romantic life, but I just keep smiling and changing the subject.

I exit the building and am circling around the path when a familiar voice comes from behind me, calling my name. I instantly recognize it as Wes. Damn, this guy just doesn't give up.

I speed up, quickening my pace as fast as I can without looking like a maniac, but Wes manages to catch up and block my way.

"What's with the glasses?" he says.

I don't answer and attempt to dodge by him, but within seconds, he's in my way again. In one swift move, he removes my sunglasses and clutches them in his hand.

"Hey!" I grab for them, but he extends his arm high in the air. Tempering my annoyance, I push up to my tiptoes and try and reach them. My head grazes his chest as I reach for my sunglasses and I catch his scent— musky, yet clean. Like fresh-squeezed lemons mixed with cedar.

"Your eyes look really beautiful in the sunlight," he says. It didn't even occur to me that the sun came out until that second. It also didn't occur to me that Wes was staring at me this whole time, studying me.

Rage courses through my body and I give up trying to get my sunglasses, planting my feet on the earth and stepping away from him.

"Do compliments offend you?" he asks, trying to suppress a laugh.

I maintain an even expression, not giving into his games or his bullshit. "You can keep the glasses," I say before attempting to storm off. He grasps my arm before I can pass. His grip is firm and unrelenting, and it pisses me off. I don't want him touching me. I don't want anyone touching me right now. Maybe ever.

I yank my arm out of his grip and he seems genuinely pained at my reaction. Well, he'll just have to deal with it.

"Okay," he says. He meets my gaze before gently sliding my glasses back onto my face. I'm surprised by his gesture, that he gave in so quickly. I assumed he'd be more stubborn and annoying.

"You want to hide, go ahead. When you don't, come find me."

And with that, he stalks off. *Come find him.* I can't deny that part of me does want to give in, to follow him, to learn his intentions.

But I've been down that road. It doesn't lead anywhere good. So I don't follow Wes, even though it nearly kills me not to.

CHAPTER TWENTY-EIGHT

HENRY

MY INSTINCTS HAVE never been wrong before.

Until my visions about Natalie, I've always been able to trust myself. It's as if this is all some cruel joke. Why didn't I consider that Natalie could have known about my abilities? Maybe she was continuing her mother's research and all of this was a test, a sick fucking test to see if she could get me to betray my entire existence for some girl I barely know.

Joke's on me, I guess. I hope she's happy. There's a clench in my chest, as if my heart is shriveling and dying. Maybe I'm better off that way.

I nearly forget where I am, caged like an animal and trapped in this concrete prison. The initial panic and pain just dissipates, and all I can process is anger. Deep, betrayed, anger. *She did this. She put me here.*

I suck in a deep breath and really fucking try to tap into the rational side of my brain. Hating Natalie—blaming Natalie—isn't doing me any damn favors.

I put myself here, unable to control my emotions like a stupid child.

"You think there was some connection? You know, between the vision you had and her mother getting…" Timothy's words trail off as if he can't grasp them. I nearly forgot he was here.

I open my mouth to answer, but the loud clang of footsteps outside the door keeps me quiet. Someone's coming, and considering what's happened to me so far, I'm not looking forward to it.

The clanging grows louder, like heavy boots stomping on those metal grates on city sidewalks.

Timothy mumbles a few words in defeat. "Med time."

The door swings open and in walks the woman who took me. Everything about her is like a machine—cold, lifeless, maybe even inhuman.

She scans me for a moment, and I swear I catch a glimmer of something in her eyes and the ghost of a smirk playing on her mouth. Maybe she's not so robotic after all. Somehow, this feels even more unsettling.

She heads straight for me, and in a flash, her rough grip locks around my wrist as she jerks me to standing. What the hell is happening? My survival instincts clobber any rationale and I rear back, breaking free of her grasp—but in a split second, she once again has a viselike grasp on my wrist. Using all my strength, I yank my arms, trying to retract from her, but she easily overpowers me. Her grip is so tight, my hand starts to go numb. I lock eyes with her, daring her to continue messing with me, but my defiance seems to breathe something into her. *She's enjoying this.* Every second of it.

Suddenly, the hood I yanked off earlier is in her hand—when

did she grab that? In one swift movement, it once again covers my face—darkness swarming all of my senses.

Adrenaline roars through my body. This is it, my chance to escape. She's strong, but Timothy is here, and there's no way she can overpower both of us. That's assuming he's going to help me. I barely know the guy, and have no clue if I can trust him, but at this point, what have I got to lose?

It's worth a try.

The chain clinks—she's unlocking me. Or is she unlocking Timothy? I wait for an excruciating moment until a second clink sounds. My muscles coil as I steel myself for a fight.

I reach up my bound hands and tear off my hood, quickly scanning my surroundings. The woman is facing away from us, marching to the door, clenching our chains in her hand like leashes. Anger scores through as I'm about to make a move, but before I can try, she's in my face, glaring at me—deliberate and calm. How did she get there so fast?

With no time to think, I flail my chained wrists, swinging right for her face—but she grabs them in one swift movement. Panic courses through my body, and it doesn't even look like she's putting in any effort.

"Détendez-vous," she says. The French word for relax, yet her hardened expression indicates I should be anything but chill right now.

She spins behind my body and shoves me forcefully out the door and up a set of stairs. The stairs are covered in metal grates, just loose enough that I wonder if they'll cave under our weight. Maybe if I stomp my foot on the edge, I can force her off-balance.

I give it a shot, shoving all my weight into the corner of the grate but it doesn't budge, just a slight wobble.

Timothy climbs up the stairs behind me until we reach a massive steel door. The woman shoves it open and I'm assaulted with blinding white light. I squint to try and make out my surroundings. There's a long corridor, flanked by rooms on each side. The smell of bleach fills the air, and it's so thick I nearly gag. Everything in this place screams mental institution. Is that where I am? Are they locking me up in here for changing a vision?

The steel doors on the opposite end of the hallway swing open and two guards I don't recognize escort a man down the hall. This man isn't restrained, but he definitely doesn't need to be. He's frail—no, worse than frail. He's wasting away like Christian Bale in that crazy movie, *The Machinist*. As we close the distance, I get a peek of his glassy, pallid eyes with purplish rims underneath—not from bruising, maybe from lack of sleep or sunlight. The guards prop him by his elbows as if he might crash to the ground and faint if they don't.

Is this a glimpse of my future? Is this what's going to happen to me? *If so, I'd rather die.*

We pass each other and I try to meet his gaze, as if he can give me some glimmer of hope or anxiety or rage or fear. But there's just… nothing. No emotion at all. Just horrid emptiness.

My mind twists with desperation. Is this the consequence of changing a vision—to be locked away in here, stripped of everything, malnourished, and imprisoned for life? Precogs are taught to be terrified of the consequences of defying our laws, and most of our campfire stories include death. But this? This is a fate so much worse than I ever imagined.

I suck in a ragged breath. There's no way I'm going down like that. I have to get out of here.

As we near the end of the hallway, I get a final shove into a room where another robotic person stares ahead, holding a tray of pills. He nods at me, I guess indicating I should take one of the cups and swallow the pills. The woman stands to my side, watching and waiting.

All of my anger slices through in one hard stroke. "You think I'm going to take your fucking pills?" I say. "You're crazy."

"You can take the pills or we'll inject you," the woman says. I'm startled to hear her speak English. My insolence slowly melts into fear at the word injection.

"Inject me with what?"

She refuses to answer, but orders under her breath, "Take the pills or we inject you. That's the only choice you have in here."

Nerves slam in my veins. I look over at Timothy, who shoots me a warning glare before pivoting his eyes down. It's clear he doesn't want to ruffle anything here, that he knows to be compliant. I'm split in two—half of me wants to get this over with and get more information from Timothy. The other half of me wants to rip every one of their heads off and get the hell out of here.

Except that won't work. I can't rely on my strength and adrenaline right now, so I knock back the pills with my bound hands and pretend to swallow them, but really hide them under my tongue.

"Open," the woman says.

I open and show her my mouth, carefully concealing the pills. She studies me, every second stretching into torture. I know I can't be the first person to not take the pills. My hand begins to quake with anticipation, but I quickly steady it. I can't let anything give me away right now.

She steps closer, and I know what she's doing. She knows I didn't swallow them. My heart thuds and I do everything I can to slow my breathing.

Then a violent crack of thunder rips through the air, piercing the tension. I'm relieved at the interruption, and I notice something strange. Her face… it's the first time she's shown true emotion. She looks…afraid.

I flick my eyes to the pill pusher. He has the exact same expression, laden with fear. Are these two robotic, frigid, barely human specimens afraid of a little thunder?

The woman motions to Timothy. "Pills. Now."

The man hands Timothy a cup of pills and he knocks them back, completely obedient.

"Move," she says, as she shoves me hard in the shoulder.

My teeth clench and I suppress the urge to elbow her in the face and roundhouse the guy. I may not be able to physically overpower these people, or whatever they are. But if they fear thunder, then they both have a weakness.

I just need to figure out how to exploit it.

⌘

Back in our room, I wait for the steel door to slam shut and the heavy bolt to lock before spitting the pills into my hands, nearly gagging on the chalky film left on my gums. I'm thankful to be so dehydrated that they didn't absorb in my saliva.

Timothy stares at me, concerned. "What are you going to do with those?"

I shrug. "I don't know, but I'm not taking them."

A dark expression spreads across his face. "But there's nowhere to hide them. They're going to know. You're gonna make it worse for yourself, trust me."

I scan the room and realize he's right. Maybe I made a grave mistake thinking I could avoid taking the pills, but there's no way I'm drugging myself—no way I'm going to cloud my judgment. Not now. I drop the pills to the ground and start crushing them up with my boot. "I'll turn them to dust and spread it in the corner. The light's so bad in here I doubt they'll notice."

Timothy shakes his head, unconvinced, as I go to work.

"Why are they drugging us anyway?" I say.

"They need to keep our powers contained."

Blood pounds in my temples. "Keep our powers contained? Like, make sure we don't have visions?"

Timothy heaves a huge sigh, and I can't tell if he's annoyed at my question or if the meds are kicking in. Either way, I don't really care what he thinks. I just want answers.

"Visions are just a baseline of our real powers," he says, his voice growing quiet and distant.

A baseline. I knew something wasn't right after I changed my vision, but hearing this shit from another precog splinters my brain. I roll my wrists, realizing how sore they're becoming from the restraints as I mull this over in my mind. "So precogs have other powers, besides visions?"

"We're not precogs," he says. Timothy's eyes flutter, and it's clear those pills have done a number on him. I'm even more grateful that I didn't take any as I watch his consciousness slip, but his words leave me in a haze of confusion, pounding me with new fears, my heart rate doubling.

Urgency rips through my veins, and I'm desperate for answers. "What do you mean, we're not precogs?"

Timothy's completely silent, but his eyes are still open with a deadened expression. What the hell kind of meds did he take?

"Hey man, wake up!" I say, dread heavy in my voice. Still nothing.

I watch his chest rise and fall, then slow to a point where I can no longer tell if he's even breathing.

"Hey! Are you okay? Answer me!"

But my pleas are met with nothing but silence. His head is now cradled against the wall, his face tipped toward mine. It's like looking in a mirror—I was supposed to take those pills too.

I can do nothing but stare at his face—blank, vacant...

... dead.

the way with a dying. Hi shot with working. Liberally saw and here aware. This is a spread and to the here doesn't the...

CHAPTER TWENTY-NINE

NATALIE

I TRY EVERYTHING possible to concentrate on homework. It's biology. I love biology. What could possibly be more interesting than life itself? I've always been inquisitive, always wanting answers for everything, dying to know why everything is the way it is. I share that trait with my mom.

It's also one of the reasons my father probably doesn't want anything to do with me. I remind him too much of her.

I slam shut my textbook and part my lips, dragging in an air of exertion. Screw DNA replication. I have zero interest in that mess right now. What I can't stop thinking about, can't stop dying to know, is more about precogs.

And, if I'm really being honest, I'm dying to know more about Wes. Why this absolute stranger who's never bothered to talk to me before, who I've never had even a microsecond of connection with, thought he should save my life.

This all loops over and over and over in my mind like the

most annoying snooze button. All my earlier bravado seems to have dissolved and now I'm just your average trope of a teenager, thinking about a guy. Again.

Ugh. I disgust myself. I press up from my desk chair. I'm exhausted, but my dorm room doesn't feel like a sanctuary right now. More like the walls are closing in, swallowing me whole.

I can't help but sneak a look in my full-length mirror at my eyes. Back to muddy brown. That gorgeous golden-green hue was all my imagination, I knew it. It's all Henry's fault, claiming that my eyes change color. His stupid lying words cloud my brain once again.

I pace back and forth, and my memory keeps slicing back to Wes and what he said about hiding. When I'm ready to stop hiding, I should come and find him. What a dick. I'm not hiding.

Or am I?

Something about that phrase, *hiding*, sticks to me—claws into my brain and seeps poison.

◈

The leaves on the ground are sticky from the rain, giving way to ugly patches of earth. Mud cakes on my white sneaks that I know I'll never be able to scrub out. Normally, this little fact would bother me because I don't like ruining new things. Sometimes I'll leave something in a box for months just so there's no chance it'll get dirty.

It takes me a good twenty minutes to reach my destination—the campus information center. It's a bizarre little brick building that couldn't really house much except a lectern with a massive student directory that looks like a worn and dusty religious scripture. It's situated under a pale, flickering yellow light—the only light in the entire space. It's eerie and I'm trembling, but I'm not sure if it's from the weather or from being in a building that will definitely be featured on a ghost hunter reality show one day.

I flip through the damp pages of the directory. It's a miracle the ink doesn't bleed together with the moisture in here. You'd think with the all the advances we've made in technology that the school could make this thing electronic—something we could access in our dorms. Except, Lockwood prides itself on all these old-world touches, harkening back to a time when things were simpler, smarter. Or so they say.

So fucking annoying.

I don't know Wes's last name, so I scan through each page—squinting to see the text under this shitty light. There are a hundred and seventy five students at Lockwood, and unfortunately. it's not broken up by class, so I have to scan the names one by one. I trace my finger down, and my heart flips in my chest when I pass his name. *Henry Thorne.*

I quickly shake it off and stay focused on the task at hand. More names… more names… and now I'm almost to the end. Serena Zundel, Langston Zuziak, Ryan Zychowski.

And that's it. No more names. Where is Wes?

Unsettled, I race out of the creepy little building and immediately spot Adip puffing on his vape. Adip knows everyone at Lockwood. He prides himself on getting to know every student, faculty member, even the maintenance staff. I run over to him. "Hey!"

"Natty Pie," he says, yanking me into a friendly hug.

"Don't call me that. You know I hate it," I say, pulling away and scrunching my face.

"My bad," he says, sucking in another puff, tendrils of smoke spilling into the cold air.

"Do you know a student named Wes?"

Adip combs his memory. "Wes? Nah, I don't think so. He goes here?"

Another strange feeling ripples through me. "Yeah."

Adip shakes his head, clueless. "Sorry, I don't know a Wes. Maybe he's a late transfer or something?"

"Maybe," I say, my words trailing off. A buzz enters my mind and static clouds my ears. It's like I'm no longer standing here with Adip, and all I can think about is Wes and the very realistic fact that he may not actually be a student at Lockwood. But if he's not a student—why is he here? And what the hell does he want with me?

"What's he look like?" Adip says.

Fragments of his face, his body, fall into my perspective. "Tall… towering, really. Thin, but built. Not overly muscular, just toned. Dark hair pulled back in a ponytail, green eyes. He dresses kinda hipster, but not in the trying too hard way. Know what I mean?"

Adip stares at me like I'm nuts and bursts out laughing. "Someone got over their breakup real fast. I thought you were into that other guy, Henry."

I swat at his arm, playful. "Shut up, it's not like that."

"What's it like then?"

I smash my lips together. I'm dying to talk to someone, anyone, about this whole mess. There are students here with the power to see the future. Someone tried to kill me. I watched Henry kill that man, but apparently it wasn't his idea.

Unfortunately, I started to fall for him.

"This Wes guy just offered to tutor me and now I can't find him."

Adip nods, knowingly. "Be careful, Natty. What if he's, like, a catfisher?"

Now it's my turn to burst out laughing. "Adip, that's ridiculous."

"It's true. You watch—that shit will be on one of those true crime podcasts."

I shake my head at his absurdity. I've been so consumed with everything (read: Henry) that I forgot how much fun I used to have just shooting the shit with Adip. He's ridiculous, in the best way, and I don't have to worry about him being a creep or hitting on me. As cliché as it sounds, he really is like a brother.

Maybe I do need to loosen up a bit, get my mind off things for a moment. "Can I get a hit of that?"

Adip whips his head to me, shocked. "No, you wanna vape?"

"Just to take the edge off. I'm having a bad day."

Adip hands me his vape pen and I take a puff. I have to admit it feels good, a tiny bit soothing, when it hits my lungs—but then I burst into a violent cough and realize that's why I don't smoke.

Adip takes the pen back and pats my back. "You hear that me and Ciel broke up?"

I nod, still wheezing too much to talk.

"I honestly don't know what that girl wants. She has a problem with everything I do."

I look over at him and roll my eyes. "Do you really care?"

"Yes, I care. I love that girl!"

I'm shocked. While it would be easy to write off his sentiment as some new relationship energy fairytale bullshit, I've never heard Adip say he loved anyone before. "Well, if you love her, why don't you just ask her what she wants?"

He stares at me, seriously confounded—as if the mere thought of asking is like I'm revealing to him I'm a flat-earther or have been sucked up in some weird sex cult.

And then, my world screeches to a halt. I spot Wes in the distance.

"I gotta go," I say, racing off before Adip can say another word.

∾

"Hey!" I call out after Wes, but he doesn't turn around. He's moving at quite a clip, and I can barely keep up with him without slipping and smashing my face.

Finally, I fall into step and grip his arm. He yanks it back and twirls around. I realize why he ignored me as he pulls out his earbuds.

"Ah, so you decided to come out of hiding, huh?" he says with a smirk.

I hate his smirk—it's so pompous. So douchey. But he looks so hot doing it. Which makes me hate it more. The cold wind curls around my body, making me shiver. "I wasn't hiding," I say, but the chatter of my teeth makes my words nearly tumble over one another. Again, he smirks. God, I want to slap it off his smug, hot face.

"You want to slap me, don't you?" he says.

Shit, how'd he know? Can precogs read minds too? Not good.

"No, I don't," I say. *I lie.* Then I muster all my chill. I just need answers—I can pretend to like this guy for a little while, right? My mom would be able to do it. She used to pretend all kinds of things to get to her story. Nothing to compromise journalistic integrity, but there are subtle ways you can adjust to people and situations. That's it. I'll just think of this as an assignment—a research assignment of sorts.

"You're surprisingly cold towards the guy who saved your life," he says.

Anger swishes through my chest, but I suck in a deep breath and paste on a smile. I mean, he's not wrong. He *did* save my life, or I guess was the catalyst for someone else saving it, so I could at least be cordial.

"I'm sorry, you're right. And I really should thank you. If it wasn't for you, I wouldn't be alive right now," I say, lacing my words with sincerity. *Who are you and what do you want?*

Wes smiles this time, looking down and... blushing? This sudden turn twists me off-balance. Is *this* guy actually insecure and shy?

"Wanna go somewhere?" he asks.

I nod, my insides screaming not to go anywhere with him, but I just can't stop myself. He's a thousand times more forthcoming than Henry ever was, and if I want the truth—I need him.

❧

Here we are, back in that deserted, abandoned classroom again. I'm seated in a cold, deeply uncomfortable metal chair staring at the paint-peeled wall ahead. Wes stands at the decrepit chalkboard, cradling an eraser like he's about to teach a class. Like he's teaching me the ways of the precognitive people. I don't like the dynamic—teacher, student. The power balance feels off, and I feel small.

I stand, asserting my ground and crossing my arms over my chest. I don't know if this is doing much, but it feels better to be on an even plane. Although he's much taller than me, it feels slightly more powerful to be standing versus seated. Wes crosses in front of the teacher's desk and perches on it, so now we're the same height. I'm not sure if he's picking up on my discomfort, or if he just wants to chill there.

"Are you a student here?" I say, mustering my most formidable tone.

"No," Wes says.

My heart bounces into my throat, and I'm stunned by his how forthcoming and direct he is. It's jarring.

"Why are you here then?"

"For you," he says.

My mouth gapes open and I'm rendered paralytic. I want to laugh in his face, tell him he's ridiculous and a liar. This is all so… bizarre.

"For me? Why?" I'm dying to know the answer, and at the same time, wanting to race out of this classroom and be blissful and naïve forever. Who am I kidding—there's no way I can ever be blissful. Not after everything that's happened.

"Because I needed to save you," he says, matter of fact. There's that word again—*save*. I hate it. I'm not a damsel in distress.

I roll his words over in my brain and they're just not adding up. This was Henry's vision, and he didn't have that vision about me until he arrived at Lockwood. So how would Wes know? Did he have a vision about Henry's vision? This is all so damn complicated, I'm not even sure I want the answers anymore.

"This doesn't make sense. How would you know what was going to happen to me before Henry had a vision?"

"I know because I was sent here to kill you."

CHAPTER THIRTY

HENRY

TIMOTHY'S DEAD.

Panic rips through me. My eyes lock onto his chest—it's definitely not moving, which means he's definitely not breathing.

A nagging thought chips away at my brain—why would they pick today to kill him? He said he's been here ninety-three days. Is day ninety-three the expiration date? Or did they kill him because of me?

Bile rises in my throat and I can't fucking stand the thought that my stupidity caused the death of an innocent person. Well, not exactly innocent, I guess. We were both technically locked in here for the same crime, for changing a vision to save someone we love.

Love. That word pierces through me. Do I love Natalie? I risked everything to save her, and maybe that's the definition of love. Or maybe that's the definition of ego. If I'm being honest, it felt good to save someone—like the hit of a drug with a high that lasts and lasts.

The pipes suddenly squeak and wail, interrupting my jostled, manic brain, as it skips between life and death and love. And, at eighteen, I'm not even old enough to really know anything about any of those things. I certainly don't have any time to waste thinking about that right now.

The minutes tick by. One. After another. After another. I've never been so aware of time, which I guess makes sense when you realize you're almost out of it. If I swallowed those pills like Timothy, I would have been dead too. I've got to find some way out of this place before I end up a corpse.

I scan the room, rolling over any possible way to get the hell out of here. My options are bleak though. First, there's the chains. Thick, unrelenting metal shackled to my limbs and locked to the floor. There's no way to break these things, so it's not even worth wasting my energy trying to figure it out.

Then, there's the escape routes—or lack of them. No windows, so… that's out. There's a door, but it's bolted from the outside and doesn't even have a handle. Even if I knew how to pick a lock—which I don't—there isn't even a damn lock to pry open.

Hatching my own escape is hopeless. Unless I can somehow conjure superpowers to rip open metal or walls, I'm stuck here until I die. What I need is for someone to open that door, unchain me, and *then* I can make an escape. Or at least try to. It's a pretty shitty plan, and dangerous. But at this point, what do I have to lose?

A chill sweeps through me as I think of loss, and Natalie clicks into my brain. Not just her, but a specific memory of the time I kissed her. When I nearly killed her. It must be yet another side effect to changing a vision, but why?

I squeeze my eyes shut, as if that will block out any memory of her. Of course, it won't, and at this point, I'm not sure there will be a time when my brain isn't hijacked by thoughts and memories of Natalie. Especially that kiss… the leaves cycloning around us…

A semblance of a plan shoots through my brain and I pop open my eyes. That day with Natalie, I was able to shift something in the atmosphere. Presumably, changing my vision unlocked some long dormant power. The same thing happened in the room earlier today, with that crack of thunder. Almost like the atmosphere was saving me, or maybe I conjured it somehow, subconsciously, to save myself.

Maybe my captors aren't scared of thunder. Maybe they're scared because they know I caused it. Like Timothy said—we're not precogs.

I might be totally insane to even chase this idea, but it's all I've got. If I can convince one of them that I caused that thunder, whether I did or not, maybe I can also convince them to unlock the door and my chains and then make a run for it. My stomach clamps with anxiety, but there's no time for fear right now. I just need to suck it up if I want to make it out of here alive.

"Hey! Help! I need help in here!" I say, screaming with every ounce of energy I can summon. I rap my chains against the floor to cause more of a spectacle. "Anyone out there? Help!"

There's nothing but silence on the other side for what seems like forever, until finally, a light clobber of footsteps pummels against the metal grates, growing louder and closer by the second.

My anxiety notches higher as the bolt cranks and the door whips open. It's the female guard, alone, and she commands the doorway, crossing her arms in frustration, fixing me with a detached but furious glare. "What do you want?" she asks in her thick French accent.

I study her for a moment, scanning every inch. Sure, her exterior looks tough—shaved head with a slight mohawk, ornate tattoos climbing out of her shirt, up her neck, and down her arms. In fact, the only part of her skin that's not inked is a patch surrounding the branded precog symbol on her forearm. But through that tough exterior, something in her eyes seems broken. Maybe even a little frightened. It's slight, but it's something I can use.

"What do you want?" she asks again, her voice laced with impatience and annoyance.

"He's dead," I say, motioning to Timothy's lifeless body.

She flicks her eyes to his body and shrugs, like I just told her we were out of coffee or something. It's unnerving.

"Are you going to do something about that?" I ask, incredulous. Maybe I was wrong about her tough exterior because she seems like the epitome of a cold-blooded killer right now.

"He can rot in here. You'll join him soon enough," she says. She pivots on her thick, black combat boots and begins to exit. I can't let her leave.

"I won't be joining him," I say, mustering defiance.

She turns back and laughs. No, she cackles. "Stupid boy. We have no use for you here."

If they have no use for me, why the hell am I here? "I think you do," I say. "I swallowed the same pills that he did, but look—I'm still alive. You know why?"

She eyes me, and a shimmer of panic flickers through her pupils.

"I'm not just a precog. I'm more."

Her staunch attitude suddenly curls into fear. "There is no more," she says, her voice slightly quivering.

"You don't know what we're capable of because they've suppressed you for your entire life. But when you change a vision, you unlock other powers. You can control things… in the atmosphere," I say.

"What did you say?" The keys in her hand rattle and I realize she's trembling. My revelation either confirmed her greatest suspicion, or her greatest fear. Either way, I'm one step closer to maybe getting the hell out of here.

"I wanted to distract you earlier, so I created the storm outside." I pause a moment for dramatic effect, letting that sink in. "You know it's true. That's why you were so scared. It's why you're shaking."

She takes a small step backwards, and I know she wants to run—but she doesn't. She could also easily kill me right now. But she doesn't.

"Why are you here?" I ask, softening my voice.

She averts her gaze and refuses to answer. I know it's not going to be easy to get her to open up, but I have to try. "Do you want to be here, doing this to people?"

Her eyes are glued to the floor and she remains silent. Her stillness makes my skin crawl. Everything about her makes my skin crawl, but I manage to stay calm. "Did you change a vision?" I say. "Is that why you're here?"

"No, of course not," she says with sudden ferocity, snapping her gaze to meet mine. "That's against our laws. It's a sin."

Okay, so she's a conformist. I can work with this. "So is this your job—to torture and kill precogs who don't conform?"

"I uphold our destiny. You chose self-centeredness and slander over truth and love."

"And you think killing and torturing people, keeping them chained up in here, is love?"

She doesn't answer, but I see the change sweep over her. Her lips sink into a frown. Her brow furrows. Her shoulders flop down and her stance grows heavy. The lines between us have blurred, and I hope they're muddied enough that I can convince her further.

"How long have you been here?" I say, shifting and calming my tone.

Tears well in her eyes as if painful memories are clawing through her brain. Hell, I can relate. Since that first vision of Natalie, it's like a frenetic trail of suffering has looped through my mind.

"I've never not been here," she says. Her voice is quiet now, guarded, gripping to her last semblance of strength.

"So you grew up… here?" I swell with actual sympathy for her. That must have been horrible to be raised here, watching people get imprisoned and tortured and executed. And I thought my life sucked.

"My mother got pregnant while she was working here for the Force."

"The Force?" My anxiety notches a bit higher. The only force I've heard of is from the *Star Wars* movies, but I'm betting that's not what she's referring to.

"That's what this place is. It's an organization designed to rehabilitate precogs who have lost their way," she says, matter of fact, as if this is common knowledge.

But her explanation makes no sense. "If this is rehab, then why did you kill him? And why were you trying to kill me?"

"There's no helping either one of you in this state. You're too far gone." Her voice is almost robotic, like she's reciting orders. I wonder how many of her thoughts are actually her own.

"How can you tell that I'm too far gone?"

"I don't give the orders, I just follow them," she says. Bingo. That's exactly what I wanted—needed—to hear.

"That's what you want to be, a follower? I didn't take you as a follower." I look at her, challenging. Her nostrils flare and I can tell something's bubbling inside of her. She's strong—she's just using her strength in the wrong fucking way for the wrong fucking cause.

"What's your name?" I ask.

"Iva," she says.

"Iva… this isn't the life you want. Trust me, there are better things for you out there."

She appears torn, and I can almost sense her coming around to my side. It's a comforting illusion, and I begin to brighten with hope. That is, until her expression turns menacing—like something snapped inside of her, giving her back her control. "What, are you trying to bond with me? I don't trust you. I know what I'm doing. I don't need you to explain the world to me."

With that, she turns to leave and there's a sudden panic in my chest. How can I stop her?

I need to prove to her that I have powers… powers that she doesn't understand. I need to make it thunder again, but I don't know how I made that happen in the first place. Or if I even *did* make it happen. It's not like I can just say "thunder" or snap my fingers and it just… magically appears.

I squeeze my eyes shut—the first thing that pops in my brain is Natalie. Always Natalie. It's just her eyes—shifting from golden brown to green. Then her hair, wild and curly. Those lips, pink and pouty and…

Then I get a strange flash. It's Natalie standing on the Lockwood campus, talking to Wes.

Wes?

I snap my eyes open, unsure if it's a figment of my imagination or an actual vision. Anger seeps through my mind at the thought of her with Wes. Was this some ploy between them? Did they work together to lock me in here? My anger surges and suddenly there's an ominous crack of thunder outside.

Iva whips back to face me, her expression full of terror. I nearly forgot she was even standing there, like I was transported into some other time or dimension for a few brief seconds—proving that what I saw of Natalie and Wes was definitely a vision. But I can't focus on that now—I need to concentrate on getting the hell out of here.

"I told you I can summon the thunder," I say to Iva. I still don't know how this all works yet, and perhaps it's just a wild coincidence that there's a storm when I most need it. "So you're not going anywhere. Sit down."

"You're mistaken in thinking you have so much power when you're over there chained up," she says, holding firm.

"I think you know how much power I have. And I think you have it too."

Her eyes widen in surprise.

"Deep down, you know I'm telling the truth. Imagine what else I can do, Iva. Imagine what else *you* can do. I know you're not here by choice. So sit down and hear me out, or I'll cause something much worse than a crack of thunder."

I wait, my heart pounding, on edge. This is my last hope. If she walks out that door, I'm dead. Panic claws up my spine as I await her decision.

After what feels like decades of a staring contest, Iva stays, bolting the door behind her for privacy. Now comes the hard part: convincing her to unchain me. And if that doesn't happen, I'll need to fight my way out of here. But I don't want to make her a casualty, not unless I absolutely have to. She didn't ask for this life, and it's not her fault she's been brainwashed since birth.

Iva's hand slips into her pocket and she begins to slide something out. I catch the gleam of metal, and fear stabs deeper into my chest. My body suddenly slicks with sweat as she pulls out a jagged knife and twirls it in her hand.

I freeze. So much for convincing her, because the conclusion is clear. Iva's going to kill me—unless I can get to her first.

CHAPTER THIRTY-ONE

NATALIE

A SHUDDER SKATES down my spine. *Wes was sent here to kill me.* Well, screw him. After everything I've been through, I'm not about to go down this way.

My instinct is to run, but instead, I stay put as if my feet are glued to the ground. If Henry's strength is any indication of how precogs roll, I won't be able outrun Wes. Plus, if I run, I'll never learn why he wanted to kill me in the first place. My heart hammers, blood chilling, as Wes and I lock into this bizarre stand-off. It's times like this I wish I wasn't raised by a journalist. My damn desire for information will always topple my survival instincts.

I scan the room for a weapon as breath coils in my chest. It's a funny thing when your body throttles into survival mode. My skin ignites, like someone's just lit a match and is slowly dragging it across my body. I'm desperate to find a weapon… not that I've ever used a weapon before. I latch my eyes onto a pencil cup filled with dusty pens that have long run out of ink, but I also spot the sharp edge of a letter opener. Problem is, it's too far away for me to grab—it's much closer to Wes. If I lunge for it, he'll get to it first.

I need to create a distraction.

I stiffen my movements in a desperate attempt for him not to catch my mental plotting. Behind me is a chalkboard with a massive amount of chalk dust bunched up the corner.

"Let me explain," he says. He takes a few cautious steps toward me as my nerves jangle. I'm out of time, and my options here are limited.

He pads forward, one step in front of the other, his arms raised as if he's holding them up in surrender. It's strange and unnerving, and I'm sure he intends it to be—to throw me off-balance and make me think he won't hurt me. That he isn't here to kill me.

Just when he gets close enough, I clasp a bunch of chalk dust in my hand and toss it in his face. The dusting puffs into the air and my vision clouds. Wes coughs in the chalky snowstorm and I know this is my only chance. I lurch for the pencil cup, knocking it over in the process. Everything inside clatters to the floor. My eyes burn and glisten from the dust as I scramble to the floor and try gripping the letter opener.

Wes grabs me by the arm just as I clasp it. I twist from his grip, slicing the sharp metal point across his bicep.

"Fuck!" he says, clutching his arm and stumbling back.

I scramble to my feet, pointing my pathetic weapon at him. Fear and frustration clang through my bones. "You want to kill me? Go ahead," I say, holding the pointy side of the letter opener dangerously close to his throat, mustering all of my menace.

"I don't want to hurt you," he says, his voice quiet, almost timid.

I press the cold metal against his throat. I'm not sure what's come over me, but it's like I can't stop. Some wicked part of me has been unlocked, unleashed even. "I don't believe you," I say.

Suddenly, his hands lock against my arms and before I can react, he spins us around and shoves me back against the wall, pressing his weight against me and yanking the letter opener from my hand. My breath quickens, choppy and ragged. He's a millisecond from stabbing me.

Except, instead of using the weapon, he lets the letter opener clang to the floor. My eyes flick back and forth to his, confused by his intentions and surprised that he didn't just end my life like he was apparently supposed to. "I told you, I'm not going to hurt you," he says.

He must think I'm a complete idiot. Wrists bound in his hands, I knee him in the groin with all my strength. He curls over in pain and I shove him out of the way. Before I can run, he grabs me around the waist and hoists me into the air, taking me down to the ground. I thrash around, trying to escape from his iron grip. "Let me go," I say through gritted teeth.

"Stop. I swear I'm not going to hurt you," he says. He sounds so damn sincere, but I can't take the chance. I press the soles of my feet against his legs and press hard. The movement is enough to distract him and I karate chop his grip on my arms. His hands loosen and I try to scramble out from under him, but he grabs me and hoists me back down, causing my body to crash on top of his.

Suddenly, footsteps clack down the hall and we both freeze. I'm not sure why—I probably should scream for help—no, I *definitely* should—but something brews inside of me, and my body stills. I have this weird compulsion to not get caught, as if I'm doing something illicit in here with Wes… and I don't want our secret to get out.

Wes remains motionless underneath me, but his eyes are wide and wet. Is he going to cry? The possibility, and sadness, of his mood locks into my heart. And then my obsession for discovering his true motive kicks in again. Damn inquisitive nature. My mom used to describe it all the time—like your emotional radar is broken, and you ignore all the red flags, all the danger, just to get the story.

The footsteps outside the door grow closer, louder, and we're motionless and silent as I straddle him. I try to calm my jagged breathing, praying whoever is passing won't hear us. I comb my gaze over him. His hair is disheveled, and his face covered in chalk looks like it's dusted in a layer of powdered sugar. His red, bee-stung lips pout through his choppy breaths.

The footsteps safely pass the door and just as I let out a small sigh of relief, Wes tips his mouth up in the corner, curving his lips into a smirk. "Do you like what you see?"

"Gross," I say as I smack my palms into his chest and climb off him. I crawl back to put distance between us, still trying to slow my breath.

"I'll admit that was pretty hot, even though I know you wanted to kill me," he says, pushing up to a sitting position and leaning against the desk. The pencil cup lies next to me on the floor and I chuck it at his head. He catches it mid-air with ease. Of course he does. I roll my eyes. I really need to stop hanging around with these precog fools.

"You're disgusting," I say.

He shoots me a look, seemingly compelled by my resistance, even amused by it. An odd shiver ping-pongs down my spine as I train my eyes on him. "Why did you try to kill me?"

"I didn't try to kill you. I told you that I saved you," he says.

An odd tingle dances on the nape of my neck. I swallow hard, realizing how dry my throat is from that stupid chalk dust. "Why would you want to kill me in the first place?" I ask, nearly choking out the words.

Wes sighs, and his brow knits as if he's carefully considering his words. He threads his hand through his hair, fixing his ponytail. When his haunted gaze meets mine, my pulse starts to pound again. What is it with these precogs that make them all so damn unsettling?

Oh right, they're either trying to kill me, or trying to save me from being killed.

After what feels like years of silence, he finally croaks out some words. "It was my family who wanted to kill you. They were ordered to."

Shock barrels into my chest. "Ordered to kill me? Why?"

"Because of your mom," he says.

My mom? His response jolts me. What could she have to do with this? I scramble to my feet. "What do you know about my mom?" I ask, not fucking around.

Wes pulls a joint from his jacket pocket. Not a vape like the other kids smoke, just a straight-up rolled joint stuffed with weed. He flicks a lighter and inhales deeply, then holds it out to me. "You could use a smoke."

"I don't smoke," I say, crossing my arms. Having a puff from Adip earlier that devolved into a coughing fit solidified that.

"Trust me. You could use a smoke."

Fuck it. I don't trust him, but I yank it from him anyway. Something tells me even I'm going to need to take the edge off what he's about to share. I inhale and the back of my throat burns. The joint illuminates and sizzles as I take another drag. No cough this time.

"Better?" His smirk is back, kicked up another notch. It's annoying as fuck.

"Tell me what you know about my mom." I thrust the joint back to him and he takes it.

"Your mom was causing a lot of trouble for our kind," he says, sucking in a drag and refusing to meet my eyes.

I inhale a deep breath, holding back my desire to kick him in his stupid, hot face. "Can you just spit it out already?" I tap my foot on the ground, impatient. "What did my mom do?"

"She was apparently writing a story on precogs, threatening to expose us," he says. An icy sensation drenches my skin. My mom wouldn't want to expose anyone unless they deserved it, unless they were up to some horrific shit.

"Why would she want to do that?" I say, my heart nearly launching out of my chest.

Wes shrugs and I close my fists with anger and fear. How could he be so fucking nonchalant about my mom? Is he completely heartless? I swallow back the tears that threaten to pour down my cheeks. I don't want to show him any weakness.

Wes takes another drag and I catch a small glimmer of emotion on his face. Remorse? Agony? I'm not sure. "You owe me an explanation," I say. He doesn't really owe me anything, but what other card can I play at this point?

"I don't get to know why. My family… we're just assassins. Orders with no explanations. I've woken up every morning for as long as I can remember with death on my mind."

His words are laced with pain, and as much as I hate him right now, there's a part of me that feels empathy for his messed-up situation.

"Have you killed anyone?" I ask, not really wanting to know the answer.

He nods. "Only one person. I mostly do the lead ups."

"Lead ups?" I ask. Talking about murder in such simplistic terms sends a bolt of fear through my body.

"Following the mark. Knowing their schedule. Knowing what

makes them tick, or doesn't..." His voice trails off and he stubs out the joint on the decrepit wooden floor before pushing himself to stand. It clicks into my brain that I was the mark, that he must have been following me this entire time. My stomach hollows and churns. I'm pretty sure I might vomit.

Then he meets my gaze and gives me a small, heart-wrenching smile. "That's life, I suppose," he says as he looks away, somber. "It wasn't even a full day of tracking you before I realized I just couldn't let you die."

Ten minutes ago, I was a heartbeat away from being killed—or nearly killing him. And now here we are, standing in silence, the air between us thick with pain and regret.

"My mom isn't alive anymore, so why do they need to kill me?" I say, my lip trembling, heart lodged in my throat.

"I have no idea, and now that I messed up your execution and got my uncle killed in the process—I'm sure there's already a hit out on me."

"That guard who attacked me was your uncle?"

Wes nods. Dread seeps through my mind, and I realize the danger we're both in. I swallow hard and think—Mom was secretive, but she always made sure someone knew the details of the story she was trying to break. An accountability partner of sorts, in case something happened to her.

And something *did* happen to her. Was the car accident that killed her not an accident after all? My blood turns to ice with this realization, and Wes looks over at me with concern. "What's up?"

Fear leeches from my body and all that's left is drive—drive to find out what the hell really happened to my mom. I tear off toward the door while Wes shouts after me. "Hey! Where are you going?"

I pause for a moment and look back at him with defiance. "If you don't have answers, then I'm going to find someone who does."

"You're never going to find out the truth. The only people who order executions belong to our authority, and they're hidden. Even I don't know who they are."

"I don't want to talk to a precog. In fact, I'm done with all of you. I'll figure it out myself." I storm out of the room and hear Wes shouting after me with pleas to wait.

Sorry Wes, you've got issues, but so do I. And I'm about to confront the one person I think might know the truth about everything.

He also happens to be the last person I want to talk to at all.

My father.

CHAPTER THIRTY-TWO

HENRY

MY EYES LOCK onto the knife in Iva's hand. She twirls it around effortlessly, like one of those stage magicians—but I'm not stupid enough to believe this is some magic trick. My heart pounds faster as she closes the distance between us, and my mind combs over all the ways I might be able to fight her off. My hands are bound tight, so I won't have much leverage as she plunges a knife down into me. My feet are probably my best option, but even my mobility there is limited since they're chained to the floor.

She's going to kill me. A chill races over my skin and I brace for her assault. She studies me for a long moment with an uncomfortable level of scrutiny, and just when I think she's about to wield that knife, she sinks onto the ground—right next to Timothy's corpse.

My entire body clenches in shock. I thought this chick was about to stab me, and now she's sitting next to me like we're old friends? Damn, this place is so weird. She looks over at me with a bored expression. She doesn't seem phased, at all, sitting there next to a dead guy.

She motions to her knife. "For protection," she says.

"Protection from what?" I say, panic crawling up my throat as the words spit out.

"From you. I'm not stupid, I know what you're doing. I know that you don't really know anything about your abilities," she says.

I gulp down the frigid, stale air as I realize she's got my number. She knows that I fed her a bunch of bullshit to stay alive, so why am I still here? Why hasn't she killed me yet? I buzz with adrenaline, realizing that maybe there's a small glimmer of something here with Iva, and that she can help me escape.

"You know, you're not what I expected," I say. I'm half lying. She is both exactly what I expected—cold, calculating, heartless, inhuman—and not at all what I imagined—curious, willing to listen. I can work with that.

"What did you expect?" she says, her thick French accent laced with contempt.

"I don't know. I guess I thought you were just some brainwashed precog robot." She bristles at my evaluation of her, and I quickly recover. "But you're not. You're smart enough to question things. I admire that."

Iva's face contorts into something that looks pained, almost human, as if my words have sliced through her heart, or triggered something she doesn't want to come to terms with. Somehow, this change in her expression makes me even more uneasy. Maybe because it makes her seem less threatening, and I need to remember that she's my enemy if I have any chance of getting out of here.

"Sometimes, something you've believed all your life gets called into question. You understand?" she says.

Yes, of course I understand. Fuck, do I understand. That's why

I'm chained up in this place—because I called into question what I've believed my entire life. And look how that turned out. I nod, indicating my connection to what she's revealing.

"Put your faith in the force," she says, getting a bit more emotional.

"What?" Is she really going to try and convert me into her creepy precog belief system? This is worse than I thought.

"That's something my father says. Always put your faith in the force."

I expect her to ask me to chant that back or something, but she doesn't. Instead, she appears almost conflicted by the statement.

"And you just believe what your father says?"

She snaps her gaze to mine, her eyes tinged with anger. "And you always believed you couldn't change a vision, right?"

Damn, she just called me out. The truth is, I never questioned Oliver about our beliefs. For most of my life, I just blindly followed what my adopted father and siblings said. I never felt I had a reason to question them, not until I had that vision about Natalie. A wave of grief hits me, but I shove it away. I can't think about Natalie right now, not when I'm in the middle of this bizarre bonding experience with Iva and the shred of possibility to get the hell out of here.

"Did you ever question your father, secretly?" I say, careful not to piss her off.

She hesitates for a while, like she's weighing her answer. Or maybe weighing if she wants to tell me the truth. "Not at first. It seemed like we had everything we needed in here. I don't know much about out there," she says. "Our father would show us news stories about people out there being murdered, beaten, and raped. About people living on the streets with no food or water. We were safe in here. We have food, and water, and everything. Why would we want to be out there?"

I take that in for a moment, realizing that she's been caged up in here for her entire life and fed whatever narrative her father wanted. "Those things happen, but the world out there isn't all bad. There are good things," I say, though I'm not sure I believe that myself.

"My sister, she didn't have faith," Iva says.

For some reason, I'm shocked to hear she has a sibling, though I can't pinpoint why. Maybe because it's another thing that makes her seem more empathetic, and not like a cold-blooded kidnapper.

"She had beliefs like you. She would sneak around and eavesdrop, try to uncover information about what we really are."

There it is again: *what we really are*. Timothy said it, too, before he died. What the hell does that mean? "And what did she find out? Anything?"

"She managed to get some article that my father didn't want us to see, something about little babies being able to breathe." Iva laughs, as if that's an absurd thing.

"What do you mean? Babies do breathe. We all have to breathe to live," I say. Is she insane? Oh right, of course she is. She grew up in some freaky precog cult and now kidnaps people for a living and holds them hostage until they're murdered. Probably even murders them with her own hands sometimes.

"No, precogs don't breathe as babies. We're born with no breath, or pulse, or heartbeat. We only have those things when we turn two," Iva says, matter of fact.

What the hell is she talking about? How can we live without breathing? Damn, her father really did a number on her. What kind of fake news is he feeding them?

"That can't be right," I say, a laugh curdling around my words.

"I'm right," she says, challenging. "I told you, I was born here. Other force members also had their babies here, and one of my jobs is to help with the nursery. None of those babies are breathing, but they are very much alive."

My stomach rolls with terror. What the fuck? So that means I was born, dead? No way. This must be a joke, or illusion. Am I hallucinating? Am I hearing this right?

"You don't believe me," Iva says. "I will show you."

ℏ

Within minutes, I'm unchained—Iva gripping my arm and yanking me down a blinding white corridor. I make a weak attempt to swallow my fear, but it sticks in my throat like a tennis ball. It's freezing, and a persistent hum rings in the distance that's torture to my eardrums. I try to keep up with her frenetic pace, but struggle with my bound hands and chained feet. Another guard I don't recognize enters the hallway and walks straight at us.

"Don't say a word," Iva threatens in a hushed whisper. I do as she says, and the guard passes by, nodding to Iva. She nods back and we keep plunging ahead, down the hall.

"You're lucky he's not your guard. He's brutal to the prisoners here. Most don't even make it to the cell," she says once the guard is out of sight.

Lucky? I guess given the circumstances.

She ushers me to a cubed room flanked entirely in glass. Inside sits just three cribs—all white—with babies inside. None of the babies are crying or making any movements at all. The whole scene sends chills down my spine.

I attempt to walk inside for a better look when Iva grabs my arm. "Wait," she says, as she presses a button on the side of a security camera I didn't even realize was there. "We've got about three minutes before someone notices this is off."

We enter into the eerie space. An air of gloom lingers and a dim light illuminates the three sterile, white cribs. I approach one of babies and notice their eyes are shut. I check the sign on the crib for a name, but it only reads P17865. Iva notices my confusion. "It's a girl. And that's our number. We're all assigned one at birth."

A number? Why didn't I know that? This makes my stomach sink, like we're all marked cattle ready for slaughter.

I gently lean over the crib for a better look. My pulse pounds as I study this tiny angelic child who appears healthy, until I notice there is no normal rise and fall of her chest. I blink a few times, sure that I must be imagining things. This baby has to be breathing. Suddenly, her eyes snap open and meet my own. A shudder wracks my body and I stumble away from the crib.

"You woke her," Iva says, disappointed.

The baby doesn't cry or make any sound. Maybe because she can't even breathe. I take another cautious peek—I can't help it. She looks right at me. Her eyes are bright and vibrant green, just like mine.

"Do you believe me now?" Iva asks.

I nod, dumbfounded. I need to stay focused on getting out of here, but everything I just learned infects my thoughts.

"I will help you escape," Iva says.

"You will?" I ask, surprised. An uneasy feeling creeps through me. This feels easy—too easy.

"Like you, my sister believed things were better out there, so she ran away and promised to come back for me if things were better. But she never came back."

"What do you think happened to her?" I ask.

"She snuck a letter to me, so I know she's alive," she says, pulling a crumpled and worn slip of paper from her pocket. "It just says I should come to the Nine O'Clock Gun."

I recognize what that is immediately. I've been there, on a trip with my family. My heart wrenches and my stomach twists as I realize I can never go back to my family, even if I wanted to. "The Nine O'Clock Gun is in Stanley Park in Vancouver, British Columbia. It's a cannon that fires off every night at nine o'clock," I say.

Iva looks at me, confused.

"It's not far over the Canadian border. You can take a train there from Seattle," I say.

"Then you will take me there," she says. "If there's a chance I can find my sister, what do I care what happens to you in the process?"

So much for bonding, but at this point, I'll take my chances. "I can take you," I say, though I don't have any idea where we are. And I have no money for a cab or ferry. And no phone to call anyone, not that I have anyone to call. But I'll figure it out. I have to.

Before I can even ask how the hell we're going to escape, Iva yanks up a metal panel on the wall and presses an alarm. The shrill sound is deafening and red lights swirl in periodic bursts throughout the room. I take one last look at the babies who don't seem affected by this commotion at all. My heart thuds against my rib cage and panic gnaws at my gut. If we don't even breathe when we're born, then… are we even human?

"Let's go, now!" Iva says, yelling over the screeching alarm. A coil of hope winds through my brain—is this real? Am I really going to escape? I quickly shove that hope away, because I know better than to get swept into some optimistic "everything will be great" viewpoint. Eternal optimism is for sociopaths with no self-awareness, and I'm no sociopath.

But against my better judgment, a slice of optimism snatches my mind and I follow Iva—bolting to freedom.

CHAPTER THIRTY-THREE

NATALIE

EVERY CLANK OF a dish and trickle of wine in this bougie restaurant becomes audible when sitting across from my father—the most awkward dinner companion ever.

I don't want to be here, and neither does he, but I'm desperate for information about the story my mother was working on before she died. And, unfortunately, my father is the only person I can think of who she might have trusted enough to tell.

"How's your soup?" he says. I haven't touched my soup, but he wouldn't know that because he's been typing incessantly on his phone since we got here. My father is one of those people who believes his time is more important than everyone else's. And if you call him out on it, he'll just say it's not true—leaving me questioning if I'm going crazy. My father, king of gaslighting.

"I'm not hungry," I say, pinning my eyes on him, heart hammering with annoyance.

He nods, still refusing to look up from his damn phone.

"Mhmmm," he says, clearly not listening. He's not even making the most basic effort to pay attention.

"I want to ask you something about Mom," I say.

That gets his attention. He snaps his head up, finally looking at me for the first time tonight. I gulp down my breath, knowing I've pissed him off—but I'm not backing down, not this time.

"You know I don't like talking about your mother," he says. *Oh yes, I do know.* My cheeks burn at his dismissal, at all the times I've attempted to share happy memories with him about Mom. He always completely shuts down—saying I'm insensitive for bringing her up, for reminding him of his great loss. As if it's not my loss too.

"I need to know what story she was working on before she died," I say, indignant. I know my father respects colleagues who stand their ground. Maybe making demands is the only way to get his help.

He ignores my request and goes back to his phone. I guess his respect is only extended to professional relationships. I shove my disappointment down because I'm used to this. I expected this from him, but this time, his indifference is a fierce smash to my heart. Frustration claws through my skin, followed by a surge of adrenaline.

"Pay attention!" I say, much louder than I intend. The restaurant patrons whip their heads around at the spectacle I've just made.

My father glares at me, disappointed, and shoves his phone into his suit jacket. He polishes off his Macallen and stares right at me. "Happy now?"

"No, I'm not happy about any of this." I scrunch my eyes shut—why is he such a nightmare? I suck in a deep breath trying to steady my nerves, and blink my eyes open. My father continues to glare at me, now even more annoyed.

"Do you know what story she was working on?" I say—nicely this time.

"Your mother never told me what she was working on," he says. I detect a bit of contempt in his voice, and wonder if Mom's career was a big reason for their turbulent marriage. I always thought it was my father's fault that they were so stormy and strained. I've never considered that mom's obsession with her work could have been a real problem. The tiniest shred of sympathy for my father swells in my heart.

"So you didn't know anything at all?"

A slight hint of knowledge passes in his eyes, but it vanishes in a second. He pulls his napkin from his lap and sets it down on the table. "I really have to get going, Natalie. I shifted my schedule around to see you last-minute and now I have a million things to finish."

He stands, abrupt, and I know he's lying. "You can stay here and order more food if you'd like. They have my credit card on file."

Without even saying goodbye, he walks swiftly out of the restaurant. Fuck that, he's not getting away. I chase after him—making yet another scene.

I catch him outside on the curb as his driver is ushering him into the back seat of the car. "Wait!" I yell, racing over. He studies me, angered by my behavior—and probably by my existence.

"Please, I know you don't want to talk about Mom, but I'm worried. I think she was working on something dangerous. And maybe it wasn't an accident that she died." I recoil a bit, blurting out more than I wanted to say.

I instantly regret coming here when my father's expression turns sinister. He always looks at me with an air of resentment, but he's never looked at me like this before. "Don't you dare say that again, you hear me?"

And with that, he gets in the car and slams the door. His driver peels off, leaving me standing on the curb, alone with my grief.

I can barely concentrate the entire ferry ride back to campus, thoughts tumbling through my brain. I want to scream, throw up, smash something. I have this sinking feeling my father knows something about all of this. Is he just trying to protect me, or is he hiding it for some other reason?

A Lockwood driver from the ferry station drops me on campus, and I mindlessly wander around the grounds. The pitch-black sky swallows the campus and it's absolutely freezing out here—the coldest night yet this fall by far. I'm too restless to go back to my room, but it's late—and there's nothing else to do this late on a Tuesday night at Lockwood.

Suddenly, the sky cracks with thunder and rain pelts down. I race inside the nearest building for cover.

The metal door smashes shut behind me, and I shiver, shaking the rain from my curls. I'm inside the treehouse building, which is a stupid name because it's not at all a treehouse. Apparently, this used to be where the biosciences were housed until they built a state-of-the-art center on the west side of campus.

I take a few steps, my shoes squishing from the rain. The building is completely dark and desolate, except for one lone light shining at the end of the corridor. Suddenly, I see a figure emerge from the illuminated space and dash across the hall. An eager tremble splashes through me, and I'm already sneaking toward the commotion to check it out. Damn curiosity, gets me every time.

As I slowly creep down the hall, I roll over all the possibilities in my twisty, dark mind. Maybe it's a student having sex with a teacher. That's probably it. *Boring.*

Or maybe it's someone pulling off a heist, stealing supplies that happen to be worth something on the black market. *Slightly more interesting.*

Or, maybe someone's got a serious operation running—like drugs, or weapons trading—and they're using this room as the base for their criminal operation. *That's a story I'd like to break.*

I pause and shake my head, fighting this investigative obsession. I don't want to be a journalist like Mom. I have other dreams—dreams that are just for me.

A loud clang in the distance jolts me from my reasoning, and I'm back on the hunt. The hallway tapers off down a small set of stairs. I slowly pad my way down the steps and twist the knob, but it's locked.

I peek in the window of the door, and I'm surprised to find a mattress, tea kettle, and a book on the floor. What the…?

Suddenly, a hand locks over my mouth and I attempt to scream, but it muffles my cries. Fear rips through me, and I manage to wrestle away from my attacker—smashing my elbow into their head.

"Ouch," he says, and I recognize a familiar male voice.

I whip around to meet Wes. He studies me, his intense green eyes visible in the stream of light coming from the room. "Goddamn. That was kind of hot," he says, with pure enjoyment.

I nail my gaze to his, challenging. "You really are gross."

"Thanks," he says, a smile creeping across his lips.

"What the hell are you doing here?"

"I could ask you the same thing," he says, and I notice a small tremble of nerves in his response that I decide to ignore.

I roll my eyes and cross my arms over my chest. Why is everything such an annoying game with him? "I got caught in the rain."

"Lucky me," he says, combing his eyes up and down my body. His gesture makes my heart race just a bit, but I'll never let him know that.

I let out an audible groan and push past him, attempting to climb back up the stairs when he clasps my hand and spins me back to him, our bodies clashing together. My heart races even faster, and I push away from him immediately. "What the hell are you doing?"

"Well, you're here, so come on in—make yourself at home," he says, slipping a key from his pocket and unlocking the door to the room.

"Wait… you live here?" I say, confused.

He nods as if I should have known this bit of information. "I'm not a student here, so I can't exactly live in campus housing. I needed somewhere to stay while I was watching you."

This revelation sends a chill up my spine, but I follow him inside the small space anyway. I can't believe he stays here. The room is mostly empty, and very dusty. Up close, the mattress is worn and covered by a few thin blankets. A book, journal, and a pen lie next to it with a small lamp. Besides the tea kettle in the corner, there doesn't seem to be much else. My gut twists with concern. As messed up as it is that Wes was initially here to follow me, to help have me killed… he didn't. And I feel terrible that he's been living in this place.

"It's freezing in here," I say, wrapping my coat tighter around my body.

"Yeah, I didn't really plan on being here this long," he says. "Didn't account for weather in Washington state, I guess. But I can't exactly go back to my family now, so… home sweet home."

We stew in awkward silence for a moment. "So did you find out any more information?" Wes asks, breaking the tension.

"No," I say, trying to cover my disappointment.

"Where'd you go?"

"Don't worry about it." I'm not ready to unveil anything about my horrible relationship with my father, or the fact that he may actually know something about my mom and this whole ordeal.

I survey the room, my shivering starting to become painful in the biting cold. "You can't sleep in here with no heat. It's like thirty degrees outside and only getting colder."

Wes shrugs. "I'll make it work. I have a blanket." I stare at the limp, thin blankets on the bed, and although he's trying to hide it, I can see him trembling.

"Come with me," I say.

❦

The rain stops and we trudge up the muddy path to my building. We enter quietly, being careful not wake anyone—especially Ciel, who is only a few doors down. I welcome Wes into my room, locking the door behind us. He looks around in awe. "This is how the Lockwood kids live, huh?"

"Haven't you seen any of the rooms before?" I say.

"Henry's, yeah, which was… not like this."

Hearing Henry's name sends a spike to my heart, and I dip my gaze away from Wes—trying to push thoughts of Henry far, far away.

"You want some tea?" I ask Wes. He scrunches up his face, as if I'm stupid for even asking.

"I don't drink tea," he says with a snark-filled laugh.

"Sorry. Let me guess, you only drink alcohol," I say, spitting back his same asshole tone.

"Nah, I've decided today to quit drinking. Straight sober," he says, his expression growing serious.

"You smoke weed, though? So not totally sober," I say, calling him on his shit.

"That's different. Weed calms my nerves. You kinda need that when you have visions all your life and your family kills people."

I bite my lip, regretting even starting this stupid battle. As I make my tea, Wes scopes out my room—pausing to stare at a photo of my mom on the wall. He removes the frame, and I rush over and snatch it from him—a strange instinct to protect it. "That's my mom."

"Can I see it again?" he asks. I nod and he studies the picture over my shoulder. "Where was this taken?"

"Umm, I think she was in France, maybe. Why?"

Wes is still studying the photo when my tea kettle boils and pops in the background, cracking the thick silence in the room.

"I know that guy. He's a precog," Wes says, pointing to a guy in the background of the photo.

My stomach sinks. "Who is it?"

"I don't know his name, but I've seen his picture before. He's a member of the authority," Wes says.

"So you think my mom was working with a member of your authority? Why would they want to be exposed if they are in charge?"

Wes shrugs, and it's clear this troubles him. I digest the information, and try to make sense of it. Did this member of the precog authority contact my mom to do a story? Or did she find him? And why?

None of it makes sense to me, at least not yet. But then, I latch onto a memory—the moment my mom gave me this photo, in this frame.

It was about three months before she died—the tail-end of summer—and I was still hot and sticky from sitting outside at our pool. My parents were fighting, as usual, and I snuck to the top of the staircase like always to eavesdrop. I couldn't help it—some teenagers spend all day taking selfies, I lurked through homes and friendships and relationships trying to smuggle information.

Mom caught me spying that day, and later gave me this framed photo. She told me to keep it with me, and if I was ever anxious, I could look at it and know she was watching over me.

At the time, I just thought it was just a way make me feel better about their fighting. But now I'm wondering if this was a premonition—did she give me this photo because she knew she was in danger?

"You okay?" Wes says.

I can't even answer him. My mind jumbles with this memory that never seemed important until now.

I trace my fingers over the ornate gold edges of the frame. She gave this to me for a reason—was it some kind of message? I follow an instinct and open the back of the frame. A slip of paper falls out and floats to the ground.

"What's that?" Wes asks.

I pick it up and unravel the note, which is unmistakably in my mother's handwriting.

"My mom hid a note in here."

Wes's eyes pop open in surprise. "Do you think it could be a clue or something?"

I read the note out loud. "I don't know. It just says, 'Nine O'Clock Gun.'"

CHAPTER THIRTY-FOUR

HENRY

THE SHRILL OF the alarm clangs in my ears.

Iva ducks behind a large piece of metal equipment and signals for me to follow. She presses her finger to her lips, and I get it—she wants me to stay quiet. Though it's not like anyone would hear us over this horrible shrieking sound.

Out of sight, we watch as a slew of robotic guards march past in unison, heading to what I imagine is an exit to this creepy fucking place. My stomach churns just thinking that every single one of these assholes was lurking here the whole time. Where the hell are they hiding? How big is this place?

And why are there no prisoners with them?

We wait for the end of the group to march out of sight before Iva hauls me across the corridor. She presses her thumb against a security pad on the door with a blinking red light. After a few seconds, the light turns green and Iva shoves the door open, yanking me inside.

I assume this is our exit plan, that there's some secret door or window we can crawl through. But once we're inside this room, it's just another damn locked box with no other escape route. Iva shuts the door, and suddenly it's quiet in what must be a soundproof room. I'm grateful for the silence, but still pissed we're wasting time.

"I thought we were getting out of here," I say, my fury rising at this detour she seems so bent on taking.

Iva whips around to face me, raw anger on her face. "I can't exactly escape with you in plain sight of all the guards. Stupid," Iva says, shaking her head at my apparently idiotic statement.

"Why is everyone out there so calm? Don't they think there's an emergency?"

"We have drills for alarms, no need to get crazy." Iva rolls her eyes at me.

The blood continues to rush back to my limbs and I realize how fucking sore I am from being bound for so long, and my legs ache. "Why aren't they taking the prisoners with them?" I say, even though I probably don't want to know the answer.

"Why would we put ourselves in danger on purpose? Bringing prisoners means they could escape, or worse."

"I thought you said this was rehab for precogs." I should shut my mouth, but I can't help it. "You're trained to just leave people in here to die?"

Iva shrugs. "Some people can't be helped."

My mind roars with rage and injustice. How can this place seriously even fucking exist? "So you're telling me that no one in here can be helped. What's the point of keeping us prisoner, then? Just to torture us, to kill us?"

Iva pauses, and I'm not sure if she's challenging her beliefs or if she just thinks I'm completely insane, but she decides to ignore my question. Iva white knuckles the knife in her hand, and I wonder if she's about to stab me.

As if she can read my mind questioning her trust, Iva shoves her knife against my neck. The cold, jagged blade threatens to pierce my skin if I make even the slightest move. "Don't even think about trying anything. I'm helping you, remember that."

I raise my hands in surrender, careful not to nick my skin on her blade. "I know, relax."

She locks eyes with mine, her face twisted into a snarl. The tension rolls between us, thick and unrelenting, until she finally breaks the stare. I instinctively rub my neck, making sure it's okay as Iva goes back to the door and peers out the small window.

"We wait until everyone's out of the building. Then we have exactly three minutes before they realize this wasn't a planned drill to get to the other end of the compound and get out before they find us."

I have no idea what that all means, but I'm committed to the plan. It's my only chance.

Footsteps echo in the hallway as Iva keeps watch. I survey the room, trying to find something, anything, to distract my mind from going crazy right now. We're in some kind of control room with a bunch of monitors on the wall. The screens flicker between security footage of different cells.

The monitors are old and dusty, and the technology is on par with its appearance. The footage on the screens is somewhat difficult to make out, but it's clear enough to see that it's of various prisoners, chained up just like I was. An old woman lying comatose on the floor. A young kid who can't be more than ten years old curled into a ball. I count about a dozen of them, and it's all so fucking grim. The deafening alarm doesn't even appear to register with any of them, but I guess they're so doped up on the drugs this place makes them take they don't even notice.

The footage flicks around and then one of the monitors stops on something bizarre. It's not footage of a cell, it's something else. Something familiar.

I squint to make out what it is, and my stomach clenches when I realize it's the Lockwood campus. What the hell? I knew those cameras still worked.

"Do you know how I can see more footage of this?" I ask Iva, motioning to the screen.

Iva twists back to me, annoyed. "Why do you want to see more footage of the cells?"

"No, not that." I press a few buttons, zooming in on the grainy video of Lockwood campus. "This footage."

"It looks like a cell to me," Iva says, turning away.

Why doesn't she see what I see? I squint my eyes for a better look, noticing a few students milling around campus... and then I see her.

Natalie. My heart slams into my chest.

And she's with Wes.

Breath lodges in my lunges as I enlarge the video, trying to get a better look. They're walking, no—they're practically running—in the dark, both of them scanning their surroundings, like they're running from something. I know where they're fucking headed—they're going to escape campus.

I'm seething with anger when Iva snaps at me. "It's clear. You stay behind me, follow my lead. You understand?"

"Yeah, I get it," I say, trying to pummel Natalie and Wes out of my brain so I can focus.

Iva glares at me, not sure if I'm full of shit. There's no way to assure her, so I don't, and we both surge ahead—out of the room and down the now-deserted corridor. Iva motions for me to keep following and we pick up the pace, eating up the distance.

I race behind her, staying focused and at the same time clocking every inch of this place. We're moving so fast I can't see inside the individual rooms, but I do spot an exit up ahead.

Suddenly, Iva makes a sharp left. "Where are we going? The exit is that way," I say, shouting over the alarm.

Iva whips back to me and grips my shirt, shoving me hard against the wall. "Do you want to escape?"

The alarm suddenly stops ringing, though the sound still echoes in my ears. Iva's not fucking around, but neither am I. My nerves are on fire, and the fact that we're not actually going to an exit makes my trust for her evaporate.

"There's an exit right there."

"If you want to leave out that exit and walk right into fifty armed guards, be my guest."

We lock eyes for a tense moment as I realize she's right. I go out that exit, and there will be fifty bullets in my chest.

"There is no more time. Do you want to escape, or stay here to die?"

She releases her iron grip on my shirt and forges ahead. I follow this time—I'm done questioning her.

We curve around a corner and break into a run, ducking down hallways, making sharp left and right turns. I'm floored by how absolutely fucking huge this place is, when…

Gunfire erupts, and Iva plummets to the ground. Holy shit. Blood seeps from her head. I have no clue where the gunshot even came from until I spot a guard in the distance. "There he is!" a male voice shouts, and suddenly, a stampede of footsteps follows.

I turn and bolt for my life, with no idea where I'm going. The footsteps behind me grow louder and closer, but no gunshots ring out. These guards could easily take me down—I'm outnumbered.

If they're not shooting, that means they must want me alive, and that's even more terrifying.

I skid around a corner out of sight and hide behind a piece of machinery, watching the group of guards race past. That should buy me a few minutes before they notice.

Once they're out of range, I race off in the other direction, taking a set of stairs three at a time. My shoes clang against the metal grating on the stairs, but I don't have time to be quiet right now.

As soon as I hit the landing, I spot a door ahead with an exit sign. My lungs burn from exertion, but I can almost taste freedom as I get closer. My feet skid from my speed and I nearly slam my body into the heavy metal door once I'm there.

I twist the knob and it's locked. There's a keypad just like the one on the door Iva opened, and I realize there's no way I'm cracking this open without a thumbprint.

Something clatters behind me, and I jerk back to find a lone guard standing behind me. His expressionless face twists into rage as he reaches for a nightstick wedged into his belt. I act fast, landing a solid punch to his face that snaps his head back. The impact knocks him off-guard for a second, and he wipes an ooze of blood from his nose. He swings back at me, but I pivot just in time for the punch to narrowly miss my ear. He digs his hands into my shoulders and shoves me into the metal door.

My head clangs against the metal, jarring my brain, but my adrenaline surges and I don't let him take me down. He raises his nightstick, and just as he's about to swing it into my face, I rear back and attack him with every ounce of force I can summon—taking us both to the ground.

I pummel my fist into his face and manage to wrestle the nightstick from his hand. I crack it into his head, knocking him out cold. Panting for air, I yank his unconscious body across the slick floor and raise his limp thumb to the security panel to try and open the door.

Please work.

It takes a few tries, but finally the lock turns green.

I step over the guard and shove open the door. The first thing that hits me is fresh air, filling up my sore lungs. It feels so fucking good to breathe again.

I surge through the doorway toward freedom.

Something smacks into the back of my head, and everything turns to black.

CHAPTER THIRTY-FIVE

NATALIE

I STIR AWAKE, forgetting for a moment where I am.

Warmth surrounds my body, and my skin flushes at how cozy and wonderful it feels. Something rustles against my neck, awakening my nerve endings and sending prickly heat down my spine.

A low rumble sounds in the distance, and I now remember that I'm moving. I tune into the low whispers of idle chatter and the train clacking against the tracks.

I snuggle deeper into the warm embrace I find myself in before snapping my head up to digest what the hell is going on.

I'm on a train.

And I was just snuggling… *with Wes.*

His arm is still curled around my neck and I yank it away, shooting him a disgusted glare. He fastens his eyes on me and chuckles as I shake off what just happened.

"How long was I asleep?"

"About an hour," he says. "I'm not complaining, though." He

shoots me a devilish grin, and I turn away and fixate my gaze out the window.

I press my face against the frigid glass, hoping it will cool some of the heat knotted through my body. Heat that I don't want to feel. Not for Wes, not for anyone.

The view of the water is stunning, lapping peacefully as the train rattles past. Wes offered me the window seat, which was nice. But I'd give up the view to not have to sit next to him and deal with his annoying behavior at all.

Wes and I snuck off campus the same way I learned he originally snuck in—by canoe. After a freezing ride across the water from Lockwood Island to a quiet suburb of Seattle, we made our way to the train station. I've never taken the train to Vancouver before, but it was a safe and fast way to get out of the city. I just need to get to the Nine O'Clock Gun and try to figure out why Mom left me that clue.

"Can I ask you a question?" Wes says, interrupting my thoughts.

I roll my eyes. I can't even imagine what he wants to know. "Sure," I say, not really meaning it.

"Were you falling for him. For Henry?"

My heart rattles at his question. Why does he want to know that? My cheeks begin to burn and I refuse to look at him. I don't need Wes picking up any cues that his question bothers me. When it comes to Henry, it's best if I just pretend I'm indifferent.

"No," I say.

A small laugh escapes Wes's mouth, and now I'm pissed. "What, you don't believe me?" I say, fighting the storm cloud of aggravation building inside.

"I didn't say that," he says, smirking. Why did I let him come with me?

"Then what's the problem with my answer?" I say, trying not to spit venom at him.

"No problem, I'm just a curious person. It'll be the death of me one day," he says.

His admission hits me square in the gut. I often feel the same way—that curiosity is my downfall. I'm almost sure I've used his exact phrasing before about myself. My body tightens and I'm a bit creeped out that Wes has the same insatiable curiosity I do. I don't feel like bonding with him, I don't want to have things in common. We're completely different people stuck on this fucked up journey together—for now anyway.

"So you weren't in love with Henry?" he says.

"No, were you?" I snap.

"Me? Nah. He's not really my type."

I shift in my seat, scooting as far away from Wes as I can. The seats are roomy—worn leather, but comfortable. I know Wes is burning his eyes into me, but I just stare out the window. Maybe he'll take the hint. *Probably not.*

"Have you ever been in love before?" he says.

My temper ratchets up. What the hell with the questions? We have more important things to deal with right now—like the fact that people want us both dead.

"Have you?" I say, not wanting to feed into his annoying curiosity—yet being a hypocrite because I'm indulging my own.

"Maybe," he says, with a sadness lacing his voice. I almost feel bad for asking, *almost.* "I'm not entirely sure."

"You would know if you were," I say. Unwelcome memories of Henry begin to flood my brain. I squeeze my eyes shut—desperate to block them out.

"So you *have* been in love," Wes says, and I realize I should have just kept my mouth shut.

"Are you going to torture me for this entire train ride?"

Getting through customs is surprisingly easy for me—they aren't kidding when they say Canadians are nice. Although, considering Wes is Canadian, and his family attempted to murder me, I may have to reconsider that belief.

Within no time, we're at the Stanley Park Seawall in Vancouver—a massive waterfront path. It's cold and rainy, and we don't have an umbrella because people who grow up in the Pacific Northwest don't carry them. I tuck the hood of my coat tighter around my head, but rain still pelts down on my face.

Despite the wet mop of hair plastered to my skin and the shivering cold, the view here is incredible—overlooking the harbor and the downtown Vancouver skyline that resembles a bunch of Legos. Wes and I wind down the path until we reach the Nine O'Clock Gun. It's not really a gun at all, but a cannon housed in a cage.

"Here it is," Wes says, unimpressed.

I search around for any clues, any indication of why Mom would want me to come here. I read the sign with historical facts and figures about the monument, but nothing sticks out. I survey all the surroundings only to find some random rocks. There are no people here besides a few joggers caught in the rain. What am I supposed to be looking for?

I lock my eyes on the cannon in the cage and make my way over. I yank on the door, but it's locked—there's no way I'm getting that open without a key. It's also fully encased, so I can't climb inside.

Suddenly, a red light above the cannon starts to blink and an alarm sounds.

Wes yells something over the alarm that I don't hear. I'm too busy examining everything for clues. Could something be etched inside the cage, maybe a message?

Wes wraps his arms around my waist and hurls me away from the cannon. I beat at his arms with my fists, annoyed that he's manhandling me, but his viselike grip is unrelenting.

"What the hell are you doing?" I say, growing more enraged.

The cannon fires, sending shockwaves through my body. I screech and instinctively tuck my body into Wes for safety. I was so wrapped up in my own shit, I didn't even consider that the alarm meant the cannon was about to fire in my face.

"What the hell?" I cover my ears from the deafening blast.

Wes laughs. "I mean, it's called the Nine O'Clock Gun for a reason." His words drip with sarcasm.

"Okay, you don't have to be such a dick about it," I say, rolling my eyes.

He leans down, our faces so close that I can feel his breath on my cheek. "If I'm such a dick, why are you still holding my hand?"

I look down, realizing he's right. *Dammit.* I yank my hand out of his grip and wipe it on my coat, as if I'm trying to erase his touch. He laughs at me again. I can't stand when he does that.

"Well, what are we supposed to do, just hang out here all night and wait for a magical clue?" he asks, tucking his hands into his coat pockets.

"How am I supposed to know? I have the same information you do," I say, annoyed. I take a mental inventory of what I've learned so far. There doesn't seem to be any clues here, that's for sure. Why would my mom leave a note about this gun? She had to know I'd come here.

"Are there people who live near here?" I say.

"Do you see anybody living here?" he says, spreading his arms to indicate that, indeed, there are no houses or signs of life. I give him the middle finger and fold my arms in protest.

"Okay, Coal Harbour is the closest neighborhood. But the

residents wouldn't identify as living near the Nine O'Clock Gun. If that's what your mom wrote in the note, then it's got to be something specific to that, don't you think?"

He's right, but what could it mean? I stare at the cannon, willing my mind to come up with something. A cannon… that goes off every single night at nine o'clock. That means something needs to happen for it to fire every night without a hitch.

"Who makes sure the cannon goes off?" I say.

"I dunno, I guess there's a historical society or something."

I quickly look up the Vancouver Historical Society on my laptop. Luckily, we're in one of the free Wifi spots Vancouver offers throughout the city. There's a website, but no contact phone number. There is an email address, and I quickly fire off a message.

"I just sent them an email. I'm not sure what to do now. I don't want to leave. What if someone gets back to me in the morning?"

"You want to stay here for the night?"

"You can head back. I'll stay," I say, looking forward to some quiet time without his distraction.

"I'm not leaving you alone," Wes says. "It's the least I can do after nearly getting you killed."

⁂

We find a nearby hotel and Wes insists on splitting the cost of a room. It's decent, with two double beds—perfect for giving us space so I don't kill him.

I tuck into bed and avert my gaze as Wes yanks off his shirt, but it's hard not to sneak a peek. His body is… rock hard. Not as bulky and strong as Henry's, but lean and muscular. I pin my eyes to my laptop, doing my best to ignore him, yet, he seems to find excuses to roam around the room. He knows exactly what he's doing. So hot. *So aggravating.*

I scroll through my email and spot a response from the historical society. "Hey, they responded," I say.

Wes walks over and sinks onto the bed next to me. Not only did I not ask him to lay in bed with me, I certainly didn't ask him to do it half-naked. *Focus, Natalie.*

We read the email together. The caretaker of the Nine O'Clock Gun is a volunteer named Ray, a retired naval officer who hand-stuffs the cannon every day with black powder around 7:30 a.m. Perfect.

"Let's hope this guy's got answers," Wes says.

I shut off my laptop and shoot Wes a glare. "Are you going to get off my bed now?"

He studies my face, then traces his fingers along my hair, tucking a strand behind my ear. I hate to admit that it sends a shiver up my spine. "I'm happy right here," he says.

I scoff and roll off the mattress, making myself comfortable in the other bed. Why does he have to be like this?

We arrive back at the Nine O'Clock Gun bright and early. At 7:30 a.m. precisely, an older man wanders up wearing a long puffy coat and coveralls. He unlocks the cage and gets to work on the cannon. I wait until he's done and then approach. "Excuse me, are you Ray?"

He nods. "That's me. Who's asking?"

"This is kind of weird, but my mom passed away and left me a note to come to this place. I don't know what it means, and I don't really know who to ask, but I was hoping you might know something." I show him the note.

As he reads it, his face twists into concern. "Who's your mother?"

"Madeline Covington."

His expression falls and I know he recognizes her name. He whips his eyes to Wes. "He your…?"

"Boyfriend," I say, cutting him off.

Wes looks over at me, surprised—trying to hide his grin. It's not like I meant it. I just thought it would be a better explanation than the real reason.

Ray tosses his gaze back and forth between us and sighs deeply. "You got yourself in some kinda trouble, huh?"

"No sir," I say, trying to keep myself composed.

"If you're here, you're in trouble," he says. He looks over at Wes again. "You sure that's your boyfriend?"

"Yeah," I say, trying to be convincing.

"Why don't you tell your boyfriend to take a walk? You can come with me. I have something your mother left for you."

Shock splashes through me. *He knew my mom.* And she left something with him, for me.

Wes approaches. "If she's going, I'm going," he says, protective.

I shoot him a glare—he better not screw this up for me. "Just go to that café we passed on the way, okay, babe? I'll meet you there when I'm done," I say, hoping he'll get the hint and just go.

Wes struggles with my demand, and I know he doesn't want me to go alone—but I need this information.

I follow Ray down the winding path, and sneak a quick glance back at Wes, who watches me with grave concern. I mouth back to him not to worry, but the truth is—maybe he should. Maybe I am putting myself in danger.

It doesn't matter.

What matters right now is that I find out what my mom is trying to tell me, because it just might save both our lives.

CHAPTER THIRTY-SIX

HENRY

WET GRASS SLOSHES under my boots as I make my way along a thick forested trail blanketed with daylight. People are everywhere—jogging, walking their dogs, sipping coffee. I squint out the sunlight to catch a glimpse of their expressions—they all seem so at peace, so fucking happy, as if everything in their lives is just perfect. Meanwhile, fury and fear war within me.

Where the fuck am I? And what am I even doing here?

I crisscross down a few random trails to get my bearings, and eventually, I'm filtered out onto a path with a breathtaking view overlooking the water and harbored ships.

I've been here before.

My brain jolts and it hits me. This is Vancouver. Stanley Park. The Seawall. Iva's voice echoes in my ears: *the Nine O'Clock Gun.*

We tried to escape… but she was shot. I made it out unscathed, clearly. But how the fuck did I get all the way here?

I shove through the crowd of happy faces and spot the Nine

O'Clock Gun in the near distance. I start to race over, and jerk to a halt when I see Natalie standing beside it. Nausea lurches in my stomach. What is she doing here? Is this a joke?

She's peering around, craning her neck. Who is she looking for... me? A dull ache begins to throb in my skull and my mind fragments with curiosity and contempt.

I plow ahead, ready to confront her and demand to know everything—about her, her mom, her real intentions.

And then I see Wes, joining her at the cannon. Anger burns through me, and I have a deep desire to attack him and toss him right over the fucking seawall. I fist my hands at my sides and wait it out, inching closer to hear what they're saying. I sidle through some tourists taking photos and lean over the railing, concealing my face with the hood of my coat.

"Tell me now," Wes says.

"I can't. I swore to him," Natalie says. There's something desperate and urgent in her tone, and I'm dying to know who she swore allegiance to. It certainly wasn't to me. The thought pulsates through my already aching head.

"Well, he's gone, so he'll never know," Wes says. "Just tell me." Holy shit. They have to be talking about me. It takes every ounce of my willpower not to turn around and knock him out right now.

"I can't do that to my mom," Natalie says. My mind twists in confusion. Her mom?

"Your mom is dead, Natalie," Wes says, followed by the loud crack of flesh hitting flesh, which can only mean one thing— Natalie just slapped him.

I crane my neck to catch a glimpse. Wes rubs his cheek, and I spot Natalie's expression—the furrowed brow, the downturned lips. A deep instinct to crush the source of her distress stirs in my gut.

"My mom suspected I'd come here with someone. She left the clue with Ray to make sure that whomever I brought with me wasn't put in danger," Natalie says.

Ray? Who the fuck is Ray? And what clue?

I continue to sneak a glance as they murmur a few words. Natalie storms off. But before she can make any headway, Wes grabs her hand and spins her back to him. She doesn't fight him off. She doesn't let go of his hand, either.

My teeth grit as I watch them lock eyes. She's looking up at him like she used to look up at me. I can't take it anymore—it hurts, and I just want it to stop.

I yank off my hood and storm over in a rabid state, my throat tightening and a burn igniting in my chest.

"Hey," I say, but neither of them looks at me. They're still locked in that stare, holding hands. I fight the urge to rip their hands apart, to tear Wes's arm square off his body.

"Hey!"

Still nothing. Not even a flick of their eyes to me. Zero acknowledgment that I'm even standing in front of them. I lean in, practically shoving my head in between their faces.

"What the fuck is going on?" Still nothing.

The world around me closes off, and I lock my hand around at Natalie's arm, attempting to pull her away—but she doesn't budge. *What the hell?*

I look around, completely disoriented by what's happening. "Why are you doing this?" I say, shouting loud enough to make a scene.

But I don't make a scene. A sea of people mill around, just minding their own business. No one notices me. No one reacts at all to my shouting. Am I going insane? How can they not see me? How can they not hear me?

My knees weaken and buckle, and a severe sense of dread climbs up my body.

≪

I snap awake with a startle, and a serious headache. My temples throb, and there's a fog in my brain I can't shake.

I'm lying on a hard floor—I think? I try to push myself up, but my arm is on pins and needles. I give it a moment for the blood to rush back and then attempt to sit again.

There's a tugging tightness as I press myself up and realize my wrists are clamped to individual chains attached to a wall. I move my feet, but they don't go far. Yup, I'm chained there too.

I suppress the panic and the scream rising in my throat, and fight to remember where I am and what the hell happened.

The room is dimly lit, illuminated only by a single ray of artificial light pouring in from the windowed steel door. My eyes struggle to interpret my surroundings as I scan the room—the white walls bleed into the same-colored floor, and it's hard to tell where the wall and floor even meet. Or maybe that's because I'm so fucking out of it. If I had to guess, I'm in some kind of solitary confinement. But why?

A searing pain rocks my skull and I reach my hands up to squeeze my temples. Something warm and wet coats my fingers. *Blood.*

I rifle through my memories—the escape. Iva getting shot. Knocking out a guard. Opening that door. Freedom…

Darkness.

Natalie swims into my consciousness, and I realize the whole scenario at the seawall must have been my imagination. I tried to escape this place, and was stupid enough to think I could. Everything with Natalie and Wes, that was just a dream—right?

Or was it a vision?

Dread climbs through my body as I consider if I had a dream or a vision. Or was it some bizarre combination of the two, because I screwed everything up by changing a vision and now nothing makes sense.

My muscles protest as I shift and try to get more comfortable. It's a ridiculous effort—I'm chained up on a hard floor with blood seeping out of my head. Comfort is not in my present, and probably not in my future. The pain in my head grows more violent, but it's better than the agony of seeing the two of them together. At this point, I'd rather be here in this prison than out there free, watching them fawn all over each other. If the precog force really wanted to torture me, they'd make me watch Wes and Natalie on a never-ending loop.

Anger slithers into my veins and I try to take my mind off things. Scanning the white cell, I notice a small red light blinking in the ceiling. That must be a security camera, and I'm one of the people being watched right now. I give the finger up to the sky. I mean, screw it. They're going to kill me anyway. Might as well tell them how I really feel.

I continue surveying the room and my eye catches something on the wall behind me. I twist around as best as I can, and squint in the shitty light to try and make out what it says.

It's a bunch of words and drawings written in red ink. Is there a pen or marker around here that I don't know about? A chill runs up my spine as I realize that's not ink—it must have been written in blood. Probably by another prisoner, or prisoners, awaiting their death sentence too.

I fight the urge to vomit as I comb my eyes over the words, trying to make sense of it all. It's a list of words. No, a list of phrases. The blood is badly faded and hard to read, as if written a long time ago.

The first word is "visions." Okay, maybe this is some list of every prisoner's doomed vision that led them here to die?

I swallow back the ache rising in my throat and continue reading. It's morbid, but I have nothing else to do here, and I need to keep my mind occupied. Besides, knowing the other visions that my fellow precogs couldn't handle might make me feel better. Doubt it, but worth a shot.

Underneath the word "visions," is the word "seduction." Okay, that's… strange. Is that supposed to be about someone's vision? Why would someone write "vision" and "seduction" on a wall before they're executed? It dawns on me that some, if not all, of the prisoners here probably lost their minds. I'll probably lose mine too.

Defeated, I keep reading anyway. After "seduction" it says, "healing from injury." Huh. Not in here, you won't.

After that, it says "heightened senses." I study the list again, committing each to memory. Vision, seduction, healing from injury, heightened senses. This isn't a story about a vision—this is a list.

My eyes race to the next set of words. It says, "greater strength." Then "agility." Then "shifting elements."

Recognition crashes into my brain—all of this is so familiar. My blood freezes as I read it again.

Vision
Seduction
Healing from injury
Heightened senses
Greater Strength
Agility
Shifting Elements

This is everything I experienced after changing a vision. Consequences—or rather, powers—that were unlocked and unleashed.

If someone else wrote this list, then I'm not alone. This somehow comforts me even within this totally fucked up situation. I suddenly wish I had Timothy here to ask if he had the same experience.

Written below the final phrase, but in a different kind of scrawl—bigger letters and brighter red—reads "human energy draining."

Human energy draining? That sounds like some vampire bullshit, like something you'd see in those movies I can't remember the name of right now.

But it doesn't say "blood draining," it says, "energy draining." Does that mean draining our own energy, or…?

My mind flips back to that moment with Natalie, the moment seared into my mind—where we kissed in the woods and she fainted. I thought she was dead. My body slicks with sweat, even though it's freezing in here.

Did I drain her energy when we kissed? Is that yet another result of changing a vision—that you'll nearly kill someone simply by making out?

After "energy draining" are the letters "C" and "A," but then the handwriting trails off. An eerie feeling slithers through my gut as I realize maybe they came for this prisoner before he or she could finish the thought.

The rest of the markings on the wall are just drawings. They're faded and must have been here for some time. I can decipher what looks like a human face with horns alongside a drawing of a woman's face. I'm not sure what it means, but something about it sends a slow, creeping fear through me.

These prisoners are trying to reveal something about who we are and the real powers we have, which extend far beyond just having visions. But you can only unlock those powers when you change a vision, which we're forbidden to do by our own authority. So why don't they want us unlocking these powers?

My mind crawls back to what Timothy said about not being a precog, and what Iva said about her sister constantly questioning what we really are.

What we really are.

Maybe I'm really not a precog. Maybe none of us are. Maybe, just maybe, we really are something more.

CHAPTER THIRTY-SEVEN

NATALIE

I CLUTCH THE note Ray gave me as I make my way back to meet Wes at the Nine O'Clock Gun. My heart fumbles as I think of my mom writing it, of her scrawling her messy-yet-somehow-readable handwriting on that piece of paper. Sure, I have other notes and cards from her, but those were all before she died. This note was for me to read… *after*.

I shiver, trying to release the thoughts from my fevered brain, but it seems they're latched there for good. In the note, my mom says she hid a box in our house. Well, in my father's house. I haven't been there in so long, I barely consider it home anymore.

I spot the Nine O'Clock Gun in the distance and scan the scene for Wes. Weird, he doesn't seem to be anywhere. An eerie feeling prickles up my neck, as if someone is watching me. I jerk my head backward, but no one is there besides a bunch of people minding their own business.

Something doesn't feel right. The air crackles with strange

energy, but I can't figure out what it is. Maybe I'm just desperate to believe that my mom is here watching over me—though I've never been one to believe in ghosts. Yet, there are people in the world who can see the future and apparently change it, so...

My thoughts splinter when Wes jogs over from the nearby park. His expression is soured with panic, and I know I freaked him out by going off alone and forcing him to stay behind. He stops short in front of me, panting with nervous energy. "What happened?"

I can't really tell him, and I know he's going to be pissed about that. "Let's just go back to Washington," I say.

"I'm not going back unless you tell me," Wes says, desperation in his tone.

"I can't. I swore to him," I say. It's not so much that I swore to Ray that I wouldn't tell a soul. It was my mom's request not to tell anyone about the note, or the box she left for me. She didn't want anyone else getting involved, or risk being hurt.

"Well Ray isn't here, so he'll never know."

"I can't do that. I'm sorry," I say. And I genuinely am sorry. I wouldn't even be here getting this clue if Wes didn't save me from his family trying to off me. "My mom doesn't want me to."

"Your mom is dead, Natalie," he says. On instinct, my hand rises and smacks him in the face. It's like I have no control over my own limbs. I look away, not even sure what to say as my anger melts into guilt. Wes huffs, raises his hands as if to say "what the fuck" without actually saying it.

"My mom suspected I'd come here with someone. She left the clue with Ray to make sure that whomever I brought with me wasn't put in danger," I say. "We have to go back. I have to follow her next clue."

"Fine. I'm going with you. We'll do it together," he says.

"We can go back to Washington together, but then we part ways. I have to handle this alone."

I begin to walk off, but Wes grabs my hand and spins me back to him. He studies my face, like he's trying to tell me something but can't form the words. "Your eyes… they're bright green right now."

I quickly avert my gaze and blink back tears. A strange sensation climbs up my body, like someone is watching again. Then, suddenly, I'm frozen—sealed up into something I don't understand. It's as if I want to move, but I'm here locked in a pocket of time with Wes. There's a tickle on my arm, like flesh is brushing against it, but nothing is touching me.

Then, as if I was lanced by something, the moment breaks—and fear sinks in. I have an urgent need to get the hell out of here, to get back to Washington, and to get away from Wes as soon as possible.

⁓

The train ride back is long and awkward. We barely speak. Well, Wes tries to speak to me, but I can't bring myself to muster a response.

At the train station, we take separate taxis. Wes turns to me before he gets in the car. "So that's just… it?"

I look at him and I'm not sure how to answer. I really need to stop all this with him. I don't want to implicate him in any way, and I need to find out the truth. That should be my focus—I can be grateful for what he's done, and at the same time, part ways.

But then I remember that he has no place to stay, and he can't go back to his family and… *damn*. How can I just cast him aside? The answer is: I can't.

"You can stay in my room. I'll be back tonight," I say.

He shrugs. "Don't worry about it. I'll figure something else out." As he slips into the taxi, he shoots me a longing glance.

I know that look—it's the look of goodbye. I know it well because it's the look my father gave me before he shipped me off to Lockwood, or to some enrichment program overseas, or really anywhere he's sent me since Mom died. He's a man of few words, and so I've learned to read his thoughts by scouring his expressions.

I guess I'm glad Wes understood that this was a goodbye of sorts. Maybe he's got a plan and can figure things out. He's made it this far in life with an assassin family, so I'm sure he's got this. Though as confident as my thoughts are, the notion of completely saying goodbye to Wes nicks at my heart.

❧

My father lives in the sprawling suburb of Bellevue, Washington. I haven't been back to my house in what feels like forever. He always signs me up for an educational or charitable program intended to puff up my college applications when I've got time off from school. If I want to become a doctor, then this is what I have to do—sacrifice time away from family. That's what he says. But if I'm being honest, we haven't felt like a family since Mom died.

As the car drops me off and I stare up at the sprawling mansion, something punches me in the gut—a waving red flag that I don't want to be back here.

I twist my key in the lock, and I'm half surprised that it even works. Then I laugh at myself. My father would never actually change the locks on me... right? The fact that I'm even questioning that tells me everything I need to know.

I enter the foyer, my shoes clacking against the cold marble—

expecting to see the same paintings and Mom's photographs lining the walls, along with all the artifacts she collected from her travels.

But they're all gone. Everything is just… gone, replaced with tacky floral paintings that look like a child barfed them up.

My heart hammers as I make my way through the house. It seems a lot messier than I remember—clothes strewn around, piles of crumpled papers, dirty dishes. Nothing beyond what a typical household might look like, but my father always prefers things pristine.

I make my way up the spiral staircase to my bedroom. Mom's note said she left something under my bed, but I can't figure out how that's possible. I've looked under my bed a million times since she died. I even used to hide under there, wondering how long it would take for my father or my nanny to find me. Spoiler alert: no one ever did. I'm not even sure they bothered to look.

I walk into my bedroom and my stomach plummets, breath whooshing from my lungs. All of my things are gone.

I race inside, frantic, scanning its replacements. Where my canopy bed used to be sits a tacky, puffy pink rug and a crib. I rip open the closet to find hundreds of frilly baby clothes. What in the ever-loving fuck is going on? Is this a dream?

My eyes latch onto a framed photo on a turquoise dresser. I snatch it up to find a photo of my father, a supermodel-thin young woman with long red hair, and *a baby*.

I process that the hell this could even mean. Is he… is she…?

I'm rattled by the insanity of it all. Does my father have an entirely new family that I don't even know about? I study the photo for clues. There's a clear diamond ring on the woman's finger hold-ing the baby. I recognize that ring. It was his grandmother's ring, passed to my father before she died, who gave it to my mother at their wedding. And now, apparently, he's given his family ring to this redheaded stranger.

Oh my God.

He shipped me off to Lockwood, and started over with a new family, a new wife, a new daughter. He completely replaced me.

That's why I barely see or hear from him. He's been trying to conceal this from me. Does his new wife even know about me? Was he seeing this woman before Mom died? How could he sneak all this by me? So much for having Mom's gift of finding out what people are hiding. My own father has a secret family and he did it all right under my nose.

I throw the framed photo at the wall and the glass smashes against the floor. I hate him. I hate him so damn much. I never want to speak to him again. I don't even want him paying for my education because that means I have some tie to him, that I owe him something.

I press my fingers to my temples, trying desperately to focus on my original reason for coming to get what my mom left me. *My mom.* I wonder what she would think about what my father did to me.

I shove the frilly fucking crib to the side and rip up the tacky throw rug. All that's left is shiny, expensive hardwood flooring— just as I'd expected. I squash the sense of defeat stirring inside and urge my brain to think. If my mom went through all of these lengths to conceal the clues, she wouldn't just leave a box out in the open. She would hide it.

I affix my gaze on the hardwood—could it be underneath? I attempt to pry one of the boards with my hands, but it won't budge. I race downstairs and grab a screwdriver from the garage, doing my best to avoid the trappings of my father and his new family laced throughout the house.

I manage to unscrew the floorboard and yank it up. There it is—a box from my mom. A flush of satisfaction washes over me as I open it to find loads of items inside—journals, newspaper clippings, photos. *Research.*

My concentration is lanced by a shrill voice coming from downstairs. "Honey!"

Shit. That must be his new wife.

I swallow back the rage coursing through my blood and clutch the box tightly as I sneak down the stairs. I catch a glimpse of her silky, long red hair and patterned yoga pants showing off her perky ass, and suppress the urge to vomit.

Even with my resilience wavering, I manage to slip out of the house undetected. I left the bedroom in shambles, so they'll know someone was in there. Maybe my father will know it was me, or maybe his secret wife will think someone tried to rob her perfect daughter's stupid pink nursery. Either way, that chapter of my life is closed.

⚘

The ferry ride back to Lockwood drags as my thoughts tumble into dark and dangerous corners. When the driver drops me at campus, an overwhelming feeling blankets my entire body—not anger, or sadness, or fury, or betrayal...but loneliness. Deep, empty loneliness.

I have no one. At least, no one that truly cares about me. My mom is dead. My father created an entirely new family and didn't even bother to tell me. We don't really have any extended family that I know of. Ciel and Adip—I mean, they're fun, but school friends don't stick around. Jack is with Josephine, and was he ever really in love with me anyway? I suspect not.

Henry pops into my mind, unwelcome, and a sharp pang slices through my gut. Sure he saved my life, but why? It wasn't even his idea. It wasn't because he cared—he was selfish and wanted to uncover information about himself. He used me, and then just left me here to deal with the consequences. He would have just ignored his vision and let me die if it hadn't been for Wes.

Wes.

Damn, I was cold to him. Here I am complaining about being alone, when I turned away the one person who maybe actually gives a shit. The person who cared enough to want to save my life. The person who was sent to kill me and completely destroyed his own life to save mine.

I race to the old science building, clutching the box tight to my chest, and spot the light at the end of the hallway. I wrench open the door to find Wes sitting up on his makeshift mattress-bed, reading. "What are you doing here?"

I can't answer him. Everything that's happened the last few hours all comes crashing down and I choke out a sob.

"Come here," he says.

My heart rattles as I carefully set down the box on the floor and climb into bed with him. He curls his arm around me and pulls me close, and I don't care if this is wrong or okay or anything in between. I just know that, right now, I don't want to be alone.

I want to be with Wes.

CHAPTER THIRTY-EIGHT

HENRY

MY STOMACH CHURNS. If I'm something more than a precog, what the hell am I?

Before my brain can process how messed up this all is, I register the faint sound of footsteps pounding from above, the ceiling groaning under their weight.

There's no denying it now—the guards are coming for me. I'm out of time, with no answers about who, or what, I really am. The clomping of boots grows louder and closer with each second.

My body jerks. I refuse to die here in this cell. This isn't about me. This is bigger than me. I need to make it out of here for every single precog who came before me, who bled out in this place while trying to get to the truth.

Footsteps grow even closer, pausing at the entrance of my cell door. A key jangles in the lock and resolve shudders through my body. There's no more time.

The heavy grind of the bolt clicks open, along with the morbid clarity that I'm about to die if I don't figure something out. I flick my gaze around the room, desperate for some shrapnel of hope.

Then my eyes lock onto the wall. There's a scripture there, but it's in different handwriting than the rest of the scrawled words. How the hell did that get there? I've been studying this wall for hours. How is it possible that I didn't see this?

Voices grumble on the other side of the door, but the guards haven't made it inside yet. The writing is so light, it's difficult to see. I blink and squint my eyes to make out each letter.

C…o…v…

The door to my cell bangs open, but I don't even bother looking at the new crop of guards swarming into the room.

C…o…v…i…

Wait… it says… *Covington?*

I'm so stunned at the sight of Natalie's last name that I barely register the guards slamming the cell door shut and locking it behind them. I'm aware that one of them is looming over me, but I can't focus on that shit right now.

My chest collapses. I can't peel my eyes away from the insignia on the wall. Why is Natalie's last name there? Am I seeing things? Maybe I'm hallucinating. When was the last time I slept? Or ate?

"Come with us," one of the guards says. *Come with us?* Yeah, dude, do your best to pry me out of here. I dare you.

My mind flashes back to Natalie. Someone wrote her last name on this wall, presumably a prisoner who was locked in here before me. Is this because of the story her mother was doing? Or is she, or someone else in her family, the reason we're locked up in here in the first place?

Or is this a call to arms? Is she the one I need to help me get out of this place? Fuck, I really don't have time to hammer this all out of my mind.

"Get up!" the other guard says.

I finally tear my gaze from the wall and meet his eyes, beady with disgust.

"Fuck you," I say.

In a flash, the guard's rough grip locks around my arms. He lurches me from the ground and physical pain slices through my body as my wrists scrape against the corroded metal of the shackles. He mumbles something to the other guard that I can't quite make out.

My determination rises above the pain. *Covington.* All of this connects back to her. I changed a vision and saved her life, and maybe the consequences of that aren't for me to die.

Maybe the result of changing a vision is that I become more powerful. And that's something the authority doesn't want—for any precog to be more powerful than them.

The other guard unlocks the shackle from the floor and my mind rifles through everything that's happened. Breaking Jack's arm. Changing the elements while kissing her. It all comes back to Natalie.

The lock clicks and the shackle snaps from the ground. The guard tightens his vicelike fists around my arms, jerking me closer to him. I study my opponents for a second—physically, these guys are way larger and stronger than I am. Each of them has a leather device strapped to their body housing multiple weapons. Attempting to fight them off isn't gonna work.

Natalie. When I'm around her, I get more power. Maybe if I think about her, I can summon something—like we're threaded in some telepathic mind fuck that no one can make sense of.

The guard who is not squeezing the life out of me heads to the door and slides the key in the lock. I'm certain they're about to escort me to whatever torture they have planned.

I squeeze my eyes shut and think of Natalie. Truthfully, it's not hard. It's harder *not* to think about her.

The bolt clicks and suddenly my body trembles with a sick shudder and Natalie's face snaps into my conscious. Those unmistakable, blazing eyes—shifting color from brown to vibrant green. Her gaze is filled with determined terror, her eyes widening each second.

My entire body shivers and clenches, completely out of my control. What the hell is happening? The guard squeezes his grip on me, white-knuckling my arms. "Hurry up," he says to the other guard.

Rain begins battering the building, hammering down on the roof. The wind picks up, lashing at the walls and the small window in the room.

Am I causing this?

The guard struggles to pry the door open, but for some reason, it won't budge. Thunder rumbles in the sky above. For a moment, it's as if I exist outside of my body. This is actually working.

I close my eyes again, picturing Natalie, and there's another crash of thunder, followed by an unrelenting downpour. The sound of glass splintering rockets through the room. We all whip our gaze to the now-cracked window. The guard who is not holding me looks at me in horror. "Devil," he says.

I'm no devil.

Or, am I? I have to be causing this to happen, unlocking some dormant powers. But I can't be a devil. No, I'm good. These guards, this whole fucking place, these are the bad people. Maybe I'm just using some sort of dark magic. These assholes deserve it.

I have no time for a crisis of morality when thunder crashes outside and the wind kicks up, shattering the window. Rain pours into the room as if a storm pipe has burst. The wind sucks into the cell like a tornado.

I shut my eyes to reconnect with Natalie, but the vibrant green in her eyes begins to fade, and life drains out of her expression. What is happening?

A surge of wind blows in and knocks me to my knees, ripping me out of the guard's grip. As he lurches to regain his grasp, he's catapulted into the air, crashing into the wall. His skull cracks against the concrete and he plummets to the ground, unconscious in a pool of blood and rainwater. *Holy shit.*

Water whips around us in a violent vortex and quickly fills the room. The conscious guard keeps yanking at the door, but it still won't budge. The only way out of the cell is through the small window near the ceiling.

Clumps of the concrete floor rip from the ground, sending shards in every direction. The other guard screams as I shield my face from the onslaught.

How do I get control of this?

The wind, water, and concrete tear at my body. I peer over my arm, shielding my face, and spot the other guard lunging at me with what looks like a nightstick. I raise my arm to stop his attack and lightening bursts from my palm, electrocuting him until his body spasms to death.

I'm rattled with shock as the force of the wind multiplies, and the water level rises at rapid speed, quickly submerging my entire body. I hold my breath as the dead bodies of the guards float around in a circle. Thrashing water and waves crash over my head.

My insides scald with the revelation that I'm about to drown. My lungs clench whatever oxygen I have left.

I have to reach that window, now.

I use every ounce of force I have left to swim to freedom, desperate to breathe. Finally, I reach the small rectangle window with ragged broken glass. I surge ahead, but the window suddenly disappears.

I whip around—realizing I'm no longer in the cell. I'm encased in something… maybe plexiglass? The water completely stills, swallowing me whole—and there is no escape in sight.

My lungs burn without oxygen and another sick shudder goes through my body. Then, a beam of light appears in the distance. A flicker of hope—maybe someone is here to save me. Please let there be someone.

I spot a figure swimming towards me. My vision blurs, but I recognize her the closer she gets.

Natalie.

She extends her hand, reaching for me.

How did she get here? Why is she here?

There's no time to think about any of that. My heart is still beating, and I'd like to keep it that way. I reach out for her hand, and just as our fingers touch, her hand twists away and she dissolves into nothing.

My terror grows and the pain in my chest nearly doubles me over. Not that it would matter if I had a heart attack. I'm drowning anyway.

I try to yell out for help, but my screams are muffled in the water. I begin to choke and sputter, dizzied and disoriented. My body seizes up… and reality swarms. This is it.

I'm dying.

I'm dying and I'll never find out the truth.

CHAPTER THIRTY-NINE

NATALIE

DARKNESS.

I shudder awake with a violent jerk. I'm soaking wet. A heaviness spreads across my chest, and I realize I'm struggling to breathe. *I'm not breathing.*

Hands grip my shoulders and warm oxygen floods into my lungs. I whirl around to find Wes lying next to me in bed. I inch out of his grasp, gripping the blanket against my clothed body—trying to piece together where I am.

Oh right, my father. Coming back to school. Collapsing in bed with Wes. The warmth leaks from my chest, leaving an aching chill in its place.

"Bad dream?" Wes asks. He strokes my back, trying to comfort me.

My father disappears from my mind and memories swirl to the forefront. Not memories of yesterday's shit show—memories of my horrific nightmare.

The pieces of my dream begin to click together—a cell. Thunder. Lightning. No, a massive storm, like a hurricane. Not that I've ever experienced a hurricane, but it seemed like one.

A wave of clarity hits me. *Henry.* He was there in my dream, locked in a cell, while I watched him slowly drown from the other side of a heavy steel door. My frenzied desire to free him finally seemed possible once the door burst open—maybe from the weight of the water. But just when I was about to reach him, I woke up.

I whirl around to face Wes, and his eyes widen at the sight of me.

"You look like a drowned rat," he says.

"Shut up," I say, jolting out of his makeshift bed/shitty floor mattress and race over to the box I left on the floor. The box my mother left for me. I was in such an existential shock last night I didn't even bother to look through the contents.

I plop down on the floor and peel off the lid, but that damn dream keeps nagging at me. It felt so real. Like it wasn't a dream… at all.

Wes joins me on the floor as I sit and stare ahead, motionless, unable to pluck that nightmare from my brain.

"You tell me to shut up, but you slept the whole night in my arms. You sure blow hot and cold, Covington."

Hot and cold. Exactly what I thought about Henry. Maybe we're more alike than I realized. I ignore Wes and sift through the box of things, mostly papers and photographs. I unfold a yellowed, wilted piece of paper to find a map.

Wes peeks over my shoulder, studying it with me. "What's that?"

"How am I supposed to know?"

He holds up his hands in surrender, and guilt claws through my veins. I didn't mean to snap at him. He's been nothing but kind to me. I should really stop giving him so much shit.

"Sorry," I say. "This is all, like, a lot."

He nods, understanding, and we both turn our focus back to what matters—the clues. The map seems to be of some kind of hospital. There's a room marked "medicine" and a few rooms marked "patient quarters."

I set it down and dig for something else in the box, pulling out an old photograph of my mom and some man I don't recognize. He's hot—like, really hot. And they seem friendly… very friendly. I flip over the photograph and it's dated with the year I was born. Huh. Maybe he's a family friend, or work friend.

"That's your mom?" Wes asks, and I nod. "You look just like her."

My heart wrenches as I stare at her smiling face. I trace my finger over the photo of her and my heart aches.

I gently set down the photo and pick up another item from the mystery box—a Polaroid photo, and a blurry one at that. My eyes strain to make out what's in the photograph until I'm finally able to see the subject. A room… no, a cell. A very familiar cell.

I shriek and instinctively throw down the photo like it's on fire.

"What's wrong?" Wes picks up the photo to study it himself.

"I saw…" I swallow, trying to steady my breath long enough to squeak out the words. "That place was in my dream. Henry was there."

Was I having a dream? Or was it a vision of something really happening?

Wes scrutinizes the photo and looks up at me. "My brother could be there too."

❧

Ten minutes later, Wes and I are racing through campus. Luckily, it's only five in the morning and no one is around, because at this point, we look like we've just murdered someone and are fleeing the scene. Not the best idea to draw attention to an assassin posing as a Lockwood student, and me… his mark. What the hell has my life become?

All the clues in my mom's box led to one thing—she was working on a story about precogs who are being detained in a facility not far from campus. Except, it wasn't much of a "facility"—more of a concentration camp where the prisoners are tortured and experimented on. My stomach wrenches at the thought of Henry trapped inside of there, especially given that he's locked up because of changing his vision to save me.

Adrenaline roars through my body as Wes and I hop on the ferry to get to this horrific place. What the hell are we going to do when we get there? From my mom's notes, this place is maximum security, and we don't even have a good plan. Or a plan, like at all.

Wes clasps my hand and I peer over at him. I've never seen him rattled before, and to be honest, it's pretty unsettling. All he wants is to get his brother back, alive, and now he might finally have the chance. I give his hand a reassuring squeeze, even though I can't be less certain that his brother, or Henry, are okay. Or even alive.

As we get off the ferry and get a taxi, winding down deserted roads to the prison, a sweeping chill comes over me. My instincts cause me to peer out the window—and I freeze in a startling surge of horror.

"Oh my God! Sir, pull over!"

The cab driver huffs and skids the car to the side of the road. I hurtle out into the frozen, damp air and stand in the middle of the deserted road, motionless.

This spot… is where my mother died.

My mind reels with the vicious truth—my mother died on her way to this place. The same place we're headed. That's why she had the map and all the other information on the location. The final piece for her big story to expose these monsters.

An accident… a car accident—or so my father said. But now I know he's the last person I should trust.

My pulse thunders in my ears and I can barely register Wes's footsteps trampling behind me. I scan the area. Empty. Gravel, flanked with massive, bright green trees. No guardrail. Completely flat land.

The sound of nature sucks back into my ears. *No guardrail.* I spin around to face Wes. "My father said my mom died here."

"Natalie, I'm so sorry."

I shake my head violently, overcome with a furious realization. "My father said her car flipped over a guardrail into a ditch. That it was an accident."

Wes cranes his neck, peering around into total confusion as I call out to the cab driver.

"Sir! Has there ever been a ditch on this road?"

He shakes his head. "Been on this route twenty years. Flat as a pancake."

My chest pounds with determination as I turn to Wes. "It wasn't an accident. They knew she was coming, and they killed her."

Suddenly, my brain grows cloudy and a sharp pain sears through my stomach. I clutch my abdomen, and a sticky, warm wetness coats my hands. My eyes drift down and I spot blood, tons of blood, coating my fingers. I try to scream but nothing comes out, and my body convulses with terror.

What the hell is happening to me?

I whip my gaze up and Wes is gone. The cab is gone. I'm out here, all alone, bleeding to death.

The ground rumbles beneath me and I catch sight of something in my peripheral. I slowly pivot to see my Mom emerging from the trees. *Wait, am I dying?*

I try to croak out some words to her, but I'm unable to speak. She stops about a foot away and studies me, but she's not filled with surprise or love or even sympathy. She just looks determined.

"You can save everyone, Natalie," she says. "You have a gift."

A gift? What gift?

I open my mouth to attempt to speak again when I notice blood seeping through her blouse—the same injury I have. Bile rises in my throat as I try to scream for help, but I'm still unable to make a sound.

Another vicious bout of thunder cracks open the sky and then… my mother disappears. I snap my gaze to my abdomen and I'm no longer bleeding. I release my trembling hands, frantic, lifting my shirt to reveal there is no cut, no mark, no injury… nothing at all.

"Natalie! Natalie!" Wes's piercing shriek rockets into my ears. I squeeze my eyes shut, the deafening volume too painful to take in.

When I open my eyes again, everything is as it was. Wes standing in front of me. The cab. The driver. The quiet road.

"What the hell just happened to you? You just froze… like some kind of robot who ran out of batteries or something."

I should want an explanation for everything that just happened. Everything that's been happening. But I can't focus on that right now. My mom's words keep looping in my cluttered mind.

You can save everyone. You have a gift.

There's one person I trust in this world—my mom. And if she says I can do something, you better damn well believe I can.

This isn't just about me, or precogs, or Wes's brother, or even Henry anymore.

This… all of this… is for her.

CHAPTER FORTY

HENRY

I FEEL MY hands first.

Blood thrums through my veins, and my muscles coil as I attempt to lift my arms. They won't budge.

Am I dead?

Everything is so dark, and I seem to be in a kind of lucid state—weightless—until memories begin to crawl back. The cell, the guards, the storm, *Natalie*. The more that seeps into my brain, the more I crack open.

Where am I?

As if completely out of my control, my body bucks and I realize that I'm restrained. Warning bells slam into my brain and I snap my eyes open, immediately blinded by a bright light.

I blink to focus, and my gaze shoots to Oliver, who is sitting in the corner of the room. Words scrape against my throat, but I'm unable to speak. *Why is he here? Is he dead too? Is this what hell looks like?*

Oliver peers over at me, and I know that look. It's the look he's given me my entire life whenever I've done something wrong.

My temper spikes—after everything I've been through, shouldn't he show some compassion? He's my dad, for fuck's sake. Foster dad, but still.

"Hello, Henry," he says. His voice is leeched with disappointment.

I open my mouth, attempting to croak out a few words. My throat is so dry it splinters as I attempt to speak. "What... happened?"

I'm still unable to move, and I strain to take in my surroundings. I appear to be fully strapped to a gurney, but I can't move much to be able to see. The room itself is empty, white, with a shitty fluorescent light buzzing above my head. There's a distinct smell of mildew and decay. I guess this is what happens when you're dead.

Oliver lets out a heavy sigh. "You surprised me, son."

What the hell does that mean? A flash of anger ricochets through my body. "Surprise you? Why am I tied up? Is this some kind of precog purgatory?" I buck again against my restraints, but they're so tight I can't budge.

"Purgatory? No, Henry. You're not dead."

Not dead? That's impossible. He's a liar. It's not like it's the first time he's lied to me. "I drowned. Of course I'm dead."

Oliver stands and approaches me slowly, with caution. His face is riddled with confusion. What's so confusing about all of this? I drowned in some superpower shit gone wrong. Now I'm dead, and was hoping I'd be numb to all this bullshit. Guess the fate of changing a vision extends into the afterlife.

"Drowned? No. You just misused your powers. It was all an illusion," Oliver says. His tone is calm and maddening.

"No, that wasn't an illusion. Two guards were killed. I saw them die."

Oliver shakes his head. "See, when you abuse your powers in a way that's forbidden, you lose control. Your consciousness is lost, and then everything goes back to the way it was."

His words hack a new kind of anger into me. "Abuse my powers? I didn't know shit about my powers because you never told me I had them."

"Language, Henry."

"*Really*? I'm tied up in some prison and you care that I'm cursing?" Adrenaline scores through me.

"I was forbidden to reveal anything to you about your full powers. It's for your own good."

My stomach lurches at his ridiculous explanation. "My own good? Chaining me up, trying to kill me, is for my own good?"

"You did this. If you had just followed the rules," he says, remaining so calm and condescending, it only spikes my anger more.

"Follow the rules like little minions, right? We all line up like idiots, and if we don't, we're tortured and killed."

I notice a flicker of aggravation in Oliver's eyes. Good. Maybe he'll feel a fraction of the shit I'm going through.

"It was for your own good, Henry. When we use our full range of powers, historically, things don't go well. We grow hungry, and begin to use them in ways that don't serve us. We must maintain order."

I'm speechless. My body jerks against the restraints, desperate to escape this hell. Oliver just stares ahead with this expression I can't read, which is somehow worse.

"Precogs have tremendous powers. But we must suppress these abilities for our own safety. No one can find out what we truly are."

His revelations click together in my impatient brain. "And what… are we?"

Oliver swallows and stays silent. Another secret, I assume. God, I hate him.

"We are Cambions."

What the hell is a Cambion? My mind grows even more hazy as he continues to explain.

"Cambions are half-demon, half-human. There are demons, dangerous beings, who live amongst us. The precog authority keeps tabs on them, tracking down when they procreate with humans, and then we take the babies before they can realize their powers and cause serious damage to themselves or others. The babies then become assigned to a foster parent, like me, who help suppress and diminish their powers so they can live in the world safely."

I can't even wrap my brain around this. All I can think of is… safe? He was assigned to keep me safe? What a hypocrite.

"What about the visions? If you take away all of our powers, why do we still have them," I say.

"Visions are the one power we've been unable to suppress. No one knows why. And, if you change a vision, that's when you start unlocking your other powers. As you've unfortunately seen."

Yeah, unfortunate is an understatement. Betrayal and resentment storms through me—my entire life, I've been lied to. And then I remember the name on the wall. *Covington*. Why was that there? An uneasy feeling creeps through my body, but I can't resist picking Oliver for more information.

"What does Natalie Covington have to do with all of this?"

Oliver studies me for a moment, his expression unreadable. "Covington?"

My fists clench and I really wish I could punch him right now. "Yeah, Natalie. The one from my vision, who I saved."

Sweat beads on Oliver's face and his eyes slant with fury. "The vision you changed… was about Natalie Covington? But we got word that the girl was dead."

"If you didn't know that I saved her life, why am I even in here?"

"An anonymous source turned you in for changing a vision. But we weren't made aware it had anything to do with the Covington girl." Oliver stares down at me, detached—almost like he's turned into some robot. Fear stabs in my chest. I don't know what's going on, but I already know it's not going to be good.

He slowly removes a flask from his jacket pocket. Is he really going to drink right now? With a heavy sigh, he begins tossing the liquid in a circle around me.

"What the hell are you doing?"

He removes a book of matches from his pocket, and it takes me a second to piece together what's happening. "I'm sorry it had to come to come to this, Henry. I loved you like my own. I came here to help you, but saving that girl is unforgivable. She can't live past eighteen or our kind will not survive."

What the hell is he talking about? His words kickstart my survival. "I won't use my powers anymore. I can get better. Just… keep me in here. I don't care about Natalie. It was all a mistake."

"I'm sorry, son. You've already unlocked a door that can't be closed."

Oliver removes a match and a commanding resolve shudders through me. Holy shit, *he's going to burn me alive.* I have to try something, anything, to appeal to his sympathy. That is, if he has any. I need to stall him, get him out of this room. I need a few moments to figure something out, or try to summon my powers again.

"You're going to burn me alive? I'm your *son*. At least if you're going to kill me, can't you do it in a more humane way?"

Oliver shakes his head, and I sense a bit of somberness in his expression. That's good, maybe I can work with that.

"I wish there was an easier way to do this, but there are only two ways to kill our kind," he says. "A dagger or burning you alive with holy oil. Trust me, the oil hurts less."

That can't be true. Timothy died from that medication. And Iva was shot. Unless… *they're still alive.*

Oliver strikes the match, and it's like a fist closes around my heart. The match doesn't ignite, which buys me a few seconds.

"Wait! If you're going to kill me, fine. But I have to know why Natalie Covington is such a threat. After everything, you owe me an explanation."

Oliver looks at me with a callous smirk. How could this terrorist dictator have been my foster dad for eighteen years? Was I that blind?

I must have gotten through to him, though, because he begins to talk. "It has to do with her mother. And Covington is not the girl's real last name."

Something shifts inside of me, and a bolt of surprise runs down my spine. "What does that matter?"

"Patrick Covington isn't Natalie's real father. Her mother married him when she was pregnant. It was a good way for her to hide."

I can't think clearly. Why would I care who Natalie's real father is? That doesn't explain anything. "Hide what?"

Oliver chuckles, an infuriating gesture that makes me wish I was the one holding the match right now so I could watch his stupid ass burn to the ground.

"Hide that neither of them are human," he says.

All of my organs reverberate inside of me and fear ices my spine. *Natalie isn't human?* "Then what is she? A precog… or Cambion… or whatever the fuck you say we are too?"

Oliver's expression turns grim as he strikes another match. This one lights. "No, she's… something else."

Oliver drops the match, and flames shoot up from the ground. He quietly exits the room without a word, or even a glance back at me, closing the door behind him.

Knives of reality stab at my body. *Natalie isn't human.*

But I'll never know what she is, or how she connects to all of this, because my own father is burning me alive.

CHAPTER FORTY-ONE

NATALIE

SMOKE.

Thick, heavy billows puff into the sky as the taxi drops Wes and I off in front of the prison… asylum… whatever the hell this horrible place is.

Adrenaline roars through me as I watch flames blaze from the building, and I race ahead. We need to get inside. *Please let Henry be alive.*

Wes grips my hand and yanks me backward. "You're not going in there."

I whip around to face him and my heart speeds. Is he kidding me? "Henry is in there. You said your own brother could be in there." I tear my arm out of his grasp and forge ahead.

Within seconds, he's blocking my way again. "There's no reason for both of us to go in. Let me."

He must be joking. "I'm going. You can come or not."

He closes the distance between us, backing my body away from the building. "No! You have too much to live for. I have nothing to go back to."

I freeze in this sad revelation, my heart clenching. I wish he hadn't said that, or didn't think that. We've been going a million miles an hour, and it's easy to forget the pain he must be in. He's an outlaw to society, and now an outlaw to his family.

"That isn't true," I say. "You have me."

He doesn't mutter a word as he crashes his mouth down on mine—hard and urgent. I can't help but gasp and melt into his embrace. He clasps his hands around my neck, gently but firmly holding me in place as he deepens the kiss. My body crackles as warmth unfurls through my bones—heat from the kiss and the fiery urgency to stop wasting time and get into the building. But I can't pull away. I'm too wrapped up in this… in him.

My legs begin to weaken, but not in that dreamy, romantic kind of way. My consciousness begins to slip. Panicked, I shove him away, gulping in air—desperate to fight off the dizziness that's consuming me. It's a familiar feeling—this happened when I kissed Henry too. My brain stitches this together—does something happen when I kiss precogs?

I can tell Wes is offended that I've pushed him away. He glares at me with a cocktail of confusion and aggravation. He opens his mouth and I'm lingering on the words he might say.

But instead of saying anything, he turns away and heads into the burning building.

"Hey!" I try desperately to scream after him, but he doesn't give me a second glance.

I begin sprinting to the building when the dizziness consumes me again. I take a moment to pause and breathe, but it's like shards of glass are lodged in my lungs. *Dammit Natalie, pull it together.*

I stumble a few paces when I hear my name being shouted from a voice I don't recognize. My stomach clenches as an uneasy feeling claws up my spine.

I slowly pivot to face on older man. I'm dying to know who he is, why he knows my name, but my instincts tell me that I don't really want to know the truth.

I stand, shuddering, as he studies me, as if I'm a test subject trapped in a glass cage. "Natalie Covington," he says. "Alive and well."

"Excuse me?" All my senses are on fire now.

He inches closer, pinning me with his gaze. "You look just like your mother. You have her eyes."

My heart throttles and every alarm bell is ringing, but I can't walk away.

"How do you know my mother?" His lips curl into a smirk. Am I amusing him? This only ignites my anger, and I demand answers. "Who are you?"

"I'm Oliver. I raised Henry from when he was a little boy. Such a shame he got involved with you."

Panicked, I try to shove past Oliver, but he plants himself in my way, gripping my arms. "You're just like your mother."

"Get off of me," I say, ferocity swelling inside.

He won't budge. I try to squirm out of his grasp, but my strength is faltering. I'm still dizzy and disoriented from that kiss.

I wriggle again, but Oliver hoists my body into his arms, dragging me away from the building. I scream, pummeling him with my fists, but I'm no match for him. And there's certainly no one out here in this dark parking lot to help.

A crack of thunder shatters my concentration, and I spot a figure in the distance. I blink furiously, trying to make out what it is. Maybe a guard? Why are they just standing in front of a burning building?

My vision smooths out and I realize…

It's my mom, again.

My body begins to sizzle like I'm charged with electricity. I stare at her, or the ghost of her, I guess. Is her presence somehow giving me power?

A current races along my skin and I use the surge to violently twist. Oliver grunts and struggles to hold me in place, but he's losing his grip. I'm becoming stronger than him.

I keep my eyes locked on my mom and I try again, thrashing around. Once I'm finally out of his slimy grasp, I use every ounce of adrenaline to shove him. He topples backward onto the ground, and I can tell he's shocked by my strength.

I flick my gaze to where my mom was standing, but she's no longer there. I could run now, maybe even outrun him, but my instinct is to stay and fight. This is what Mom would do—she never ran away from anything.

In a split second, Oliver is up and he slams into me, sending me flying backward into a heap against the ground. White-hot rage explodes into my brain as I spring back to my feet.

Oliver studies me again. "Do you already… know what you are?"

What I am? Yeah, I know what I am. I'm an eighteen-year-old high school senior who wants to get rid of creepy assholes like you.

But I don't answer him. He doesn't deserve any explanation. If he wants to know who, or what, I am—he can figure it out on his own. I'm sick of this ridiculous back and forth bullshit. "What do you want with me?"

He tucks his hand into his coat pocket and takes a deep sigh. His demeanor suddenly changes, like he's decided to be cool and collected now instead of an old guy attacking a girl. "You look just like her."

"Yeah, you said that already," I say, my words slicing back.

He shakes his head, stepping closer to me, and I stand my ground. I haven't run yet, I'm not about to now.

"I mean, you look just like her... right before she turned nineteen."

He yanks a dagger from his pocket and my eyes barely catch the gleaming metal before he attempts to plunge it into my stomach.

Power surges through my body and static crackles under my skin as I manage to grip his hand before the blade can pierce my skin. As our flesh makes contact, an electric current sparks between us—and not the good kind. Oliver yelps and snaps back, losing his grip on the blade.

The knife crashes to the ground and I'm able to grab it in a split second. I'm not sure what the hell is going on, but I've never been this agile or powerful in my life. This is the first time that Oliver's looked genuinely frightened. I hiss at him while stabbing the blade into the air. "Stay back!"

He raises his hands in surrender and that shit-eating smirk is back on his face. "That won't kill me, you know. That blade will only kill your kind."

Is this guy on drugs? "My kind? You mean, humans?"

It's then that he breaks into maniacal laughter. He must be crazy. No, psychotic. Maybe he's not on drugs, and that's the problem.

"You really don't know, do you?" he says. "What a shame that your mom never told you what's to happen before *you* turn nineteen."

I tighten my grip around the handle of the blade, holding in my rage by feeling the intricacy of it in my hand—there must be some markings or carvings on the handle. If he breathes another word, another lie, about my mom—it's going to be really hard not to stab him.

His expression morphs into anger and he lunges at me. Before I can even think, my hand twists the blade and slices into his stomach. Another electric current surges out of me and through the metal piercing his flesh. Oliver writhes as I stand there, trembling, almost like I'm watching from above—as if it's not actually me who's stabbed him.

The electricity suddenly stops, like a circuit trip, and Oliver's body slumps—nearly knocking us both over. He flops to the ground with the dagger still lodged in his stomach and lands on his back.

The world grinds to a halt as I stare down at his dead body. Holy shit, I stabbed him.

And then the bigger realization sinks in.

I killed someone.

CHAPTER FORTY-TWO

HENRY

SMOKE CROWDS MY lungs and I wonder how many breaths I have left before I die here in this morgue.

I need to summon my powers, but how? I've done it before by thinking of Natalie, but it's a little difficult to concentrate on her when my skin is practically melting from my flesh.

It's getting harder to breathe by the second. Getting harder to think. I writhe and slash against my restraints, but they won't budge.

Fucking Oliver. Some father he was. If I ever get out of here, I'll make sure his fate is even worse than leaving your own son to burn alive and die. That, I'm certain of.

A clang rings somewhere in the distance, and I wonder if it's just something that's fallen over in this room. These restraints make it impossible to see beyond what's right in front of me.

But the footsteps continue and I realize someone must be here. A lifeline.

I attempt a weak shout for help through my burning lungs. "Help!"

The footsteps get louder. Someone is definitely here. I just hope it's someone who can actually save me and not kill me. At this point, my odds aren't great. But I'm hedging on complete desperation and this is the only chance I've got right now.

Wes comes crashing into the room, looking like a wolf ready to attack. I have no clue why he's here, but his arrival hacks at least a shred of hope into me.

I expect him to grab the fire extinguisher or at least throw a cup of water on the flames, but he just stands there, frozen.

"You wanna help me over here?"

He gives me nothing. He's over there looking like a frozen puppet.

"Yo!" I attempt to yell, but my words collapse into a guttural cough.

Why isn't he moving? I follow his eyeline, trying to crane my neck enough with these damn restraints to see.

Then the hard realization hits.

On a gurney in the corner of the room is his brother. Well, what looks like the corpse of his brother.

Wes turns to face me and I expect him to be gutted, but instead he's angry. Not just angry—but burning with rage. "What did you do to him?"

Me? "What did *I* do? What the hell are you talking about?" I choke again. "I didn't do anything. We were both prisoners. They killed him. Or tried to."

"Who is 'they?'"

My temper spikes and I'm losing patience. "The guards. Look, man, can you get me out of here? We're both going to burn alive."

The pain behind his eyes vanishes and is replaced by a vindictive glare. "You didn't try to save him?"

Is he serious right now? "Save him? I couldn't do anything. Do you see me strapped up here?"

Wes shakes his head, his hands clench into fists. "But you're alive. And he's… clearly not. Did you sell him out to the authority?"

It's becoming clearer that Wes has zero intention of helping me. Power thrums under his words, and he seems to be on some vengeance ego trip. I can't even muster sympathy for him at this point. "Fuck you."

Wes storms out of the room, and I scream after him. "Hey. Hey! You can't leave me in here!"

It's like a hammer against my skull. Wes has left me here to die.

A million feelings slam together, tearing through me. I squeeze my eyes shut and Natalie's face appears. It's the same vision I had about her before, in the woods, except I'm the one lying on the cold dirt, bleeding out. Natalie strokes her finger along my cheek. "I told you, you can't save me, Henry."

Something cracks inside of me and my body begins violently twisting and contorting, like I'm having a seizure. Maybe this is what happens when you die.

Thunder crashes outside to the tune of my body, as if my movements are in sync with the weather. Then a strange feeling of freedom washes over me. *Now am I dead?*

I blink open my eyes to find that I'm very much alive, except the flames are now fanning away from my body. And my restraints are broken.

A burning ignites in my chest. I'm actually free. I swing my legs off the gurney and give it a moment to orient myself. There's a clear pathway to the door, like some invisible bodyguard is holding the flames away. I don't understand it, but I don't care. I just need to get the hell out of here.

I burst outside, choking and gagging from the smoke. I trudge forward until I notice Wes standing in the distance. He's not alone.

Numbness skates down my spine, replaced with revulsion as soon as I spot Natalie… in his arms.

Everything within me acts on instinct, as if my very survival depends on this moment. I lurch ahead, ignoring the horrific pain in my lungs. Wes seems about ready to jump out of his skin when he sees me. *Didn't think I'd survive, did you, asshole?*

Natalie stares at me in disbelief as she pulls away from Wes. "You're alive."

Yeah, no thanks to you and your little boyfriend. I shove her back. "Get away from me." *I saved you, and you ruined my life.*

I twist all my rage to Wes, clenching my fist and punching him as hard as I can.

He crashes to the ground and I follow, pummeling him in the face. Natalie's screams play out like background music, but I don't let up. Wes makes a weak attempt to fight back, but he's no match for me right now—physical or otherwise.

Then something locks around my throat and tosses me back. My body smashes onto the concrete. *What the hell was that?*

I rock forward and snap upright, trying to quickly regain my vision and composure to glimpse my competitor. Shock rattles my mind when I realize the person who just tossed me like a rag doll… was Natalie.

She shakes her head, seemingly as shocked as I am. How the hell did she just do that?

Then I remember what Oliver said, about her not being human. The memory is like a fist closing around my heart. What *is* she then? And how does that connect to what I am?

Cambion.

Oliver's admission burns in my mind. I can still feel the band of friction around my throat, pulsing where she grabbed me. I slowly push to stand, and look over at Wes. His body lies on the ground, bloody and broken, and he's not moving. Even though he looks dead, I want to claw at him again—take out every inch of my fury on him. But I can't trust Natalie. If she's that strong, I can't risk what else she might do.

Natalie collapses next to his body, checking to see if he's breathing. I don't bother to stick around and find out.

I turn my back and walk away from them. I don't know where I am, or where I'm going, but anywhere is better than here.

I need to get away from precogs, from my past, and even farther away from Natalie Covington. Or whatever her real name is.

I make my way down a long stretch of bumpy soil. The rain kicks in, a drop here and there, and then a loud crack of thunder teasing a storm. I have a strange sense of helplessness and hope as I trudge ahead and finally manage to reach an open road.

One decision, one terrible decision, to save a girl I didn't even know. That one decision ruined my entire life.

But I'll survive—I've done so up until this point—as long as I keep to myself. As long as I trust no one and never let anyone in, because that's when you end up in so much pain you start to wonder if it's better to be dead than to be alive.

As the gleam of headlights comes into view and I hitch my thumb in the air, I make a promise to myself.

This will be the last time I ever think about Natalie Covington.

BONUS CHAPTER: CHAPTER FORTY-THREE

WES

One month later

SOMETIMES I WONDER what my life would be like if I wasn't tossed such a delicious twist of fate.

Natalie Covington.

At first, she was just a name. Someone my uncle sent me to track while he cosplayed as a Lockwood guard. He got to stand around in that ridiculous uniform, I got to spend time watching Natalie. I was certainly on the winning side of that arrangement.

I yank off my eye patch and blink until the vision in my left eye comes back into focus. Yes, I can see just fine, but Natalie doesn't need to know that. She believes that Henry permanently damaged my eye, which seems to endear her to me. I'll keep up this charade for as long as I can.

Natalie didn't leave my side while I was in the hospital, and hasn't left it since. She came up with an entire scheme to make me a legit student here at Lockwood. I'm now a bona fide member of the Lockwood elite, hitting up polo matches and expensive parties. I went from homeless assassin to hot commodity in a matter of months. All thanks to her.

Natalie. She makes me feel alive, which is astounding considering I grew up surrounded by death. I was raised by a hitman, my uncle. He fixated his training on me since my brother turned out to be completely useless at it.

Yet another delicious twist of fate: my uncle became my first kill.

Henry may have changed his vision and knocked my uncle unconscious, but I had to step in and finish the job. I hid in the trees and watched as Henry threw a rock at his head, proving to me that he's even stupider than I thought. A rock will not kill a precog, nor will most normal ways of taking someone's life.

Natalie doesn't need to know that I stretched the truth about my eye injury, *Okay, I lied about it.* She doesn't need to know that I'm the one who actually killed my uncle. She also doesn't need to know that I'm not Canadian. Or that I was the one who staged my uncle's room at Lockwood to make it look like he was a deranged stalker so the police would quickly close the case.

There are other things she doesn't need know, too. Secrets that are better kept hidden, even in my own mind.

I strip off the rest of my clothes and climb into the shower, letting the hot water rush over my body—truly one of my favorite parts of the day. Living as an outlaw for so long, I never knew when I'd have time for a shower. Most of the time, I was sneaking into public bathrooms and splashing water and soap where needed, or taking a baby wipe "shower," which sucks even more. Now I'm in Henry's old dorm room, taking his place as a student and as the guy in Natalie's heart. Exactly where I belong. This is how I deserve to live. I used to be surrounded by decay and now with Natalie, it's like I have an IV drip of vitality.

I twist off the faucet and grab a towel before stepping out of the steam into the frigid air. Damn, that shower felt amazing. But not as amazing as it will feel being with Natalie in about an hour. Holding her hand in public. Tracing my fingers along her spine or anywhere else she'll let me. Kissing her, which doesn't last long considering that act quite literally scrapes the life away from her. *We're working on that.*

I pull on a beige sweater and navy-blue khaki pants. This is not a great look for me. Not a great look for anyone, really, but it seems to be the preferred uniform for rich, preppy dickheads. And I gotta blend in if I want to stay with Natalie, so preppy dickhead it is.

I groan, slipping this stupid eye patch back on, If I need to fake an injury and keep up a web of lies to make sure Natalie and I are together forever, then fine.

I'll do whatever it takes to make sure she's mine.

NATALIE

CHAMPAGNE GLASSES CLINK in front of my face.

I raise my glass to toast just a moment too late. Ciel makes a face. "Natty, where are you? It's like you disappeared into some dark place in your brain."

I shake off my thoughts, which isn't easy to do nowadays.

Wes reaches over and clasps my hand in my lap. He leans in, whispering in my ear and grazing his lips against it. "You okay?"

I nod and paste on a smile for him.

I float my gaze around the table. Ciel and Adip—who have rekindled their romance, yet again—nuzzle together, constantly and inappropriately touching at every opportunity. Then there's Jack and Josephine, whom I'm weirdly happy ended up together. I guess it's easier when you experience the pang of love, and know that your ex-boyfriend wasn't it.

My eyes pin to Wes, who grins back at me. A tightness clenches my stomach, but it's not at all unfamiliar.

Being around someone like Wes, playing the perfect girlfriend to extract information, isn't exactly easy. But it would make my mom proud—my investigative skills are at an all-time high.

I scrape my fork around the plate of lemony cod over roasted vegetables, pretending to eat. I smile and fake a laugh to the group, pretending to be happy—pretending to care.

But it's all a façade. People have always underestimated me my entire life. My father. Jack. And now Wes. He really thinks I don't know that his eye patch is fucking fake. He truly believes that I would be dumb enough to fall for his romance cluttered in lies.

Make no mistake, Wes is here at Lockwood because of me. Because if I ever want to find out the truth about my past, to continue my mother's legacy, to discover what I really am, I need more information on the precogs. Henry is gone, and I haven't heard a word from him. Not a sighting, an email, handwritten letter, or anything. He just vanished.

My heart clenches with a stab of pain anytime I think of him, but I'm learning that this is life. When you let yourself truly feel, you get hurt every time.

So here I am, in some relation*shit* with Wes. He's hot, so there's that. And he's such a good liar that sometimes I wonder if he really buys the bullshit he's serving. Sometimes, I even buy it myself.

But none of that matters. I need Wes—to find out more about my mother's investigation, what she knew, why it's so dangerous… and the truth about who—or what—I really am. Henry's creepy foster dad said something will happen before I turn nineteen. Well, I've got less than a year before that happens.

Wes tucks a strand of hair behind my ear and plants a soft kiss on my lips. I pull back, biting my lip, pretending to enjoy this.

"You're killing me, Covington," he says. Okay, truthfully, I like messing with him. He *is* hot, and why shouldn't I have a little fun?

He thinks he's playing me, but really—I'm playing him.

At least until I find out the truth. About me. About my mom. About precogs.

About *Henry*.

THE END.

The story continues in book two of the heart-pounding Lockwood Trilogy, UNRAVEL.

Dear Reader:

Thank you so much for giving CONTROL: Book One of the Lockwood Trilogy a chance! If you enjoyed following the twists and turns of Natalie and Henry's story, I'd be so grateful if you could rate and review it online!

If you want a sneak peek at book two, UNRAVEL, that features Wes and Natalie's point of view (with a healthy dose of Henry - #Hatalie fans don't worry!) turn the page…

*A sneak preview of UNRAVEL -
Book Two in the Lockwood Trilogy*

UNRAVEL

CHAPTER ONE

NATALIE

I HATE HOW *he consumes me.*

Wes' tongue pries my mouth open. His hips push into me and my body unravels in a soft moan, sinking deeper into the mattress. I don't want this to feel so damn good…

It's been thirty-three days since the incident. Thirty-three days since I figured out I have some kind of powers. Thirty-three days since I learned my mother wasn't killed in a random accident, but likely at the hands of the precog authority.

Thirty-three days since I last saw Henry.

Henry Thorne. Disgust and desire whirl through my body, weaving through my insides, stirring around my heart. I stopped him from beating the life out of Wes and he had the nerve to get angry with me. What did I ever do to him—besides protect his secret and do everything in my power to save him?

Wes traces his palm along my side, grazing over my chest, dusting his fingers around my neck without applying pressure. He doesn't need to. For some inexplicable reason when I kiss a precog, I lose consciousness. It happened with Henry.

And I hate that I can never forget that kiss. It's seared into my memory. It feels pathetic and at the same time, necessary. Because thinking about Henry has really helped me push through these make-out sessions with Wes.

Heat spreads through my body when I think about Henry and no matter what I try, I can't shake it.

Wes and I have been practicing… for thirty-three days.

My head falls back as my consciousness begins to slip.

I used to nearly pass out after a brief moment of making out. Now we can kiss for almost thirty minutes before I reach the brink of blacking out. I look at it like training for a boxing match. If, or when, I need to fight for my life again, I can at least survive romantic warfare.

"You're getting better at this," Wes says. More like, he growls. His words wrap around my body, making every part of me clench. My lungs beg for air and he notices, moving his lips to my neck, lightly brushing up to my ear.

I need to keep up this charade with him if I want answers. He's the only precog I know besides Henry. And certainly the only precog who'll give me access to information about them, information that can lead me closer to truth about my mom. About me.

About Henry.

I mentally slap myself as Wes' hand skates up under my shirt.

Henry hasn't shown up at school since the incident at that precog prison, or whatever the hell that place was. He also hasn't tried to get in touch. Sure we don't have cell phones at Lockwood, but we do have a school email address. Or he could take five minutes to send a letter. Maybe he thinks it's too risky or maybe he hates me. And, if so, why? The last I saw him things were good, before he was taken away by their authority. Maybe they've shifted his perspective on life. *On me.*

Henry Thorne. What reason does he have to be angry with me? And why I do I care so much? *I hate that I care so much.*

This mix of emotions stirs something inside me—hate and longing and anxiety and pleasure skitter over my flesh. I don't understand what I'm feeling.

Wes picks up on the desirous parts of my behavior, tightening his grip on my skin, deepening our kiss.

My lungs start to seize and my mind begins to darken. "Stop," I say, nearly breathless.

Wes immediately backs off. "Sorry, did I take it too far?"

"No. It was… great." I push myself up onto my hands.

Wes curls me into his arms, twisting his fingers gently into my hair, stroking my scalp, planting a kiss on top of my head. "I love you, Natalie."

My heart ricochets into my throat. *Love?* No, he can't love me. This is all a game. He lies to me. I lie to him. He's wearing an eye patch after all, faking an injury, thinking I'm some idiot who will swoon and feel bad for him. I'm only sticking around for clues and information. Okay, and let's face it, because it's also fun to make out with him. Even when I'm thinking about Henry.

Speechless, I inch away from Wes' body. Disappointment paints his face. "I don't know what to say."

"You don't have to say it back. It's only been a month, but I couldn't hold it in anymore."

I paste on a grin, acting flattered. He takes that as a cue, leaning into me, pressing his lips against mine, spreading an instant tingling sensation through every corner of my body.

"I need a break," I say, climbing out of my bed. "Do you want some tea or something?"

Wes shoots me a look. "Covington, when do I ever want tea?"

"Right, sorry." I cross over to the kettle, feeling Wes' gaze boring into me from behind. I can't let him get too suspicious. Maybe I should just lie and tell him I love him.

Suddenly, a siren wails in the distance. It's deafening, piercing my brain.

"What the hell is that?" I peer out the window as Wes joins me at my side. Dozens of Lockwood students rush out of the buildings into the courtyard down below.

"A fire alarm?" Wes says.

But I know it's not that. We had several annoying fire drills the first day at Lockwood, before Wes got here.

The ominous wail continues and I get the feeling that something is very, very wrong.

ACKNOWLEDGEMENTS

I'm a huge fan of entertainment you might refer to as "guilty pleasures." Though I don't believe we should ever feel guilty about experiencing pleasure.

I had so much fun writing CONTROL—a twisty, soapy tale about messy relationships and situations. I really hope you enjoyed reading this story as much as I enjoyed creating it.

To my husband, Gary, thank you for always supporting my writing and helping me brainstorm the wildest ideas. None of this would be possible without you.

To Susan Hyatt for getting this book out of a sad desk basket and encouraging me to put it out into the world, even when it felt scary.

To Dawn Ius, my friend and developmental editor, who loves salacious stories as much as I do, and who always makes my writing better.

To Jessica McKelden, whose line edit caught so many details I'd missed (d'oh!)

To Alexandra Franzen, Shenee Howard, Lisa Fabrega, Nicole Antoinette, Jessie Rosen, Shelley Cohen, and all my friends who supported and encouraged me along this wild ride. I'm forever grateful.

To my mom for always taking me to the library as a kid, letting me watch soap operas, and for not noticing when I stole your romance novels. Ha!

To my beta readers, thank you for your invaluable feedback and for cheering this story on to the very end!

To Washington state, my beautiful home that partially inspired this story.

To anyone who writes/creates Turkish dizis (quite literally the best TV shows out there.)

To everyone who makes unapologetic, not-so-guilty pleasure entertainment. I'm obsessed with you.

ABOUT THE AUTHOR

Melissa Cassera is a professional screenwriter and the bestselling author of angsty, twisty romances with a soft spot for the morally gray. She is also the writer of 11 movies for *Lifetime Network*, including "The Obsession Thrillogy," the network's first trilogy of movies.

When Melissa isn't writing twists you won't see coming, she can be found drinking too much coffee, playing at the lake with her dogs, or getting lost in the romance section of a bookstore.

Join Melissa Cassera's author mailing list for exclusive sneak peeks and giveaways: https://melissacassera.com/control/

Melissa's Instagram: https://www.instagram.com/melissa.cassera/

Melissa's TikTok: https://www.tiktok.com/@melissacassera